About the Author

I am a father of three who lives in Worcestershire. My hobbies include mountain walking, big boat sailing, and amateur archaeology.

The Chaos and the Randomness

Nick Evetts

The Chaos and the Randomness

Vanguard Press

A CIP catalogue record for this title is
available from the British Library.

ISBN 978 1 80016 911 1

This is a work of fiction. Names, characters, businesses, places, events and
incidents are either the product of the author's imagination or used in a
fictitious manner. Any resemblance to actual persons, living or dead, or
actual events is purely coincidental.

*Vanguard Press is an imprint of
Pegasus Elliot Mackenzie Publishers Ltd.*
www.pegasuspublishers.com

First Published in 2024

**Vanguard Press
Sheraton House Castle Park
Cambridge England**

Printed & Bound in Great Britain

For Cheryl. With thanks for her patience.

"The monster in the barrow
The dragon in the mere
The chaos and the
Randomness that hold humanity prisoner..."

Introduction

This is a novel set in the English Civil War as it draws to its first conclusion in 1645.

It tells the story of a disparate but hopelessly entangled group of people as they strive to survive and live their lives through a tumultuous time in English history.

There is no more tragic a war than a Civil War when a nation turns inward and savages itself. I have tried to dispel from the readers' minds the ingrained stereotypes of gay laughing flamboyantly dressed Cavaliers and hymn-singing pious Roundheads. As we have watched the tragedies of Bosnia and Rwanda unfold on our television screens in our own time, we know civil war is not like that at all.

The scars of the ECW are with us still almost four hundred years later. They persist in our allegiances to political parties, in our perceived status in society and in our attitudes to royalty. The story of what happened then is still pertinent today.

However, this is a novel, not a historical textbook and, as such, students of the period may find mistakes. These are mine and mine alone. My intention was to portray to the reader a 'feel' of the time and what it was like to be alive then. To illustrate what it means to be a human being has not changed much at all in the intervening years. In the main, I have used modern language to avoid detracting from the dialogue with any 'gadzookery.'

Nick Evetts

Chapter One

Shrewsbury.

The first four prisoners had already been crudely bound, their arms pulled tightly behind their backs, course hemp rope biting deep into their wrists. They stood in a sullen group, fearful faces gazing hopelessly around them. Their faces wore the blank hopeless expressions of creatures who have realised that resistance is futile, and only obedience may hold any hope of salvation.

Executions were always a messy affair; it was a defence to maintain a brisk professional approach and get it over with as quickly as possible. It was to be here in this cobbled square, surrounded by half-timbered buildings that they were to die. Behind them, the gatehouse of Shrewsbury castle reared up sand coloured and stark against the grey sky. The smoke from within showed that the fires begun in the night attack smouldered still. The acrid smell of the thick dirty smoke was still strong, carried by the listless breeze.

In the centre of the square, raised on a hastily constructed dais, stood the gallows, hurriedly prepared this morning, the unweathered wood still smelling of sap. The main spar would undoubtedly bow under the weight of the four men. There were no crowds, no hordes of citizens, shouting and chattering excitedly, fed by roving hucksters. Here there were only soldiers, both on and off duty, who out of interest or want of something better to do had strolled up to watch. Faces appeared at mullioned windows overlooking the square, but these would be the only inhabitants of a Shrewsbury under a strict curfew that would witness the executions.

Lieutenant Jacob Sedgwick switched his gaze from the tragic scene and glanced down at the warrant he held, his lips moving silently as he read the names there mentioned. Names that in some cases sounded outlandish to him but, here and there, were names sounding much like those of his own men. Such was the nature of civil war, he mused. Rerolling the warrant, he shook his head in exasperation. He understood that an example must be made, but this was a heartless affair, watching a man choke his life away at the end of a rope. The protruding tongue, the bulging eyes and the inevitable distasteful moment when bowels opened.

"It must be made clear," his commanding officer had said during the peremptory 'drumhead' trial earlier on, "That no true bred Englishman of whatever beliefs will tolerate the use of foreign mercenaries in this conflict. Perhaps Prince Rupert will take note."

Sedgewick knew that the unfortunate Irish prisoners had been taken to the open ground behind the castle in the last hour and made to dig a hole which they knew was their own mass grave. "At least my lads were saved that chore," he mused.

The soldiers attending to the execution worked quickly. Chivvied unceremoniously onto the dais, the prisoners' hats, belts, and boots were quickly removed and thrown into a pile.

Whatever few pathetic personal items they possessed were also taken, in fact, one was wailing as blood dripped from a torn ear lobe as an earring was summarily ripped off by an overzealous trooper. The troopers' faces, wind-burned and leathery under their broad-brimmed hats were set and rigid with an effort to show no emotion. Men, as in all conflicts, were not indifferent to the things they did, even under orders. They made the usual disparaging remarks about the men they were working on, remarks they had made many times before, but the harsh laughter eased the tension. The faces of the prisoners remained unchanged as most were probably unable to understand a word that was said, being conversant only in Irish or even Gaelic.

Sedgewick barked out a command for silence and turned away to look back at the gatehouse, from which the next group of bound prisoners was emerging, escorted by two more troopers who casually cradled their muskets as if they carried a child.

Behind this sad procession, Sedgewick knew, was another group and then a fourth, and so on. He raised his leather gauntleted hand to rub the bridge of his nose and sighed. This was no fit work for soldiers.

The hanging of prisoners was a recent development in this civil war in which Englishmen fought Englishman. It had started out as a mock gentlemen's war with chivalric acts on both sides and prisoners exchanged with rapidity. Now after three years of fighting, the conflict had become harsher and more bitter. Too many families had lost husbands, fathers, or sons to the fighting, and the numbers of civilian men, women, and children who had lost their lives left little room anymore for honour or pleasantries.

This new order to summarily hang all Irish prisoners taken, Irishmen brought over by Royalist commanders to fight for the King, reflected a fear felt by many that once mercenaries were used in any number the conflict would degenerate into the larger, more terrifying conflict in mainland Europe, now entering its twenty-seventh year.

"Jacob," a strident voice intruded on Sedgewick's thoughts. Turning he gazed at the burly figure of his comrade in arms, Lieutenant Nathaniel Collingwood, striding across the square towards him boots drubbing. Since Sedgewick's promotion from a somewhat junior lieutenant to 'Aide' to Colonel Mytton, relations between these two comrades in arms had been somewhat strained. The experienced, arrogant, and some years older Collingwood, with his lengthy, and dedicated service with Colonel Mytton had considered the post his by right, and he had accepted his colleague's good fortune with ill-concealed annoyance. Did he but know it was his bluff approach to life and complete lack of tact that had ruled him out of promotion in Mytton's eyes?

The haughty face under the brimmed and feathered hat registered his disdain for the task at hand. The hard blue eyes swept the scene with an imperious glance and returned to Sedgewick. With a gesture that was habit, he smoothed the Van Dyke beard that was immaculately trimmed and which gave his face the elongated appearance favoured by the elite officer class of both sides in this war.

"The old man wants to see you immediately," the nasal voice drawled. "He is down the passageway there," he jerked his head at the alleyway from which he had just emerged. "Stone-built place, our banners hanging outside. It's called the Blue Boar if you can believe it." He laughed easily, then seeing Jacob's blank look, "You have read some scribblings of the playwright Shakespeare?"

Jacob shook his head. Collingwood spread his hands in exaggerated mock dismay.

"No matter. He's been dead for thirty years anyway." He reached forward and snatched the rolled warrant from his friend's hand. "I should hurry, his mood is not good. I, God save us all, am to take over here".

Sedgwick nodded, glad to be quit of the thankless task, turned and strode off smartly across the square his boots drubbing the cobblestones. Entering the alleyway, he spied almost immediately the limp hanging banners outside a decrepit-looking building and headed for it. As he entered the inn, he heard from the square behind him loud jeering and catcalls that signified the first unfortunate four were gasping and thrashing their lives away. He hurried inside.

Colonel Mytton was working industriously as he had for some hours. Having viewed the large number of prisoners taken, and supervised their incarceration, this slightly-built stooping man with curling dark hair now flecked with grey, had called a meeting of his senior officers and carefully briefed them on the garrisoning of the town. Ever a studious, serious man, Mytton was forty-eight but looked ten years older, his only nod to contemporary style being his shaped and curled pencil-thin moustache. Whilst most of his senior staff retired to grab a little sleep, he had moved to his makeshift quarters to write his report.

Pale, grey light filtered through the partially drawn curtains, lancing the gloom. A guttering candle flickered and smoked on the desk in front of him. All furniture had been stacked against the far wall and a table and chair from the kitchen had been placed near the window. In one corner, piled in a heap, were his boots, breastplate, scabbarded sword and hat. He sat in stockinged feet, stockings which were in need of repair. His slashed leather jacket hanging from the back of his chair likewise showed signs of hard use.

His slight frame was hunched forward as he wrote, his head bent in total concentration, lifting only to dip his quill pen into the ink pot. He appeared totally oblivious to the cheering and noise from outside. He lifted his head, chewing his lip, as he struggled to construct a difficult sentence. He was anxious that his report was accurate and reflected his thought processes in the recent action. The screwed-up papers that surrounded his feet attested to his earlier efforts.

His task this morning was to compose a report to the so-called 'Committee of Both Kingdoms' in London, describing with some pride the taking last night, February 22nd, of Shrewsbury town and castle, for parliament, with a mixture of dash, cunning, and treachery.

The Governor of Shrewsbury, Colonel Sir Michael Ernle, one of the 'Irish Colonels', had been a sick man for some time. With discipline lax, his men had become slovenly and inept. Some had actually contacted one of Mytton's officers selling information for coin. Last night, taking advantage of the reported absence of many of the garrison on campaign, Mytton had seized the chance and attacked.

A strong force, under cover of darkness, crossed the river by boat and managed, with the help of Royalist traitors, to open the gates. The parliamentary main force flooded into the city before the sleepy, unprepared guards were aware of what was happening.

Mytton reached for a fresh sheet of parchment, laid

it on the desk in front of him and, quill in hand, broodingly chewed his lip. The next paragraph would have to be tactfully constructed to attach no blame to himself.

It was unfortunate that he was roused from his bed by the tumult, as his retreating troops frantically sought to escape from the pursuing, hot-headed roundheads. Ernle had been hacked to death as he stood a bewildered figure in his nightshirt. Try as he might, Mytton could not identify one officer or trooper under his command who had witnessed this atrocity.

The voice of Jacob Sedgewick rudely interrupted his thoughts, "Sir!"

Irritably Mytton looked up at the soberly-dressed young officer with long curled brown hair who stood before him.

"What is it?"

"Forgive me, sir, but I understand you sent for me."

Mytton recovering himself, leaned back in his chair and placed his quill on the desk. "You witnessed the executions?"

Jacob stared at the wall above his commander's head. "No, sir. Lieutenant Collingwood said you wished to see me immediately. I... "

"Yes?"

"The first group dropped as I reached here, sir, I... heard the cheers."

"The cheers?" Mytton's frown deepened.

"Yes, sir. The men watching, there were quite a few when I left".

The Colonel's lips compressed with anger. "I wanted no gawking idiots present. I thought I made that clear. These are military executions, not a sideshow." My own fault, he mused, I should have had the gallows set up outside the city walls instead of in the square. I'll remember next time.

His eyes were sore and red-rimmed; smoke from the action, followed by hours of writing by candlelight. He stared at Jacob's face for some moments then down to his papers.

"You know, of course, why this is being done?"

"I believe so, sir."

Mytton searched the younger man's face for signs of sarcasm but found none. "It is to dissuade our opponents from the use of foreign mercenaries in this struggle." He shifted his gaze to peer briefly out of the mullioned window and then back to his young aid.

"Praise the Lord that this conflict, heinous as it is, has as yet not developed into that which rages across Europe." His eyes lowered to the neat stack of scribblings on the desk before him, and absently he straightened the small pile. "You have a relation of some sort in the foreign wars, do you not?"

Jacobs's eyes flickered down to his Colonel's face and then back to the wall. "Yes, sir, my elder brother." How on earth did the old man know that?

"How does he fare?" Mytton's voice was gentler if

such a thing was possible "Have you heard from him recently? Does he tell you what is going on over there?"

The silence stretched on. Distantly, more cheering could be heard. "I have not heard from him for some considerable time, sir." Jacob's tone was non-committal.

There was another short silence as the Colonel surveyed the young face above him. This lad had promise and he intended, if he could, to advance him where possible. He valued integrity and loyalty in his closest staff officers and felt he would receive both from this gentleman farmer's son. Realising he was not going to receive an answer, he once more picked up the quill and fiddled with it.

"How long?" The Colonel's voice was softer. There was a slight pause.

"Ten years, sir."

Myttons face showed his surprise as he looked up into the face of the younger man, and he immediately looked back down again lest his eyes betray his conclusions about the fate of his aide's relative. He peered down at the writing in front of him as the silence lengthened.

"I see."

Again, he straightened the small pile of writing paper in front of him covered in his small, neat script. Clearing his throat, he shrugged and dismissed this line of questioning. It was after all none of his business. He had more pressing matters.

"Well, Sedgwick, I am afraid that for the moment you are leaving us." He permitted himself a dry smile. "I have a task for you."

"Yes, sir".

Moravia. February 1645

They moved in just after dawn when the village would be barely awake, always the best time for maximum shock effect and fear, a trick learnt over long, bitter years.

The picture was idyllic; rolling snow-covered hills, and frost-rimed pine forest surrounded the settlement. Small, thatched cottages and wooden shacks nestled for comfort around the stark grey stone church, its undamaged onion-shaped spire a rarity. Smoke from freshly lit hearths curled lazily upwards in the still morning air. A harmless domestic smoke, so different from the stench-ridden smoke of war. Chickens scrabbled the muddy square, hunting for seeds or refuse, keeping a wary eye on the half-starved mongrel stalking them.

From his vantage point on the hill above, a tall rangy man, his dark clothes worn and tattered, irritably scratched at a scab on the neck of his thin, unkempt horse and surveyed the scene. His breath was steam in the morning air and he muttered to himself a stream of unintelligible invective and obscenity, through which permeated the words, "Come on, Come on." He was watching his men close in on the unsuspecting village, crawling or running, bent double from one stone wall or hedge to the next, their stealth borne of the professionalism of long practice. Hawks, vicious and relentless, closing in on unsuspecting doves.

His horse coughed hugely, the sound tremendous in the silence, and he swore again concerned at the slowness of the progress below him. As if in answer to his plea, a crescendo of shots rent the air, followed by the splintering of wood as doors and window shutters were barged or hacked down. The usual din of female screams and shocked male oaths brought an ugly smile to the rider's face. His lads, knowing their trade, wasted little time on niceties.

In an unconscious habitual movement, he fingered the huge scar that ran from hairline to chin down the left side of his face. The memento of a scrape with a Danish pike-man some years ago. When the weather turned cold, it ached with a dull throbbing intensity. His face was long and gaunt and the slate grey eyes set deep; the left one half-closed from the scar, lending him a permanent sinister leer. His hair, cut collar-length short for ease, had once been a ruddy bronze, but now the colour had faded and was heavily streaked with grey as if he had rubbed ash-covered fingers through it. Cupping his hands, he blew on them, then replaced his gauntlets, pulled his fraying grey cloak more tightly around him, adjusted his battered wide-brimmed hat, and rode slowly down the hill. The horse slithered and slid on the wet snow-covered slope, drawing further curses. Reaching level ground at the base of the hill, he rode slowly up what passed for the main street, his horse carefully avoiding the icy puddles. The chaos around him seemed not to interest him; he had seen it many times before. His men, enthusiastically going about their work, glanced only sporadically at him as he passed, eager to be seen plying their trade. They were afraid of him.

He stopped in front of the main doors of the church and disinterestedly looked up at the spire, before dismounting with the air of someone about to start a long day's work.

His men, from long practice, worked quickly, tattered, half-starved, efficient scarecrows of war. Already the women and children had been shoved or bludgeoned into a quietly moaning group and the men of the village, sullen, and unco-operative, into another. Only two troopers stood guard over them. The faces of the unfortunate villagers showed little fight, only the dull resignation of despair. This had happened before, it would happen again, many times. The look was common enough in Europe at this moment in time. Around them, their homes were being thoroughly ransacked by these tough human locusts that had descended on them.

The soldiers had no uniform of dress, the clothes

25

were from a dozen different countries, added to, and modified over the years of killing, giving them a look of competence and menace. Their hungry or diseased faces were somehow more frightening than robust healthy ones.

Every morsel of food that could be found, which was not much, was being carefully loaded into sacks, destined for the bellies of the twenty-thousand-strong army of Sweden's King Gustavus Adolfus, camped not ten miles away, near Brunn. Here and there a fire had started but, apart from taking care to avoid the leaping flames, the soldiers ignored them, whilst the helpless villages stood impotently and watched their homes burn.

A huge, florid thickset man, his thinning blond hair grimy with cinders and sweat, strode towards the remote gaunt figure standing in front of the church.

"Not much, Captain," he barked. "If there's anything else, it's well-hidden, we can't find it".

His thick accent betrayed his Dutch birth. He stood with his hands braced on his leather-clad hips breathing deeply from his recent exertion.

The Captain pondered for some moments and his eyes strayed to the clumps of villagers.

"Sort out the head man from that lot and bring him in here." Abruptly he turned and entered the church.

The bare interior was dark and quiet after the din outside. He strode up to the makeshift altar, his boots ringing on the stone floor, and rested his outstretched arms on it. Above him, a crude stained-glass window, amazingly almost intact, portrayed Daniel and the Lion's Den, the dim light shining through the coloured glass fragments making a multi-coloured mask of his face. He whistled softly through his teeth, a tuneless whistle; he'd long ago forgotten music. The tramping of booted feet behind him broke into his thoughts and he turned.

The prisoner was trussed like a chicken hung between two ragged, but powerful Danes. One of them had an old rusting crested Morion helmet which had been dislodged from his head and was suspended by leather twine down between his shoulder blades. The prisoner was a short, wiry man, his homespun shirt frayed through long use. He gave off the aroma of dung, sweat and fear. His head hung forward and all the Captain could see was lank, greasy black hair. His hands were tied brutally tight behind his back, so when the Danes shoved him forward, he tripped and sank almost lazily to his knees.

The Captain gazed down. "Your name?"

Slowly the man raised his head, one eye was closed and his lips were swollen and bruised. Blood ran from his nose and mouth and dripped onto his shirt. Slowly, his tongue brushed across his battered lips, and he leaned slightly forward and spat blood on to the floor.

The Captain's face hardened with irritation. "Why so rough?"

The soldiers stood like statues, pitiless eyes staring

from wooden faces. The blond Dutch sergeant spoke for them.

"He gave us a bit of a fight, Captain".

The Captain squatted down in front of the prisoner. "I asked your name."

The man did not appear to have heard, he made no move or sound. One of the Danes kicked him in the back, drawing a sharp cry.

"Says his name is Haussmann," interjected the Sergeant casually, "begs us not to kill him for his wife's sake."

"His wife's sake?"

The Sergeant nodded. "Heavily pregnant, ready to drop at any time."

One of the Danes chuckled and would have made a remark, but he was silenced by a look from the Captain.

"Well, Haussmann," the Captain began speaking to the top of the peasant's head. "You have already proved you are a brave man. Don't prove you are a fool also. Tell us where the rest of the food is."

Still, the man did not speak; it was as if he did not understand. Outside there was a sudden crackle of noise as one of the cottages collapsed. Smoke and cinders wafted in through the half-open church door.

"Answer me!" rapped the Captain.

In a fluid movement, the Sergeant stepped behind Haussmann, jerked back his head by the hair and rammed his knee up into his back. The man gave a cry of pain.

"We have no more," he croaked in a weary, thin voice, "the soldiers who came last week took everything we had left."

The Captain's eyes looked bored. "Indeed? What soldiers were they?"

The man made a sound that might have been the ghost of a laugh, or a groan. "Who knows, they were soldiers, that is all I know".

Viciously the Sergeant pulled the head back further until the neck was painfully stretched and his eyes rolled in their sockets.

"He's lying," he snarled. "There's more, there's always more. These carrion have more hiding places than a squirrel."

"Ease up a little," rasped the Captain, his tone hard.

As the grip on his head was loosened the man slumped forward retching painfully. A small rivulet of blood and vomit ran down his chin and dripped on to the flagstones. The Captain crouched closer and lifted the wretch's head with his gauntleted hand.

"Listen well, farmer," his voice was low, almost friendly. "I do not wish to kill you, believe that, but we must have food, you understand? There has to be more, or you and your people would not still be here. No?"

The pain-wracked, bloodshot eyes of the man stared back at him and still, he said nothing.

"One last time will I ask," whispered the Captain as if he were speaking to a child. "Tell me where the rest of the food is hidden or you hang right now before the eyes of your wife and friends?"

An expression that could have been loathing flickered across the peasant's face but still, he said nothing.

Losing patience, the Captain stood and turning, rested his hands once more on the alter. "Take this fool out and hang him."

Grinning hugely at the thought of a little excitement, the men gathered up the prisoner as if he were a bundle of clothes and hurried him down the length of the church and out through the double doors.

The Captain gazed up once again at the stained-glass window. He believed the wretch; there was no more food. But he led a multi-racial group of mercenaries: Poles, Swedes, Danes, Scots, Italians and many more. All of them rapists, murderers; professionals. They were afraid of him because of his skill with arms and his ruthless efficiency in keeping them alive but to show compassion or weakness at all would mean his own death before the next night fell.

His men were typical of every soldier in this conflict that was now almost thirty years old. Called a religious war but manipulated by politicians and self-serving princes, it had long since devastated Europe. The ruling houses of most European states still maintained their petty bickerings, fuelled by misplaced religious fervour, whilst in their name, huge hungry armies of mercenaries trundled back and forth across the land, leaving death, destruction, famine, and plague in their wake.

Sighing, he held up his spread hands to the weak daylight. He could see the outline of every bone through the thin flesh. It had not been a successful day. Perhaps it would be better tomorrow.

He emerged from the church to the mixture of jeers, catcalls, and screams that meant the sentence was being carried out. He turned his head and watched the writhing, jerking figure suspended from a small tree. As he watched, an old man surged forward and, grabbing the dangling man's legs, hauled down as hard as he could. It was an act of mercy he had seen many times before, usually done by a close friend or a family member, as it hastened the end of suffering.

The air was full of the sound of wailing; the loudest and most plaintive coming from a heavily pregnant woman surrounded by what must be her immediate family.

The Captain became aware of his Sergeant standing next to him.

"He said nothing?"

"No, sir."

"Anyone else?"

From behind a large barn came a pistol shot. Panic erupted as soldiers and peasants ran in all directions. Only the Captain and his Sergeant stood still, peering through the smoke. He watched as three figures approached him.

One of his own men was struggling weakly as he

was hustled forward by a large Italian and one of the Poles in his command.

The struggling man was known to the Captain as a recently recruited Scot. He eyed him with distaste. He did not like Hagen and, long association with men such as he, had warned him there might be consequences to accepting him into his troop.

"Well?"

The Italian spoke, wrenching at the Scot's thin sandy hair as he spoke, "He rape this little girl, Captain. Only this big." He indicated his knee. "He rapes her then he shoots her." He spat a stream of Italian invective at his prisoner. Then slapped his face backhanded.

The Captain stepped in front of the Scot, "You know my orders, Hagen."

The Scot nodded and then smirked like a naughty child. His face was soot grimed. The Captain's eyes were flint.

"Which were?"

The Scot's lilt was still strong. "No killing or raping on raids unless you order, Captain."

There was a time when he would have reasoned with the idiot but that was all finished long ago. Patience, reasonable behaviour and compassion; all those things from another life were not present in this place, at this time and had not been for many a year.

In one quick movement, the Captain withdrew a flintlock pistol from his broad leather belt, cocked it, and fired point-blank into the Scotsman's crotch.

As the Scotsman's arms were released, he flopped

like a broken doll at the Captain's feet. He screamed like an animal as he clasped both hands to his groin and watched the thick blood pulsing between his fingers. Then, as if performing an acrobatic trick, he began to roll around the yard, head over heels like a hoop.

Turning from the spectacle, the Captain spoke to his Sergeant, "Get them ready to move."

"Yes, Captain."

"And finish that." He indicated the moaning, bloodied heap still rolling in the mud. Orders were rapped out and two men drew knives and finished the erstwhile rapist where he lay. Casually, they began stripping his clothes and boots. These would be auctioned off when they arrived back at camp.

The Sergeant started to move away and then obviously felt some remark was necessary. "He asked for it, Captain, what you did was fair".

"Was it?" said the Captain. "I believed him. There is no more food here."

Briefly, the sergeant looked puzzled, then realised the Captain was referring to Haussmann, the peasant.

"No sorry, Captain. I meant Hagen there."

The Captain said nothing but gathered up his reins and prepared to mount his horse.

The Sergeant stepped closer, his Dutch accent thick with contempt. His breath foul from a mouthful of black and rotting teeth.

"As far as that's concerned, Captain," he nodded his head at the body hanging from the tree. "I believed him too. There never was any more food; I was in the troop that was here last week."

He leaned forward peering at his commander. "Does it matter?"

The Captain gazed at him for a long moment, his face unreadable. "Probably not," he said. Relieved by the correct answer, the florid Sergeant turned and tramped away.

The Captain mounted his horse and re-arranged his tattered cloak around him. A mounted bugler edged his horse next to him in case his services were required, his almost circular crude horn slung from his saddle. But the Captain merely glanced around the village for the last time and moved off. They rode away up the snow-covered slopes carrying the meagre scraps of food in sacks slung from their saddles. Behind them, the smoke and the cries rose up together to the lead-coloured sky.

Chapter Two

Taunton / Brunn, March / April 1645

The sunlight speared through cracks in the wooden shutters, shafting in bright bars across the dingy room. It dimly illuminated the bare floorboards and flaking plaster of the small room. The only furniture, a tattered four-poster bed, resided squarely at its centre, surrounded now with hastily discarded clothes in untidy heaps. An overturned jug, still dripping occasional drops of wine, nestled against one wall where it had rolled. Flies droned heavily through the air, thick with tobacco smoke and the smell of sweat.

The girl emerged from the tumbled sheets, rubbed fingers through her tousled hair and rolled slowly onto her back, careful not to disturb her still-sleeping partner. Easing down the grubby sheet, she gingerly inspected her bruised and bitten breasts, hissing involuntarily as her fingers probed a sore spot. Fearing that even this small sound might awaken the man next to her, she turned and surveyed her bedfellow.

George, Lord Goring, slept on, every breath pushing a strand of his long brown hair away from his face. The face which, when awake and alert could appear stunningly handsome, even cruel, was in this unguarded moment, childlike and showed signs of wear and tear. Strain and fatigue had carved deep lines into the flesh. The nose, long and slim, nevertheless had a faint blue tinge, evidence of prolonged wine abuse. High command in the Royalist army in this year of our Lord 1645, was not a brew designed to make a man look younger.

The girl shifted position slightly, causing the sheets beneath her to ruck up under her buttocks. Without conscious thought, she eased herself further away from him. She was trying to reconcile this quietly sleeping figure with the demon of last night.

Drunk and tired, he had been voracious in his needs, criticizing her roundly if she failed to perform to his satisfaction at his every request. Once he had hit her and, although had apologised immediately, her fear had made her more submissive. She had heard that behaviour like this was to be expected from this man, but she had also heard that he was occasionally extremely generous in the cold light of morning. Chances such as this did not happen often in the small Somerset town of Taunton where she plied her sexual trade and she had hopes that her labours would reap a rich reward.

The man who lay next to her was, at thirty-seven, possibly the greatest cavalry commander in the Royalist army, with the possible exception of Prince Rupert. Decisive, daring and fearless in battle, his character was nevertheless marred by a darker reputation for cruelty and harshness, both with his own troops and civilians. Troops under his command often left stories of rapine and plunder to mark their passing. A notorious drinker and womaniser, he could, when he wished, be the most courteous and affable of the King's advisors. A member of the King's inner council, it was said he held great sway with His Majesty. A fact that did not, it was rumoured, endear him to Prince Rupert, the King's nephew.

He walked with a limp, a permanent reminder of an ankle wound received whilst serving for five years in the Dutch wars. Consequently, when on campaign, it was rare to see him afoot. On his return from the wars, he had been made Governor of Portsmouth but, at the outbreak of hostilities in England, had raised his banner for his monarch. During the last three years, he had proved to be startlingly successful as a cavalry commander and strategist. Such success had brought with it a meteoric rise to power and now, on this March morning in 1645, he was The King's General of Horse in the southwest.

He snorted suddenly, breaking the rhythm of his breathing, and opened bleary eyes. His glance took in the naked woman next to him, then flicked away as he sat up and ran fingers through his hair, swearing quietly. Finally, he spoke to the woman without looking at her.

"Who are you?" His harsh voice sounded bored.

He stretched his arms up above his head, hearing

the joints crack. She remained silent, seeing all her dreams founder. He remembered nothing.

Turning irritably, he snapped, "Well?"

"My name is Margaret, sir." She risked a gap-toothed smile. "You requested me last night. You recall?"

He turned away, swearing obscenely again under his breath. If she did but know it, he was acutely embarrassed, having faced this situation many times before. The feeling of the ridiculous, when one awoke in the cold light of day, sharing one's bed with a complete stranger who had probably seen you in every idiotic position of lust. He wanted to be rid of her and quickly. His head ached and he felt nauseous. The smell of sweat and stale sex was potent.

He raised his head and called out. With a suddenness that indicated someone had been waiting just outside, the rickety wooden door to the room crashed open and an immaculate foppish young man in long folded-over riding boots and broad-brimmed hat strode in.

"Sir?" The voice was nasal and well-bred.

Goring rubbed the bridge of his nose and spoke through closed eyes, "Get this out of here."

Too stunned to protest, the woman was silent as she and her bundled-up clothes were hastily ejected from the room. Crossing to the window, the young aide flung open the shutters and the harsh winter sunlight flooded the room, drawing a low groan from the man sitting in the bed. The sounds of the army filtered into the room. Men shouted, horses whinnied, somewhere a blacksmith hammered at metal and, sporadically, near at hand or far away, a cannon boomed. The siege of Taunton dragged on. The strong defences of the town still stubbornly denying the surrounding Royalist army.

Crossing back to the door, the young man risked a sideways glance at his commanding officer. It was always wise to assess the mood of this man before speaking.

"Shall I give her some money, sir?" The younger man's eyes betrayed nothing.

Goring looked up sharply but. seeing no implied criticism in his aide's expression, looked away to the window.

"Yes," he said. Then as an after-thought, "and, Lieutenant… "

"Sir?"

"Impress on her the need for… discretion." He turned to glance at the young man. "Impress it strongly."

The foppish young man's eyes were bleak. "Yes, sir".

Goring held up his hand in a signal to stop the door being closed. "Assemble my staff downstairs as quickly as possible, we move north today."

A note of anticipation and pleasure coloured the response. "Yes, sir, immediately." The door slammed behind him and boots clumped off down the corridor, accompanied by petulant female protests.

Throwing the grubby sheets to one side, Goring stood, stretched and began to gather up his garments.

They left two hours later, Goring at the head of two thousand of the finest cavalry in the land. Dressed almost exactly like their counterparts in the Parliamentary ranks; buff coats, thigh-length boots, breastplates, gauntlets, and a variety of head-ware, they presented an impressive and reassuring picture to the infantry left behind to continue the siege, as they jingled out of camp.

During the last hour, the senior staff officers had been briefed in Goring's own earthy style of the situation as it presently stood. Earlier in the month, His Majesty King Charles, the first of that name, had indicated his intention to move the substantial train of artillery from its headquarters at Oxford to join Prince Rupert at Hereford. Gaining news of this, Colonel Cromwell, who had been operating in the area, promptly swept the whole area clean of draught horses. So now Rupert had been summoned east to Oxford with every heavy horse that could be found, and Goring had been summoned north to free the King of Cromwell's attentions.

As they rode out, the young Lieutenant ruminated again on the chameleon-like qualities of his master. All traces of the drunkard of last night, or the slightly embarrassed wreck of this morning, had vanished. From the brisk business-like briefing to the cool professional tour of inspection prior to their departure, he was now the embodiment of his legend; brilliant, decisive and ice cool. The men riding with him were in high spirits, not only because they were freed from the 'mess' around Taunton, but also because of the man who led them. As children feel safe with an adult, they felt safe and confident with him and, reflected the Lieutenant, it was a confidence borne of a long association with this incredible character and the results of his actions. As the silver trumpets rang out, the whole cavalcade swung into a jaunty trot.

Two days later, Goring surprised a large body of cavalry from both Cromwell's and Fairfax's regiments as they crossed the River Isis. In an explosive thirty minutes, he savaged them terribly, killing large numbers and scattering the rest. Pausing only to regroup and bury his dead, he rode on to meet his King.

Brunn. Moravia.

The Captain lay for long moments after waking, staring fixedly at the rough wood planking above him. Weariness as ever lay upon him like a cloak. How long had it been since he felt energy or happiness? He could not remember. He did not even think about such things, they were of the long distant past. From the moment he opened his eyes in the morning until he closed them again to blessed unconsciousness at night, every minute was a battle to be won, to stay alive. He yawned hugely and sat up, then snorted contemptuously at himself for the self-pity.

Once again through a restless night, the dreams had come. Dreams he knew well now but could not control. He did not want them and had willed himself not to have them, but to no avail. His childhood featured more often lately, one in particular, was especially disturbing. He was sitting on the stone-flagged floor in the kitchen with his family whilst his father read from the family Bible. Remembering it now, he could still see the old man's bald head gleaming in the candle-light and hear his guttural voice, thick with the local accent. He could vividly recall the smell of his tobacco smoke as it curled lazily from his habitual clay pipe. The picture was idyllic but then, as always happened, a beautiful young girl, in seconds, was stretched out on the kitchen table, screaming as soldiers climbed all over her.

This was when the Captain always awoke with a jerk, covered in sweat and trembling. Thinking about it now brought a small mew of anxiety. He closed his eyes to blot out the memory.

A heavy roll of thunder brought him fully awake and he shrugged on his battered boots and stood. A leak had allowed a constant drip of rain to fall on to the blanket on which he lay; he felt the dampness of his leather jerkin even through his homespun shirt. He had slept fully-clothed as ever. Save only his boots, no item of clothing had been removed for many months except for the daily necessity of lowering his breeches.

Smoothing down his hair and his jacket with the same movement, he crossed the dingy ramshackle hut that was home at present, thrust aside the hanging blanket that served as a door and surveyed the day.

The Swedish army, complete with its huge herd of mercenaries, lay spread before him encircling the besieged city of Brunn. In every direction as far as he could see, was a vast shanty town of tattered tents, wooden shacks, and scratch-built huts. The whole sewage-smelling, smoky litter of it, floating on a sea of clinging mud. Women and children squelched by in larger numbers than the soldiers. Hardly surprising when they outnumbered the fighting men by two to one.

The Captain knuckled the last vestiges of sleep from his eyes and spat into the mud at his feet.

"You want some broth, Captain?"

Van Meer, the huge florid sergeant, was at his master's side, ever watchful, like the trustworthy dog he was. The Captain nodded looking up from the mud. Idly, he watched as the big man shouldered his way amongst the groups of squatting women and filled a wooden bowl from the black cauldron that hung over the nearest fire. Giving it to his Captain, he reached into a leather bag suspended from his belt and produced a hunk of black bread that he dropped into the broth.

The Captain grunted his thanks and sipped unappreciatively at the thin steaming brew. His gaze moved sideways as a movement caught his eye and he was greeted to the sight of the heaving buttocks of the

Italian as he straddled his 'woman' on a pile of straw. There was no such thing as privacy in camp. One took one's pleasures where one could. Her muddy legs were wrapped around his back. His comrades, who sat a few feet away playing dice, paid little attention.

Tilting the bowl, the Captain consumed half of its contents in one gulp that scorched his tongue. He jerked his head at the heaving couple in the straw.

"Stop him now, we move when I have finished this."

Stony-faced, the Dutch man strode over to the heaving Italian and prodded him between the legs with his boot.

"Up!" he shouted. "All of you. Up! Make ready, we move soon." The words were spoken in the patois of the camps; a mixture of a dozen languages and accents, all merged into some sort of intelligible pattern.

"Captain," a mountain of a man strode as far as it was possible through the mud and debris towards the hut. Flamboyant but filthy clothes and an eye patch gave the figure a rakish appearance.

"Are you going out again?"

The Captain nodded. "Can I come too?"

Throwing the remains of the bowl into the hut, the Captain shrugged.

"If you wish, MacDonald. Come or don't come."

"Then I'll come." They were friends these two; if friends could be had in this place.

Two hours later they were approaching another village. This time it was in a clearing in a stretch of thick, dark, dripping forest. Constant rain had made the ground underfoot soggy, a wet dank carpet of leaves that concealed puddles and tree roots alike. The cold was a wet clinging thing that soaked into men's clothes. Some of the men were riding their thin underfed horses. Those without horses jogged and kept up as best they could or hitched a partial ride by hanging onto their comrade's stirrups. They carried a variety of murderous weapons, halberds with their curved vicious heads on a pole, axes and swords of many types, some had muskets or even pistols, occasionally only a converted farm implement. It depended on what they had found or stolen over the years.

They were close, only perhaps one hundred yards from the village, when a crescendo of pistol shots and shouting rent the air. The Captain held up his gauntleted hand and the whole troop halted silently. Turning in his saddle he uttered a low call.

"Schenk."

A Saxon trooper, leather jacket, riding boots, and a floppy hat, manoeuvred his nag forward. "Yes, Captain?"

"Was anyone else coming out this way today?"

"No, Captain." The trooper jerked at the reins of his sidling horse and gazed at his leader. The Captain's grey eyes stared levelly back.

"You're sure?"

Nervously, the German looked around at his mates, then back to the Captain. "Yes. No one, I swear."

The sounds through the trees were confusing now. More shots, screams and the smell of smoke were on the wind.

"Croats," said the big flamboyant man riding next to the Captain.

"Yes," growled the Captain. "Croats." Involuntarily his spurs nicked his horse and it jerked.

David MacDonald glanced over at the man he called a friend and was uneasy. The word 'Croats' always seemed to bring an immediate reaction from the Captain. He had heard some stories and rumours, but never dared to ask his friend about them.

The Captain's face had become a mask, lifeless, save for the glittering pitiless eyes. His scar stood out ugly and purple in the poor light.

Croats was the general term given to all eastern European or Balkan cavalry used by the Imperialist armies mainly for scouting and foraging. They received no pay but survived on booty and pillage. Executed out of hand when captured, they were treated as little better than vermin.

"Not worth a fight, Captain," said Macdonald. "Only a stinking village. There's plenty more."
The Italian who had run beside the Captain's horse this morning holding on to the saddle, looked up. He wore a Spanish crested morion helmet that he had stripped off a corpse months ago. It was far too big for him but he

had tied it on with twine under his chin.

"Nothing in it for us, Captain, plenty women elsewhere."

Seeming not to hear, the Captain turned in his saddle checking the men behind him.
"Van Meer, Rossi, Schenk, Bellini, Muller and three others with me. Macdonald will take the rest of you, circle, and come in from the other side. Drive them on to us."

There was a murmur of discontent from the group, silenced by a hard look. Only a mad man would take on the Captain.

"You're going to do this then?" questioned Macdonald, his voice incredulous.

The Captain glanced at him and gave a thin mirthless laugh. "Only the dead find peace."

Macdonald blew out his cheeks but, seeing the look on his friend's face, decided not to argue. He dismounted and tied his horse to a bush, before drawing his sword and a pistol.

"I'm cold," he said flatly.

"We arc all cold," said the Captain. "This village will warm us."

Turning, Macdonald trudged off through the undergrowth, followed by the men assigned to go with him. Turning, he gave a shouted whisper,

"God with you, Captain."

The Captain stared back and seemed amused. "The world is the devil's," he said, "ask him for protection."

Impatiently, he gestured them away.

With amusement, he noticed some of his men genuflect at this blasphemy. As the minutes ticked by, every soldier prepared for the coming fight. Belts were tightened and weapons checked. Each man in the formed line checked the ground at his feet to ensure he did not slip. Somewhere in the group one of the men farted hugely. No one laughed as the tension was too high. However experienced they are, a man does not risk his life laughing.

Suddenly, a fresh fusillade of shots erupted, shattering the now comparative silence. Men shouted or cried out in a variety of languages, their voices echoing through the trees. Then, with a crashing and shouting, the fleeing Croats burst through the undergrowth, straight into the line of seasoned killers awaiting them.

Aiming with deliberate care, the Captain shot a large Croat in the belly, relishing the thought of how long it would take him to die. One Croat, who had managed to mount his horse, clung desperately to it as it careered and bucked out of control with fear. He ran straight onto the upraised halberd of Van Meer, who heaved him out of the saddle and hacked his head off. Shouts and guttural curses. A Croat with Asiatic features used his horse to flatten Schenk. He dismounted and stood slashing frantically at the heaving body beneath him. A shot rang out and he sat down heavily, his face surprised by the fount of blood that gushed from his neck. A one-armed Spaniard who had gone with

Macdonald, appeared from the bushes behind him and split his head to the jaw with a meat cleaver.

Rossi ran across the Captain's front, chasing a limping Croat who had long black plaited hair. Rossi's helmet had fallen off and banged his back as he ran, held on by twine. Catching his man, he tripped him with his musket then, as the Croat lay winded, placed his musket to his head and fired. The head exploded in a welter of blood and brains.

With the arrival of Macdonald's men, the butchery was soon over. The Captain was down on all fours fighting to regain his senses after a lucky blow from behind by a musket barrel, when he became aware of Langstrom, one of the Swedes, standing over him.

"Captain, can you come?"

Groggily he stood up, shaking his head like a drunk. Wiping the clotted blood off his blade, he sheathed it.

"Come where?"

"The Scotsman, Captain, he's down."

Before the Swede had finished speaking, the tall gaunt Captain was striding away towards what was left of the village. It resembled an abattoir. Dead and dying peasants, men, women and children, littered the floor. Buildings were burning. In the mud lay the corpse of a woman, her legs spread and hanging from her ripped stomach was the red and slimy foetus she had been carrying. Many of the dead men were together in a pile where they had been thrown. Valuable powder had not been used, but their battered heads were squashy where they had been bludgeoned to death.

The air reeked of the acrid smell of smoke and gunpowder.

A grizzled little Dane was kneeling and clumsily holding Macdonald's head up. The Scotsman was in terrible pain. A huge hole in his chest pumped blood and his left arm had been all but hacked off. With one glance, the Captain knew that his friend was finished. He knelt beside the fallen man.

Macdonald's eyes were already beginning to glaze but, realising who was kneeling beside him, he rallied with an effort and tried to smile.

"Told you this was a bad idea," he hissed as a spasm of pain racked him. "Bastard Croats, bastard war. Never thought it would happen to me." He turned his head away. He was dying and he was ashamed, he wanted it over.

The Captain gently turned the big head back to face him and fought for something to say. Macdonald shook his head.

"Leave it," he muttered. "There's nothing... " He jerked as another spasm shook him. "Christ, Ethan... " The last words tailed off into a scream. His heels drummed the earth and a gout of blood and froth spurted from his mouth. Then his body went limp and he slumped back dead.

The Captain did not move. He continued to stare at his dead friend, his face inscrutable.

"See you later, Davey," he whispered. Then,

leaning forward, he closed the wide-staring eyes with his fingers.

A hand touched his shoulder. "Not now," he snarled, snatching the hand and shoving it away.

"Sorry, Captain." It was Van Meer, attentive as always.

The Captain shook himself and, glancing one final time at the Scotsman, turned. "Do we look for food now, Captain, or leave it?"

The Captain replaced his hat and walked off, calling over his shoulder, "Of course. That's what we came for, is it not?" He swore loudly at the lowering sky and then, regaining control of his emotions, he stopped and fingered his scar as if in thought. "Put the bodies of Schenk and Macdonald in one of the remaining huts and burn them."

"Yes, Captain."

An animal-like scream pierced the smoke-ridden air and crows started from a tree nearby. The Captain looked questioningly at Van Meer.

The Dutchman gestured to the corpse-strewn village. "They had their games, Captain, now we have ours."

He led his Captain around a smouldering barn. A sharpened stake six feet in length had been rammed into the ground and straddled on top of it, writhing in agony, was a captured Croat, whose arms were secured behind his back. Rossi, the Italian, hauled on one leg, whilst one of the Danes hauled on the other. The unfortunate Croat screamed again as the sharpened stake disappeared quickly up his anus.

Laughter came from many of the soldiers around who were methodically sorting boots and clothing from the dead peasants.

Beside the Captain, Van Meer chuckled, "So the world turns, Captain."

The one-armed Spaniard, freckled with blood and gore, appeared behind them munching on a piece of black bread from his pouch. He gestured with the bread towards the writhing Croat.

"I've seen them last for two days like that," he said conversationally. The Captain was looking at him, a strange look that made him uncomfortable.

"You don't believe in God then, Captain?"

"God?" said the Captain. "God's dead, we killed him a long time ago."

The Spaniard snorted. "What does it matter? I was at Nordlingen. I saw the thousands who died there and I asked myself, what did it matter what they believed? The crows still had their eyes."

The Captain nodded, almost to himself, then turned and walked away. Behind him, he heard the Spaniard say something to Van Meer and both men laughed.

Finding his horse where a trooper had left it, he mounted and rode slowly to the edge of the village. Dark was approaching and because of this, the fires seemed to be burning more brightly. He stopped and, turning his horse, gazed at the scene. His men still flitted like ghouls through the murk as the buildings burnt on. Somewhere down there, the Croat screamed in agony again to a cacophony of cheers and catcalls. Old memories filtered into his mind, like smoke through wood, and he thought of who he was for the first time in many years. Suddenly he had had enough. He had seen enough. Too much. Enough.

He turned away and, unseen by anyone, rode slowly away through the trees. After ten long years, Captain Ethan Sedgwick was going home.

Chapter Three

Woodstock / Gloucestershire

His Majesty Charles Stuart King of England, Scotland, and Wales stood at the tall, elegant window and gazed out at the steady drizzle as it fell from a grey sky onto the immaculate garden lawns of the Palace of Woodstock. His large, expressive, sad eyes were distant and unconsciously, he chewed his lip, deep in thought. Educated to believe that his status was sanctified and ordained by God, life now both puzzled and angered him. How could his people be at war with their own monarch? Surely purgatory awaited such creatures.

Sadness was the overriding emotion, but his enemies must be brought to heel and that task was proving to be a far more difficult and onerous undertaking than the hotter-headed of his 'advisors' had predicted four long years ago.

Behind him they argued on, all standing. In deference to their diminutive monarch, they leaned against or paced around the large intricately carved, highly-polished wooden table that dominated the room. A table now littered with maps. Although they bickered and sniped, no one had as yet raised their voice, conscious as they were to the presence of their silent brooding King. The inner council was in session.

The soldiers amongst the group were alone in the subdued, practical nature of their clothing, which stood out markedly against the dandified peacocks of the civilians. It was fashionable amongst these men to affect a mincing gait and appear somewhat effeminate. Jackets and breeches of bright velvets and silks were slashed in sleeves or body, to reveal silk shirts beneath. Large widely-brimmed hats, some sporting gay feathers, accentuated the vigorous head movements as the wearers agreed or disagreed with a point made. Lace was seen at collar or cuffs, and even sprouted from boot tops. Highly polished, thigh-length boots of soft leather were worn, so that they folded down over themselves above the knee, the square-toed soles often painted red. However, one must not be fooled as the King knew; whilst the clothes were affected and often effeminately flamboyant, the gentlemen who wore them most certainly were not.

As he gazed out of the huge, mullioned window, itself a marvel, he idly watched an old man in dowdy clothes stride slowly across the lawn, his arms rhythmically swinging the scythe from side-to-side, trimming a further fraction from the already neatly trimmed grass. He almost envied the wretch the simplicity of his days, but God had selected him for higher things, so dismissing the thought, he abruptly turned and surveyed his council.

"So, gentlemen, have you yet decided on the advice you would proffer concerning our future course of action?" His stammer was now almost unnoticeable but his soft voice nevertheless carried the whiplash of authority that cut like a knife through the hubbub of voices, and silence descended. Small and slight in stature, he dominated the room.

Moving slowly to the table, the sad eyes that had so entranced Rubens and Van Dyke, swept the assembled group, resting briefly on each man's face. They all felt the force of his gaze and lowered their own eyes.

Charles was irritated by the lack of any cohesive guidance from his council, which after many hours, still it appeared, could not agree on fundamental decisions. His tetch of annoyance was an unusual sign of feeling from this imperious man. It saddened him to once again be talking of war in this most beautiful and his favourite of rooms. Figures painted by Titian, Raphael and Tintoretto gazed down impassively from the brocaded walls but offered no help.

The silence lengthened as members of the council glanced uncertainly at each other. A servant's footsteps in another part of the palace could be clearly heard. Around the table, someone stifled a cough.

Once again, the King swept the group. "Am I to believe that your discussions have once again proved fruitless? Have you nothing to help your King with his decisions? Decisions, gentlemen, that should be yours."

This mildest of rebukes, at last, elicited a reply.

Striding around the table but stopping well short of the King so as not to draw attention to his height of over six feet, His Highness Prince Rupert of the Rhine, the King's nephew, began in the heavily-accented English that betrayed his German birth and his current annoyance,

"Your Grace, I fear we continue to find ourselves in disagreement." He turned his handsome saturnine head to the murmur of discontent behind him, a chilly stare bringing silence.

"Or rather I and two others find ourselves at odds with the general consensus of opinion." The King stared at his nephew but remained silent and it was some moments before the young man realised that he was expected to elaborate.

"If Your Majesty would be so kind," he gestured towards the table. Charles moved closer, the assembled lords parting before him like the bow wave before a ship.

"Briefly, sir," began Rupert, still careful to keep his distance from the tiny monarch, "I will outline the situation, although I am sure Your Majesty is conversant with it."

Quickly and concisely, he précised what all those present knew. Parliament lately realising the importance of Taunton, had ordered Lord Fairfax, the commander in chief of the parliamentary army in the south, to hasten to relieve the battered town. Only two days ago he had left Windsor with upwards of eleven thousand men. It was a tiny section of this host that had been dealt with so harshly by Goring. The prince arriving with his own force from the west, was advocating that their joint assemblage, together with the King's army encamped around Oxford, be used to strike a significant blow to their enemies.

"Parliament," he instructed, "will expect us to move southwest to intercept Fairfax and give them battle." There was a loud murmur of agreement from the assembled Lords, silenced by a stern look from the King.

"That would seem, dear Nephew, to be the correct stratagem."

"With respect, Sire, I do not think so. We have a God-given chance with such a host assembled, to strike at the greatest danger to our cause and your Majesty's person."

The King's head was bent forward studying the map. "Which is?"

Rupert's finger stabbed at the map. "The Scots army of the parliament, as we speak, is besieging Pontefract." His eyes were alight, his enthusiasm a palpable thing.

"Think of it, Sir, this foul iniquity, this army from the north and, more dangerously, this most professional of armies, on the very soil of your realm!" His fist banged the table, "and we have a chance to meet it in a fair fight, to destroy it!"

"Reckless," someone in the group spoke loudly and there was a concerted murmur of agreement. The King held up a diffident hand for silence. He had slept badly and his huge eyes were sunken in their sockets. He was missing his beloved wife and help meet Queen Henrietta Maria who, following the birth of their latest daughter, had relocated to France as the fighting in England became fiercer and more savage. He refused to admit, even to himself, that he feared the inevitable outcome of this cursed war and prayed to his God every night for guidance. It rankled that, to this day, his beloved consort, whom he insisted be called Queen Mary, had not been given a coronation as she was catholic. With an effort, he gathered his thoughts to concentrate on the matter at hand. He gazed slowly around,

"Who else here supports Prince Rupert's plan?"

"I do, Your Majesty.". A thicker, coarser version of Rupert shouldered his way forward, more flamboyantly dressed, but obviously a close relative of the prince.

The King inclined his head, the flicker of a smile at the corners of his mouth. "I acknowledge that The Prince Maurice supports his brother in all things." There was a snigger from the group.

Maurice coloured at the barb. "Nevertheless, Sire, I believe the plan to be sound."

"I also support it, Your Majesty." A thick Yorkshire accent sounded strangely out of place in this setting. A tall cadaverous middle-aged figure stepped forward and inclined his head in deference. The dowdy clothes and bluff manner named him a soldier. The King raised his eyebrows in surprise. Sir Marmaduke Langdale, the straight-speaking colonel, and commander of cavalry, had not hitherto been a supporter of Prince Rupert but rather, in fact, a constant critic.

The huge eyes stared at Langdale. "And what reason, pray,, can you give me Sir Marmaduke, to recommend the scheme?" The stammer, however slight, had for the moment disappeared.

"Sir, it is well known that the army of Leven is at present sorely depleted. He has had to send many of his best troops back to Scotland to help in the fight against our good servant, the Marquis of Montrose. Never has he been so weak." He opened his hands in entreaty. "Surely it is a God-given chance to strike?"

The King held a kerchief to his nose and sniffed. "Could it not be, Sir Marmaduke, that the Northern Horse under your command is famously reluctant to join fighting further than a day's march from their own lands? And that is purely for that reason you support my nephew in this?"

Langdale coloured instantly. "Your Majesty, I do protest."
A thin, mirthless smile crossed his monarch's face but, before he could reply, another voice interjected,

"Your Majesty, may I speak?"

The King turned slightly. "Ah, Lord Goring, pray, give us the benefit of your advice?"

Goring stepped forward to his Kings side. Rupert stiffened and glowered hotly but said nothing. The figure of Goring was markedly different from the bedraggled man who had led his troops away from Taunton. His hair and goatee beard were immaculately groomed, his matching jacket and breeches were of green brocade, slashed to reveal yellow silk beneath, perfume wafted from him and a pearl earring swung from his left ear.

He bowed slightly. "With Your Majesty's permission." He straightened and his gaze wandered from the King to Rupert and the assembly. "Sir, most of us believe that it is the army with Fairfax that is the single most dangerous threat to our cause at this moment. If we move south to intercept him immediately, we cut him off from London. His only decision then will be to fight on our terms and fight us with his 'new' army, inexperienced and raw, or move further into the southwest of the realm which, as you know, is wholly sympathetic to our cause. Eventually, he will be cornered. Either way, he must fight, he will have to.

Whether he is ready or no."

There was a chorus of agreement from most of the men around the table. Again, with only a slight hand gesture, the King received silence. He pondered for some moments, gently stroking his small beard.

"Dear Nephew," he began at last. "I fear I find myself in agreement with these men in this matter. The plan herein outlined," he gestured towards Goring, "would seem to be the most expedient in these troublous times."

Rupert was clearly fighting to maintain his bearing. He was unused to having his decisions questioned.

"Your Majesty, I still most strenuously disagree." His German accent was pronounced due to his agitation. "It is true that this army of Fairfax's presents a danger and will undoubtedly become more dangerous the longer it is unmolested, but what has been the greatest danger these two years and more? The Scots," he answered himself.

"Could it not be?" interrupted Goring, with a courtier's smoothness "That His Grace the Prince is, forgive my impertinence, allowing personal prejudice to cloud his otherwise impeccable military knowledge and judgement?"

Rupert rounded on him, "How so?"
Goring spread his arms in a conciliatory gesture. "We all are aware and I am sure, sympathise, when we acknowledge that it was largely due to the presence of Scottish troops in the Parliamentary ranks at Marston Moor that the Prince was so soundly beaten that day…"

"How dare you!" exploded Rupert, taking a step forward.
"Enough." Though the voice was soft, the King's voice crackled with authority. In the ensuing silence, the ticking of the clock on the huge mantelpiece was loud.

"My Lord Goring," began the King. "We consider your last remark to be incendiary and also to be insulting to our nephew, the Prince Rupert. You will withdraw it at once. I will not have members of my inner council arguing like guttersnipes in my presence." His anger was plain, which was an unusual sight for those who spent time with him. "You will, therefore," he continued, "apologise."

Goring, ever the courtier, bowed low. "Your pardon, Your Majesty, Your Grace. I do humbly proffer my apologies. In the heat of debate, my tongue was my enemy."

The King nodded imperceptibly. Rupert looked not at all mollified and continued to glower.

"And now, my Lords," said the King, suddenly weary of this stalemate. "We will adjourn this meeting whilst I consider the proposals herein discussed. My decision will be made known to you." The diminutive figure once more adopted the aloof, distant pose indicating that he was no longer available for approach. His heels sounded hollowly on the floorboards as he stalked out of the room. All bowed low at his passing.

Rupert straightened, glared around at everyone, and hurriedly followed his uncle.

The council was not again resumed. Instead, orders and directives were carried by messenger to all concerned. Charles had made his decision, despite further passionate entreaties from his nephew, and it was implemented with speed.

Goring was despatched back to Taunton with his Western Horse because, it was rumoured, Rupert demanded it. Shortly afterward, Rupert and the King gathered their respective staffs around them, joined the army and began the march which, after a series of events, would lead them to their destiny at a small Northamptonshire village called Naseby.

Gloucestershire.

Jacob Sedgewick leaned against his grazing horse and, having taken a long swig from his leather water bottle, wiped his mouth with the back of his hand and replaced the stopper. Somewhere to his right, a lark sang shrilly and he peered up at the cloudless blue sky attempting to locate the hovering bird. Failing, he turned and reslung the water bottle from his saddle. The horse, head bent to the damp grass, chewed stolidly on. It had earned its rest, he mused, having been ridden hard. The sweat was drying stiffly on its bay-coloured coat. Its horsey smell very strong.

It was a perfect spring morning, the sort April occasionally throws up between days of showers. There was a sharpness in the air and he was glad of the thickness of his doublet. He remembered days like this back on the family farm, back before the world had gone mad.

How long was that now? He gave up trying to remember and, making a sudden decision, hauled his horse's head up by the reins, quickly mounted and heeled the horse into a trot. He must be on his way, he carried despatches. He was somewhere north of

Gloucester that he knew, but he planned to ask directions at the next hamlet that he came to.

It was pleasant to be away from the army; the noise and the smells, the urgent rasped commands, the lack of privacy. He was enjoying the experience of passing down quiet country lanes or wooded tracks, accompanied by only his thoughts. His mood was of quiet enjoyment, marred only by the need for constant vigilance. There was always the chance of encountering a Royalist patrol. Although this was Parliament country, one never could be sure.

He had been away from Shrewsbury now for some weeks. The despatches Mytton had given him that grey February morning were for delivery in person to the House of Commons.

London had shocked and surprised him. He had expected a place dowdy and quiet, made so by long years of war. Instead, he had found it garish and noisy. Walking down jostling noisy streets, deafened by the screech and scrape of wheels on cobbles and by bawling hucksters, one could almost forget that anything was amiss in the Kingdom. True, there were a great many soldiers on the streets, either marching by in serious serried ranks, arrogantly shoving the people out of the way as they tramped by, or in groups of off-duty men, strolling by, or gathered outside alehouses, their chatter and laughter loud. The cosmopolitan appearance of the grey city by the Thames had surprised him. It was his first visit and he was shocked to hear snatches of conversation in a dozen different languages spoken in the streets: Dutch, French, Spanish, German and even African.

True, some of the market stalls that were everywhere had fewer items to sell, but this only served to increase the voracity and sales pitch of the merchants, eager to sell their products. Spices from the east, tea and opium from India, Tobacco from the new world, salt, and furs from Muscovy. Jacob had been shocked to notice the great number of prostitutes on the streets. Their lewd suggestions muttered or bawled at this young, obviously inexperienced, young officer were quite shocking to him when he first heard them, but he had grown used to such approaches very quickly. The committee of both Kingdoms frowned on the trade and were harsh on arrested malefactors, but they were spectacularly ineffectual in policing the women, who laughed and continued to thrive in a London whose male population had more than trebled because of the war.

Such was the overcrowding, that he had only been able to find less than comfortable accommodation at a small, unkempt and overcrowded inn quite near Westminster. Here, he had whiled away several days awaiting the promised reply to his delivered despatches. His enquiry to the frosty aide as to how long his wait would be, had been met with an imperious stare.

"When it is written. Now away with you."

Eventually, after many days, the morning had come when roused from his sleep by the landlord, to be told there was a "Gentlemen from the Commons to see him and be quick about it," he had descended the rickety narrow staircase to meet the immaculate young man who waited for him with not one, but two despatches tied with scarlet ribbons.

"You will not proceed directly to Shrewsbury town," the haughty young man had spoken down his nose. "It will be necessary for you to make a detour."

Jacob was jerked from his reverie as his horse stumbled. Cursing the beast ineffectually, he dismounted and lifted the beast's front right leg, satisfying himself that the hoof was sound and able to continue. He straightened up and removed his hat. It was getting warm. He wiped his brow with the back of his gauntlet and peered around at the surrounding brush. Nothing. A small fitful breeze ruffled his long brown hair and he replaced his hat and remounted.

The extra despatch he carried was to be delivered to the ferocious Governor of Gloucester, General Edward Massey. Someone in London had considered that Gloucester was on the way back to Shrewsbury. He shook his head in mock despair and once again heeled his horse forward. Two hours later, he jogged into the next village and the war reared its ugly head once more.

He sat his fidgeting horse patiently, toying with the reins, unsure whether to remain mounted or step down. The sentry trooper at the edge of the village with causal insolence had told him to 'wait here' as he strode off in search of an officer. Jacob looked about him with a mixture of resignation and disbelief. The calm permanence of the Gloucestershire village had been fractured as the war came to visit the half-timbered street. Two of the cottages had sustained damage; one smouldered still from the fire only recently quelled. The smoke from it was still strong enough to sting the eyes as it blew fitfully away. A tree on the distant village green was festooned with a grim fruit, as three freshly hung corpses turned lazily at the end of their ropes. The people of the village stood around in clumps, talking animatedly, gazing at the fire and the corpses with equal horror. One old man wailed loudly to his neighbours as he stared at the ruins of the house he had been born in.

The whole village was alive with buff-coated parliamentarian troopers, their thigh-length riding boots, breastplates, and helmets signifying they were cavalry. They moved about with grim efficient purpose as they attempted to restore order. Looking to his right, Jacob watched a young trooper lead his broken-legged and limping horse a little distance and, after calming him with a few soft words, shoot him with his wheel-lock pistol. The horse went down, dead before it hit the ground. The trooper turned and stumbled away, tears streaming down his wind-burnt face. 'Why is it,' mused Jacob as he watched, 'that in the... midst of all this, a man cries for his horse?'

"Climb down." The sharply delivered order came from his left. A bald sergeant stood at his stirrup. Behind him stood the sentry. "I said, climb down," he repeated. "I'm damned if I'm going to crick my neck talking to you up there."

Jacob dismounted.

"Your name?" said the Sergeant.

"Lieutenant Sedgewick of Colonel Mytton's regiment with despatches from London for General Massey in Gloucester." The Sergeant stiffened and regarded him with new interest.

"You can prove that?"

Jacob withdrew the sweat-stained rolled despatched from beneath his jerkin, the wax seals clearly evident.

The Sergeant's eyes, more respectful now, moved from the seals and back to Jacob's face.

"Well... Sir, you're in luck, the General's not in Gloucester, he's here. Follow me."

They strode off towards a large half-timbered house at the end of the street, outside of which a number of horses were held by a bored-looking trooper.

"What happened here, Sergeant?" Jacob's head moved from side-to-side as he spoke, taking in the scene.

"Clubman," said the Sergeant, dismissively. "Wrong place, wrong time for them." He snorted in derision. "We were passing through as they were at it. Short work for us." He nodded grimly at the festooned tree. "Those are the ringleaders."

Clubmen were becoming increasingly common throughout England. Groups of villagers banded together to form loose associations or vigilantes. Initially to protect their own but many, on deciding they had a little power, took to a bit of rape and plunder on their own account. There had been a number of notorious incidents during the last year in the southern counties. They were always ruthlessly dealt with if caught.

"They had only just started," continued the Sergeant. "Raped an old widow in that cottage there," he indicated the dwelling. "She almost died from what they were doing."

They swung left and filed through a rickety wooden doorway into a narrow hall. The Sergeant indicated he should wait there and stumped off, up the stairs. He returned almost immediately with a middle-aged man, whose face was pocked with acne.

"Sedgewick?" Jacob nodded. "This way." Together they climbed the stairs.

As they neared the top, a tall figure with thinning black hair appeared. His head leaned forward from stooped shoulders and a large beaked nose was topped by cold, cruel eyes which raked Jacob from head to foot. The Captain next to him stiffened.

The man's voice when he spoke was high pitched and nasal but bore authority. This man emitted casual authority.

"You are Sedgewick?"

Jacob nodded, "Yes, Sir."

Once more the hard eyes raked him with disdain and

something else that Jacob could not define.

"This way."

They marched down the hall and up another flight of stairs, stopping before a narrow door. The tall man turned and leaned down towards Jacob, his thin hair framing the pale face like drapes

"Report to me when the General dismisses you, I am Major Wilmott." He rapped loudly on the door and, hearing a muffled, 'Come' turned and, without another word, moved away down the stairs.

Jacob entered the surprisingly large room; bare polished floorboards creaked beneath his feet. The figure that turned from the window fitted the stories Jacob had heard of this man.

As tall as the Major but with shoulders much broader, General Edward Massey was a commanding presence. Piercing dark eyes were set in a tanned aquiline face. Cascades of curly brown hair touched with grey, fell to his shoulders. His doublet was entirely of leather, slashed in arms and body, with lighter leather peering through. The leather was heavily scarred and marked but cleaned and buffed to a sheen. A man of his rank could obviously afford better but, no doubt, it suited his vanity to be seen in the immaculate but worn clothes of a soldier. A voluminous orange sash, denoting his rank in the army of parliament, looped over his right shoulder and was knotted in a tight bow on his left hip. The vitality and strength of purpose that emanated from him were palpable. Jacob was well aware of the military reputation of this man. His ferocious defence of Gloucester against the full army of King Charles last year had been an inspiration to Parliament. He had learnt his trade in the foreign wars and was a protégé of General William Waller, known as 'The Night Owl' who esteemed and trusted him.

Massey glanced only briefly at Jacob before holding out his hand. It was some moments before the younger man realised he was being asked for the despatch. With a muttered word of apology, he withdrew one of the scrolls and handed it over.

Signalling Jacob to sit on the small stool to his right, Massey once more turned to the window and, breaking the wax seals, unrolled the missive. As he stood reading, bathed in the sunlight from the mullioned window, Jacob was able surreptitiously to study him. He knew the Royalists feared this man as they feared the devil himself. From the very outset of the war, his daring, cunning, dash, and ruthless discipline had won him success after success.

Based in the impregnable and largely walled city of Gloucester, he had led his command far and wide in the border country of Wales and England and beyond, always appearing where he was least expected, his raids spreading panic and fear through the King's ranks. Watching the man reading before him and noting the intelligent expressive face and the commanding physical presence, Jacob found himself thanking God that this man was on his side.

Massey finished reading and re-rolled the parchment before casually throwing it onto the small bed in the corner. His voice when he spoke was deep and rich, echoing in this room.

"So, you are with Mytton?" Jacob stood.

"Yes, Sir."

Leaning back against the window casement, Massey folded his arms. "Give me your assessment of the situation in that area." Jacob described to the best of his knowledge the situation and finished with a brief outline of the happenings just prior to his leaving for London.

Massey nodded to himself and looked at the floor. "That was bravely done," he growled. "To hang that Irish scum without trial or explanation. I would have done the same. Although I hear Rupert has hanged thirteen good Englishman in reprisal. The man is a scoundrel. You cannot compare English Parliamentary soldiers with that Irish rabble. The King must be insane to think a creature such as his nephew would bring ought but harm to his cause."

Jacob, feeling that he was required to make a comment but unable to think of anything to say, merely nodded and grunted an assent.

"We must choke at the source and completely without mercy any attempt to involve the large-scale use of mercenaries in this conflict. Witness the complete devastation of the European wars during the last twenty years to evidence the consequences of such an action."

Jacob uncomfortably thought of the Scots army in the north of England who had entered the war to fight for parliament. Their savagery, a byword, and all in the pay of Westminster who turned a blind eye. With a start, he realised Massey was gazing at him and probably knew what he was thinking.

"Thank you," said Massey dismissively. "That will be all."

Jacob stood, gave a sketchy salute and was almost at the door before he was halted.

"Stay." Massey glanced at the young man. "You will remain with us for a short while. I must send despatches myself to your Colonel."

"Yes, Sir." As he closed the door behind him, Massey was once again staring out of the window.

Chapter Four

Western Germany / Gloucestershire, Early spring,
1645

Ethan Sedgewick sat moodily beneath the dark frosty
trees, drawing meagre warmth and comfort from the
small fire that he had built against the night's bitter cold.
His huge threadbare cloak was wrapped tightly around
him but still, sporadically, he shivered.

Branches hung above him in the dark, edged as they
were by the meagre light of the fire looking like huge
bony frost-rimed fingers reaching down to him.

Nearby, just visible in the dim light, his horse
pulled stolidly at the meagre grass that poked through
the frosty ground. He had run out of oats two days ago
and now wondered how long the beast would last. How
long had he had this one? He could not remember. He
had tried not to remember anything for so long now it
was a habit, a way of life. Forget about the past, nothing
to spare for the future, and a full belly covered the
present.

Somewhere in the distance, a wolf howled, he paid
it little heed, he had heard many during these last days,
but the horse raised its head and whickered. He listened

for it again on the whispering fitful wind, but no more sound came.

There had been many nights such as this since he left the ruined village outside Brunn and turned his head for home. Home! What did that mean? Where was it? Instinctively he had set his face for England, but why, he was still unsure. If anyone, friends or family were still alive back there, they probably thought him long dead. His father and his young brother. He could not really remember their faces now, just a blurred image, the occasional sound of their voices had flitted through his consciousness over the years, but he had put those thoughts aside. All those years ago it had seemed the kindest thing not to send any message home, even if such a thing was possible. Like most things now, he was not sure. Like a man who has been unconscious for many years and was now awakening, his mind was foggy, his thoughts chaotic. He was realising slowly who he was and what he had seen and done.

Some days ago, musing on this, he had concluded that the single fact he was certain of was that he was not sure of anything anymore. The thought had amused him as he rode along and he had laughed out loud. The sound guttural and cracked.

Anyone watching him pass by would have seen a tall, rangy man in worn clothes on a battered horse. The scarred face and grim unfriendly aura that surrounded him would have deterred anyone who may have thought to approach. He was a man to step wide of.

Occasionally, he muttered to himself like someone deranged, deep in some long-ago conversation, oblivious to the world, his eyes glazed. Occasionally, when different, long-dead thoughts surfaced in his tired and befuddled mind, he would smile and reach a hand forward as if to stroke someone's face. Then he would remember with a grimace, things kept locked deep down inside him, where they could not surface. Feelings so raw that he often drew in his breath with a hiss as if he had probed with his fingers at a wound, and he would force memories back deep down from whence they had come. Locked in, for that way lay madness.

He had been a creature of war for years. The simple task of staying alive was all-consuming. He had long ago become immured to the death, destruction, atrocities, plague and chaos that were his every day. He was a soldier in this war without end, and these things were an inescapable consequence of his trade. But during these last weeks, as he moved ever westward, he had seen, almost with the blinking eyes from which a blindfold has just been removed, the ashes of Europe. The terror of the farmers, the merchants, the traders and townsfolk who had somehow thus far lived through it. The scarred, pinched faces and the hopeless eyes in the gaunt faces of children with swollen famine-induced bellies. The ruined villages and the empty fields where crops rotted. The burnt and fire-scarred churches, the gallows at almost every crossroads, ripe with rotting human fruit. Killed for some forgotten reason or even just for their religion. Hardened to the killing and suffering for years, he viewed it now with weary disdain. Even a man such as he had become was not without loathing.

There had been a morning when a recurring nightmare from his past had awoken him screaming from a fitful sleep and he realised hope had died. He had sat for long minutes with the barrel of his pistol in his mouth. It would be so easy; oblivion, restful precious oblivion and an end to the torment. As the sun rose and the world awoke around him, he had stared death in the face but found himself too eloquent in the art of self-preservation. He could not pull the trigger.

Dimly, as self-awareness had slowly returned, he realised that he was no longer the young man that his father or brother would recognise. The scarred, emaciated face from which hard, weary eyes stared at the world, the prematurely greying hair and the worn, and ragged clothes were just an outward appearance. The difference was deeper, more primal. Now he was a shadow of the person he had been, a worn-out husk, harsh, even cruel. Men did not spend ten years in hell and come out of it the same. He was shocked by this thought when it had first occurred to him, but the shock had passed and he faced the future, whatever it would bring, with grim amusement. For now, he would just get home.

Throwing another twig on the fire, he scanned by habit the edge of the clearing. Thus far he had avoided contact with soldiers of any kind, but the threat was ever-present. Somewhere out there the wolf howled again, closer now. He was not perturbed. He knew it would not come near a fire. Nevertheless, he placed his pistol where he could easily reach it, lay down and closed his eyes.

He was almost relieved to be awoken. The old terrible dream with its locked-down memories was once more tormenting him. What had caused him to wake he did not know, but he trusted his senses, honed as they were to self-preservation over long years. Keeping his eyes closed and remaining motionless he listened, blotting out the wind and the sounds of his horse. The slithering footfalls from the treecovered slope behind him were so soft that stealth must be the intention. The footfalls were not of boots but something softer.

Only one person so far as he could judge, but that was enough. 'Fires keep away wolves,' he thought, 'but attracts other predators.'

The hairs on the nape of his neck stood rigid, as the footsteps padded slowly into the clearing. Still, he did not move, the blood pounded in his ears as he fought to control his breathing. The wind sighing in the trees above him almost drowned out the stealthily approaching steps. He knew he must move now, if the intruder had a pistol he would die as soon as he moved, but there was no other choice, so he prepared to die.

In a fluid movement, he grabbed his pistol lying beside him and rolled directly across the fire, feeling the hot sear of it on his body. Rolling into a crouch, he levelled the pistol at the shadowy figure standing near where he had lain.

"No! My son, for our Blessed Lord's sake, no!"

In the glow of the small fire, Ethan could make out the shape of a thin black-robed figure, his empty hands held out in supplication. 'A priest,' he thought. He made no distinction, a priest was a man and men killed.

His voice was harsh and cracked, "Priest, you almost met your God face-to-face."

The priest did not move but stretched his hands wide in a gesture of surrender.

"I'm sorry, my son." He squatted warily nearer the fire, his eyes still on the Captain. "It was not my intention to startle you, as God is my witness." He stretched dirty hands towards the meagre flame. "I was up there," he gestured with his head at the slope behind him. "I was hiding from the troop of horsemen that passed by earlier, when I saw your fire." He sighed hugely, "and the need to take warmth overcame all else."

Ethan lowered his pistol slowly; he did not wish the priest to see that his hand trembled still. Stepping forward, he crouched down before the fire and added a few more twigs. His eyes did not once leave the figure in the filthy cassock.

"I'm told it is very hot in hell, priest, and you could well be finding the truth of it, coming upon me like that without warning."

The priest nodded imperceptibly and drew the back of his filthy hand across his eyes. "You think we are all, without exception, bound for hell, my son?" His thin ferrety face was heavily pockmarked from some earlier skin affliction, and his mouth was a riot of blackened teeth.

Sedgwick snorted contemptuously. "We are there already, my friend, but mayhap the region inhabited by the Devil is a little warmer." He sat back and placed his pistol on the frosted ground next to him. He sniggered mirthlessly at his own humour and gazed across the fire at his visitor. "What baffles me, priest," he said, his eyes dark hollows in his shadowed face, "Is that, despite everything, there are millions of people who still believe God loves us." He shook his head and lapsed back into brooding silence.

Gazing back, the priest did not like what he saw. A gaunt, scarred scarecrow of a man in travel-worn clothes, but recent lightning-quick movements showed a familiarity with action and possibly violence that was obviously borne of long practice.

"I do not take such casual blasphemy lightly, my son. I see no reason to hold religion to ridicule because the world has gone mad."

Sedgewick's eyes liquid with dislike and anger jerked up to the priest's face. "You hypocrite!" he snarled, "what do you think this mess feeds on but religious fanaticism? The princes and politicians started it, but the poor fools who do the fighting, and I include people like Wallenstein and Prince Bernard, continue to be fed this hell's brew of religious intolerance and fervour to feed the madness." He raised his finger at the priest and glared at him across the flames. "We've killed religion, holy man, murdered it along with all the countless thousands who have died. So don't quote your nonsense at me or I'll give you a blade to chew on."

Sudden passion spent, he stared back down at the fire. The priest, appalled by the sudden ferocity, kept his mouth shut and rubbed angrily at his forehead where this frightening man had pointed.

The silence lengthened as each man kept his thoughts. The wind sighed and the small fire crackled. Somewhere far away the priest thought he heard gunfire on the wind and glanced up to see if his companion had heard it also. The Captain's head was cocked to one side as he listened.

"Someone else's war," the harsh voice said.

After a long time, the priest cleared his throat to speak, "My son, would it be possible… do you have… Could you perhaps spare me a little food?"

Sedgewick did not answer but after a few moments, rose and took something from his saddle bag. Squatting once more, he tossed the Priest a small piece of hard, black bread.

"All I can spare."

The man in the tattered cassock sat and closed his eyes, munching on the morsel, relishing each small mouthful. The act of eating giving him intense, almost sexual pleasure. His last food had been three days ago given to him by a small family at the roadside who, although starving themselves, had like naive children, given him half of the food they had when he asked for it. He stretched pale bony legs from under his robe and the hammer-toed dirty feet in the battered sandals almost touched the flames.

Sedgewick sat deep in his thoughts absently rubbing his scar. He knew the creature who sat opposite and his kind ruled the world. It was a fool who thought otherwise. He realised his outburst had been that of a child. God and religion had not been killed, of course not. Both would gain immeasurably from the war. The victors would claim that God had fought at their side and the losers would seek solace in him. Men would continue to blame themselves for all that was bad and praise God for all that was good. Around and around his thoughts went as he stared into the flames. His chaotic horror-filled mind darting here and there as it had for weeks arguing, reasoning, and always there was the woman's face tenderly smiling at him through the pain, and the tiny child's hands touching his face. *NO! Stop those thoughts, don't let them in.*

Every day as he rode, his life seemed more meaningless, more futile. All those he had killed, all whom he had seen killed. The pointless barbarism. The millions who had died or been maimed or starved or expired of plague. For what? He loathed the robed figure sitting opposite him chomping noisily on his bread. So self-satisfied, so assured of his catechism, so smug in his supposed knowledge of God.

A woman's voice spoke soothingly to him, her face close to his, "Ethan, be at peace. You cannot cure the ills of the world, my love." She had said it to him many times. *No, NO more! Force that voice down to the depths of his soul where he kept it; safe and hidden.*

He looked up at the priest, his hatred an insane intense thing. He could kill him easily, snuff him out as he would a bed bug. He had killed like that often, it would be so easy, feel so good.

He regained control of himself and shivered. Looking up at the dark sky, he stretched up his arms until his shoulders cracked, then rose and, without a glance at the priest, walked over to his saddle and blanket, lay down and fell into a fitful sleep.

It was early dawn when he awoke. The soft milky glow of the coming dawn infused a cold white light onto the clearing, the clear sky had a milky radiance. The wind was stronger and the bending groaning trees thrashed wildly above him. He realised he was cold and noticed before he moved that his thin blanket had slipped off his shoulders. Suddenly he remembered his visitor and glanced towards the fire. Immediately he stiffened. The priest was creeping slowly towards him, the pistol in his hand. His eyes were riveted on Sedgewick, like a cat stalking a mouse. Some sixth sense had alerted the Captain to the danger even whilst he slept. Cursing himself for a fool, he realised that in his anguish of spirit last night, he had left the pistol on the ground near the fire. Such mistakes cost lives, now he would pay. Instinctively, without conscious thought, Sedgewick rolled over and leapt forward. The sudden movement saved his life. The priest, unused to firearms, fired hurriedly and misjudged. The ball ripped a slice out of Sedgewick's ear, drawing a yelp of pain. Throwing the pistol down, the priest turned to run but was far too slow. Sedgewick was on him in an instant. His left hand closed around the priest's scrawny throat, his nails drawing blood from the soft papery skin. This close he could smell the man's fetid breath as he tried to speak.

"Please, a mistake, I beg of you... "

Sedgewick's eyes were bleak, his voice gravel. "The mistake that killed you, Priest." He had encountered many men like this in the last years. This long war, with its endless killing and cruelty, its religious intolerance, famine and plague had driven many to the verges of insanity. The twitching of the priest's head and hands last night should have warned him. His horse and clothes and whatever meagre food he had on him were invaluable to such a wretch.

Holding the struggling man down with his left hand, he reached with his right to the huge knife in the belt behind his back and, with one fluid movement, drove it into the stomach of the squirming body beneath him. Thought was not present, just a survival instinct and pitiless self-preservation honed over long hard years. The priest screamed and writhed trying to move away from the burning probing steel, but Sedgewick was relentless.

Gathering his strength, he stared down into the bulging terror-stricken eyes and sawed the blade upwards feeling the flesh tear and muscle pop, until steel snagged on bone as it hit the base of the ribcage.

He bared his teeth like a dog and laughed into the dying man's face. He watched the eyes beneath him glaze and begin to fade and felt the priest's body go slack. Standing, he leaned down and wiped the clotted blood from the blade onto the dirty cassock then straightening, he coldly watched the dying man.

There was no sound now; the fatally wounded holy man was beyond that, only a slight gurgling came from between his lips tinged with a bloody froth. He gazed helplessly up at Sedgewick and tried to speak, but could not. Something like sadness passed across his eyes and then they set in death and all movement ceased.

Kneeling, Ethan wiped the thick clotted blood from the blade onto the dirty cassock once more then standing, stretched as if from a hard day's work and walked to his horse.

Unhurriedly, he broke his camp, saddled his horse and mounting, rode away past the corpse without a backward glance. Before long, the already-bloated crows began to gather and feast on the body he left behind.

Herefordshire: May 1645

Mary Honeywell swayed from side-to-side and grunted with effort as she made her way across the dung-strewn yard of her family's farm. The heavy wooden yoke across her shoulders was weighted at either end by the slopping contents of the full milk buckets she carried, the rewards for her efforts during most of this morning. She bit her lip in concentration as she fought to maintain her balance and not spill any of the precious contents onto the ground.

The air in the yard, protected as it was on three sides by farmhouse, barn and cowshed, was still and heavy and reeked of animal smells. The drone of insects was loud in the still air and the noonday sun was warm. She hardly noticed the background sounds that she had known all her young life. The low of a cow in the barn, the chittering of the hens that strutted about the yard in search of grain and the tinkling of the small brook behind the barn. She was hungry and was keenly aware of the baking smell that came from the farmhouse kitchen she was headed for.

She had been working as usual since well before dawn. Long before the sun heaved itself up over the horison to warm the dew from the grass, she had been clearing the drainage ditch in the far pasture, her long blond hair that, when loose, hung well below her slim waist, was neatly braided and tucked up primly under her calico bonnet. Her russet homespun skirts were hitched up and tucked into her belt to keep the mud from them, and evidence of the digging earlier could be seen in the mud that spattered her shins and clung to the wooden clogs she wore on her small feet. She looked much younger than her twenty-three years with her frown of concentration and the mud stain on the end of her small, upturned nose.

Her father and elder brother had been impressed into the Royalist army a year ago and, since then, life for Mary and her mother left alone to try to keep the farm going, had not been easy. Her mother, robbed in a single day of her husband and son and with no idea if she would ever see them again, had at first fallen to pieces. The initial impotence and anger had given way to lethargy, and it had taken Mary many weeks of gentle cajoling and reassurance to bring her back to some sense of normality. Now, keeping her despair locked deep inside, her mother maintained an outward semblance of what had been before. Mary, bred to hard work from the cradle, was coping reasonably well with the heavier work, helped only by a village boy who was paid with food for his family, whilst her mother took care of the lighter chores and ran the house. In this way, the farm for the moment maintained some sort of working life.

Against the background of everyday farm sounds the sudden musket shot from the front of the house sounded thunderous. Stunned, Mary stopped abruptly, slopping milk onto the dung-spattered floor. Her heart was beating hugely and briefly, she wondered if she had imagined it. At the start of this civil war, her family had daily expected soldiers to come and ransack the farm but as the years went by, they gradually came to believe that these fears were groundless. The troops that had taken her father and brother had come in the night, silently. Since that time, Mary and her mother were always alert for the feared musket shot and now, here it was.

Further sounds now reached her ears, a ragged cheer and men's laughter. Dropping the yoke and buckets, heedless of the spilt and wasted milk, Mary ran towards the commotion.

Rounding the front of the house, she saw that her mother was there before her. Dressed exactly like Mary but with grey wispy hair protruding from under her cap she stood like some demented witch, flour caking her arms to the elbows screaming and gesticulating at the three troopers who leaned casually on their muskets grinning at her. At their feet and still bleeding profusely was the twitching carcass of the farm's one remaining goat, the huge wound in its head already collecting flies. The tallest of the men, a big loutish fellow with long greasy lank brown hair was casually reloading his musket, a gap-toothed grin creasing his dull face. He seemed completely oblivious to the tirade from the woman in front of him, as he concentrated on his task. Slung from the wide leather belt that crossed over his left shoulder and down to his waist, were twelve small flasks, each one holding a powder charge, wadding, and a lead ball. As there were twelve of them, they were called apostles, and every musketeer in the armies wore such a belt. Using the ramrod, he packed down the charge into the long barrel of his weapon expertly. All three men seemed to be finding the situation amusing, but their expressions changed abruptly as Mary arrived. A wariness came into their eyes, together with an obvious appreciation of her beauty and figure.

"What's happening here?" Her voice surprisingly deep for a young woman sounded more confident than she felt.

"Mary," her mother turned to her as a child would to a parent, her lower lip quivering with a mixture of fear and rage, "They've killed the goat. Our last one, the very last... " She broke down, and Mary placed a protective arm around her. Through the sobs, her mother continued, "If my husband were here," she said, her voice muffled through the tears, "You would not dare to do this."

All three troopers laughed. "Yes, but he's not, is he, woman, and you're all alone. Reckon even if he was, he could not do much against the three of us." He leaned his head forward, leering at the women, "Do you?"

"You threaten like the gutter rat you are," spat back Mary, her anger welling inside her like a living thing.

"Oh," said one of the other men, "She has teeth." All three seemed to find this remark and Mary's anger amusing. The tall man hefted his now reloaded musket and stepped forward, seeking to intimidate the women.

"And what are you going to do, little miss?" It was a trick he had used many times before, using his height as a weapon. Invariably it worked. This time it did not.

More from anger than bravery, Mary stood like a rock, her grey eyes holding and returning the gaze of the lout. This close she could smell him, the mixture of sweat, leather, metal oil and gunpowder was palpable. Her voice trembled with fear and rage.

"You, I imagine, are from the garrison at Gloucester. I'm told Governor Massey takes a harsh line with his troops who molest civilians. Is that not true?"

It was not strictly true, Massey being an avid plunderer, but the name of their commanding officer and his known fanaticism where the discipline of his troops was concerned, brought a look of caution to the men's faces. They had not for the first time, decided on a little plundering for themselves whilst on patrol, this was not part of the plan. Those you were robbing were not meant to threaten you with reprisal. The unspoken question flashed across their faces as they glanced at each other. 'Could this vixen be silenced?'

Catching their look, Mary decided to push forward her brief and tentative advantage. She knew this was fraught with peril, but her anger was palpable, "Or shall you add the crime of murder to your sins?"

"Now listen," the smallest of the three men stepped forward and seeking to defuse the situation, hefted the carcass of the goat onto his shoulder. "We don't want no trouble. We'll just take this here goat to feed our poor starving bellies and be on our way." Taking the hint from his mate, the tall lout stepped back and started to move away.

"Yes 'tis only a poor stringy thing anyway, not worth troubling about, we'll just go." They began to move away, passing ribald comments and laughing nervously, seeking to hide their sudden embarrassment.

Mary did not move or speak, she was trembling with fear, and anger and knew only too well how much worse this could have been. She wanted to shout a further challenge or insult but dared not. Her mother still sobbed in her arms like a frightened child. Behind Mary, the young farm boy appeared and stared open-mouthed at the soldiers.

At the turn in the track, just before they disappeared into the woods that surrounded the holding, the tall lout turned and grinned cheekily, his bravado and fragile confidence restored, "Maybe we'll come back and see you again." His mates both chuckled.

Mary watched them go, her knees beginning to shake with relief and she let out a sob herself. Her mother raised her head and realised what was happening. They were taking her goat, something else stolen by soldiers. First, her husband and her son, now this, it was too much. Her rage swelled up again and obliterated her fear. Pulling away from Mary she began to run after them.

"You filthy, filthy swine," she screamed. "Give that back."

Taken by surprise, Mary started after her but was shocked to a standstill by another thunderous report from the musket that the tall soldier had levelled at the charging old woman. Walking away angry and embarrassed, the trooper had reacted without thinking to the unexpected threat from behind him. The heavy lead ball caught the old lady full in the chest, shattering her breastbone. She was flung ten feet backwards to fall like a broken doll in the dusty track. Dead before she hit the ground, her old fragile face bore a look of shocked surprise.

In the silence that followed as the echoes of the shot died away, nobody moved. A flock of birds clattered noisily from the nearby trees startled from their perches. Mary, the youth and the soldiers stood in a frozen tableau as the smoke from the musket gradually dissipated and wafted away. Gathering her wits, Mary ran to squat down beside her mother.

"Lord, save us," said the trooper with the goat's carcass on his shoulder, "What have you done?"

His mate turned around, smoke still oozing from the barrel of his musket. "Why did she do that?" he said. "We was leaving, no need for that. Why did she do it?" He was clearly shocked himself but gathering his wits, he turned to walk towards Mary and the broken body on the ground.

Suddenly everything changed. A horse and rider seeming huge in the confined space, crashed through the undergrowth, shocking by the suddenness of their appearance. The horse hauled to an abrupt stop and sat on its haunches its front legs sawing the air, its eyes wide and terrified. The rider, in a blur of movement, brought the large basket hilt of his drawn sword down on the head of the standing trooper who dropped like a stone, blood pouring from a deep gash in his scalp. His spent musket clattered onto the dusty track. With difficulty, the rider fought the panicked horse to a standstill and as it stood quivering, his commanding voice rang out,

"Ground your muskets!" The remaining two soldiers did as they were told, their mouths still open wide like fly traps unable to believe the suddenness of what they had just witnessed. Their weapons clattered onto the ground.

"I am going to dismount," continued the rider. "Do not move!" Sheathing his sword and drawing a pistol from the holster on his saddle, the rider dismounted. The teenage trooper holding the goat, let it slip to the floor and quietly began to cry. Moving over to Mary, the rider rested a leather-gloved hand on her shoulder.

"Mistress?" There was no reply.

"The rider knelt down beside her, vacantly she turned her head to stare at him. He had seen this look of shock many times before and recognised it for what it was. Unconsciously he drew in his breath at her beauty. As, standing slowly, she seemed to shake herself awake and peered at him again.

"Why? My mother. Why?" she whispered.

Let's go into the house, mistress," he said gently. "I'll bring… your mother."

He was surprised by the frailty of the old woman as he lifted her body. Skin and bone, disguised by voluminous skirts. As he followed Mary, he turned to bark at the two troopers who still stood motionless.

"You two, follow me and if your mate still lives, carry him with you. One of you bring my horse."

Chapter Five

Herefordshire / Taunton

Parson Roberts, a small plump man with a straggle of white unruly hair exploding from the brimmed hat that was too big for him, stood in front of the huge fireplace warming his back as he spoke. His clothes in general were black and shabby, but clean. The black stockings that fell from his knee to his cumbersome shoes were threadbare but again, clean.

"She's in a state of shock, my son," he intoned to Jacob, who lounged on the corner of the huge wooden kitchen table, one of his legs swinging idly. "I have seen it often unfortunately in these God-forsaken times." He turned and knocked his clay pipe against the iron bar from which hung a gently boiling kettle, emptying the ash into the grate.

Earlier the frightened and wide-eyed farm boy had been sent to fetch some help from the nearby village and had returned with the Parson and the Parson's wife.

The kitchen was a cosy place, incongruously reminding Jacob of his childhood. Flagstones on the floor, old black timbered mantle-piece, pewter and copper cooking pots, jugs on shelves and window ledge.

"Will she recover?" queried Jacob.

"Oh, yes," assured the little man." Lord willing. It is common enough. A good night's sleep will help and she is young and strong. But as God is my witness, this was an appalling crime." He produced a piece of cloth from somewhere and wiped his nose. "I baptised her only yesterday it seems," he announced, "And I am her godfather."

He stepped towards the table and casually broke off a piece of the still-warm loaf of bread that was there. He chewed with obvious relish before a thought occurred to him.

"Martha must just have taken this out of the oven when they came," he said uncomfortably. Not liking the thought, he hastily swallowed and sat down in the chair opposite Jacob.

"Might one enquire," he began timidly, nodding at Jacob's obvious military clothing, "Where your allegiance lies?"

Caught off-guard by the blatant bald question, Jacob bridled, "No, you may not." Seeing the frightened expression that crossed the little man of God's face, he relented somewhat, "Does it matter anymore?"

The Parson sighed, "I do not know, my son, I just wish it would end. For the love of God." He rubbed his eyes and decided to change the subject. "It was fortuitous you were near and heard the shot. Had they had time to consider their position, I doubt Mary would have been left alive to tell the tale." Again, he rubbed his eyes and tutted, "Such wickedness. What has happened to the world?" He gazed uncertainly across the table, not seeing Jacob but peering into an uncertain future in a world he no longer understood. "You were on the Gloucester to Ledbury Road, I take it, to get here so quickly?"

Jacob nodded absently, "Yes."

"That road is frequented by both Royalist and Parliamentarian patrols," persisted the little man.

"Is it so?"

"It is."

Jacob chuckled mirthlessly at the obvious fishing exercise and looked the Parson in the eye. "Very well," he acquiesced. "I am in the service of Parliament, my friend. Forgive me, I realise that for such as you it is wise to ascertain allegiances before you open your mouth." He became serious once more. "It would not do for a member of the clergy to be punished for uttering seditious statements, would it?"

Outside, it had started to rain and the pattering on the mullioned windows sounded comforting. The gentle raindrops and the crackle of the apple wood in the small fire in the grate were sounds of peace, not war. A pinecone in amongst the logs flared as the flames found it, looking like a fiery flower.

He half stood and helped himself to a grab of the still-warm bread. "My name is Jacob Sedgewick, sir, and I am an officer in the armies of Parliament and am on my way from Gloucester to rejoin my Regiment further north."

The Parson relaxed a little as he eyed the younger man. "Thank you, my son. It is true that in these terrible times, it is always advisable to know the affiliations of one whom one is in conversation with. In this way we avoid, shall we say, swampy ground."

"Indeed it does, Parson, indeed it does." Despite himself, Jacob found himself liking this portly little man with his twinkling eyes that spoke of humour. Sitting and talking with a civilian in the warmth of a farmhouse kitchen brought back memories of a simpler, happier time.

"I was passing nearby and heard the shot, I arrived just as the old woman died," he continued, picking a flake of mud from his long boots. "The rest you know."

The Parson stood slowly and resumed his stance before the hearth, gently rubbing his back. "Yes I do and may I say it is refreshing to meet someone willing to place themselves in danger for another. Many would have ridden on without bothering to investigate. Others… " he hesitated, "may even have joined in the crime."

Jacob found time to be annoyed at the inference of indifference of all military men to the plight of the local people. "There's plenty still who would help, Parson…?"

"Roberts," said the little man, "My name is Obadiah Roberts." He began once more to fill his clay pipe. "Forgive me, but of late I have seen few examples of man's goodness. Perhaps we are all made harsher by this war. Amongst my flock, such as it is, there are many good people but there are also some who have changed… for the worst." He bent his head sighing and continued to load his pipe.

Jacob did not answer but gazed at the rain on the window. Idly he watched the droplets run down the thick discoloured panes his deep-set hazel eyes pensive. He nodded sagely.

"Amongst the men of my command are some who relish violence for its own sake, but there are also many who are decent men, committed men who believe in their calling."

"It may be different when seen through the eyes of a soldier," continued the Parson, "But I live and work amongst the people, and not the rich people, but the poor, hardworking souls of this benighted realm. I have seen how they have suffered and continue to suffer. They see regiments pass by, marching hither and thither, stealing, despoiling, and worse, whilst they just want to be left alone." He looked down at his wrinkled, gnarled hands as they held his pipe and tobacco, noticing with irritation the liver spots. With a conscious effort he stopped them shaking as they did nowadays when he became angry. His voice had risen and was strident. "Once they probably did care who ruled this land of ours and were convinced or even passionate about the cause of one side or the other, but now I believe, after nearly four years, they just want it all to stop."

This was a long speech for him, as a country parson working amongst farmers and peasants, he kept his thoughts usually to himself, and he drew in a long breath to steady himself before resuming his task.

Jacob had sat silently letting the man vent his anger, now he saw that, as quickly as it had come, it had subsided, leaving the Parson deeply embarrassed. "I'm sorry, my son," said Roberts. "Small thanks for what you did today, to be lectured by an old and helpless man."

Jacob smiled and dismissed the apology with a shake of his hand. He stood and, walking to the open door, leaned on the jamb. He folded his arms and watched the swallows as they swooped and dived after flies in the evening light. The rain had stopped as quickly as it had started, and a fitful setting sun shone through a break in the clouds. 'He's right,' he thought. 'This old man behind me at the hearth, the dead woman laid out on the parlour table, the young woman upstairs sleeping restlessly, they are all victims. Wars are for kings, princes and politicians. The trouble is they are fought by ordinary people, men and woman who should be living their productive lives in peace and happiness, rearing children, laughing and loving, not killing and dying.'

Without turning, he spoke into the fading dusk, the poor light lending him a certain anonymity allowing him to speak as he had not before. To elucidate his thoughts was somehow cathartic. "I come from a farm just like this, maybe a little larger, but essentially the same. My elder brother found it not at all to his liking, too boring for a young man such as he and left us for the foreign wars a long time ago. He has probably been in his grave for years. My father never spoke of it, but I saw the anguish in his eyes. Mother had died many years before, now his eldest boy had gone." This lengthy statement had come unbidden and, perceptive as he was, the old Parson realised it was a well-rehearsed monologue that this young officer must have spoken to himself many times.

Jacob stopped and blew out his cheeks. He heard the Parson come up to stand beside him in the doorway and together they watched the dying day. A bat twittered in the gloom and he felt rather than saw the fluttering shape as it swooped past him chasing the midges.

"We kept the farm going, but then I came home one day to find the house ransacked and my father dead. Neighbours said it had been soldiers after plunder, but soldiers from where or for whom they fought they did not know. Just soldiers." He watched as a bat flitted out of the gloom again and disappeared into the eaves of the house. "So, I joined the army of Parliament. I was quite well-educated, father had insisted, and a land-owner of sorts, so rank came quickly. I thought it was safer to be a soldier than not."

He turned his head to peer down at the little man in black. "Does that make sense to you?"

"Yes," replied Roberts, "and no." He drew his hand

across his face and shook his head in despair. "I don't know. In times like these each man must follow his own conscience and trust his path is the right one." He cleared his throat and glanced at the taller man beside him. "If you will allow an old man, my son, I have thought a great deal about this and I think I know why the war continues."

Jacobs's voice was soft, "Why?"

"Because,," continued the Parson "when this war is over, if it ever is truly over, the men in control, who have the governance of us, will have risen to political power and influence through military service. So, there will always be an excuse for the war to be continued by those who do not think they have risen far enough. They will invent reasons to carry on the struggle for their own advancement."

Jacob leaned away from the door jamb and stood straight, his hands balling into fists, clenching and unclenching.

"If I thought that," he snarled, voice loud and harsh. "If I thought that… "

"What," said the Parson, studying Jacob's face intently, "What could you do?"

"Nothing," said Jacob as he realised the truth, his voice wavering with spent emotion and his head sank as he leaned back on the door jamb. Presently. he spoke again. "I suppose," he said, forming his thoughts as he spoke, "Since Marston Moor battle, perhaps even before that, the King and his advisors must realise that they have no chance of winning, only of prolonging the inevitable." He peered out at the gloom of the evening, speaking almost to himself. "Equally," he continued, "If the fools running our side would for once work together instead of pursuing their own little careers we could finish it in weeks." He gave a small harsh laugh, "and, of course, there's Cromwell, always there, always brow-beating anyone who disagrees with him, prating on about doing God's work. Dear Christ, as if killing is ever God's work." He sighed. "So it goes on and the poor fools like the poor wretch out there on the track, who could have died where he stood, or the old woman on the parlour table, they pay the price and reckoning, and always will." It was a long speech for him and he gave a deprecating half-laugh to hide his embarrassment.

Together they stood in the fading light, each deep in his own thoughts. "So, your brother is in the foreign wars?" The Parson broke the silence.

"No," said Jacob, turning once more to look at the Parson. "He must have died long since, God save him."

"And you miss him still." Roberts eyes were sharp, missing nothing.

"Father begged him to stay, but he would have none of it and, yes, he was my big brother, I miss him."

"But you've no real proof he is dead?" said the Parson, his eyes intent on the younger man's face. In the deepening dark he could only really discern the eyes.

Jacob stood upright and turned back into the kitchen, the tone of his voice signifying the conversation was over. "No, I've no proof."

The sound of the latch on the door from the stairs turned both their heads. A small plump woman, with the kind of face that tells the world she has everything under control, bustled into the kitchen. Her grey homespun dress had a collar and cuff edged with a snippet of lace, and her white apron was spotless. "She'll sleep the night through now, I gave her a draught, that is if you," she jabbed an accusing finger at her husband, "and this gentleman can keep your voices down."

The henpecked little Parson nodded and gave a weak smile. "We are well reprimanded, my dear."

"I'm going to wash Martha's body down now. Obadiah, we'll be staying the night," she bustled on into the small parlour, the small latch door closing behind her.

"My wife, Bridget," chuckled the old Parson ruefully. "I fear she bullies me terribly." His eyes wrinkled with suppressed laughter. "But perhaps we old men all deserve it."

Jacob gathered up his cloak and belongings from the table. "Well, Parson, I'll take my leave. I will sleep in the barn with our three beauties and take them back to Gloucester in the morning. I will be gone before you are awake so I will say goodbye now."

"Wait," said the Parson and striding up to Jacob took his hand between his own. "The Lord God and all his Angels keep you safe, Jacob Sedgewick," he intoned in a raised voice.

Jacob gave a little embarrassed half-laugh not sure how to respond. Finally, he settled on,

"May he look after you also, Parson Roberts," and rested his hand briefly on the old man's shoulder. Solemnly they shook hands and Jacob tramped away across the yard into the gloom. The Parson watched him go, his face unreadable and he continued to stand there long after Jacob had disappeared.

Taunton, Somerset 1645.

They sat playing cards heedless of the damp and the mud and impervious to the thin drizzle which continued to waft across the lines in grey sheets. The cloying mud soaked into their footwear and oozed from tattered boots. It stained their clothes, found its inevitable way into their scraps of food and sucked and clawed at them whenever they moved.

It had been raining now for seven days, raining without prejudice on besieged and besiegers alike. Was it not for the privations of constant hunger brought on by blockaded supplies, the men of Parliament within the walls of Taunton with at least some shelter to be found, would count themselves luckier than their Royalist counterparts who crouched like hunting dogs outside of the town's formidable defences, squelching and sodden in their maze of muddy siege trenches and gun emplacements. Some of these unfortunates, it was true, had died of exposure and a few, it was rumoured, had drowned in muddy swamps having unwittingly fallen and without the strength to claw themselves out. The common soldiery and the officer core alike were all heartily sick of Taunton town and morale amongst the Royalist army was low. Still, they sat and peered at each other across a wasteland of mud. The boredom alleviated by the occasional attack against the walls.

Sporadically, the bombardment of the town by cannon and mortar continued drawing the self-deprecating joke amongst the Royalist soldiery that they were used to living at the wrong end of a skittles alley. Robert Blake commanded Taunton for Parliament, as he had throughout the previous siege, and he had gradually fortified old walls and earthen ramparts punctuated by small but sturdy forts.

Sir John Berkely was in command of His Majesty's forces surrounding the town, the charismatic and gifted soldier, Sir Richard Grenville, who had been left in charge by the departing Goring having been badly wounded in an earlier sortie. Sir John was not a gifted soldier, his tactics were dour and unimaginative. Thus, with each failed attack, the death toll grew and morale slipped a little further.

Eight of them squatted or sprawled in a circle around the small, upturned barrel that served as a card table. They were long since drenched through and ceased to pay it any heed. Their homespun and woollen clothing retaining cold rain like a sponge. They all bore the unshaven, hopeless look of hungry tramps.

Martin Honeywell and his burly son, John, sat as ever close together sharing what meagre warmth could be had from a single worn blanket and their own body heat. They wore their battered morion-style helmets as of habit for what protection from the weather they gave, although the retaining leather thongs that, when in use, secured the headpiece under the chin, now hung down on their shoulders. The impression of vagrants was heightened by Martin's grey straggling hair and the fingerless gloves that had somehow survived the years campaigning since he and his son's impressment. Both men were stocky, although of late, the elder Martin had it seemed, decreased in size when compared to his son. They looked much alike with their open peasant faces, although the thick black hair and scraggy beard of John contrasted with the wasted shrewish look developed by his father of late.

The breeches of all eight men although of varying colours looked uniform under the general covering of mud. Stockings and shoes were likewise coated.

Behind them stacked in the usual pyramid was each man's fourteen-foot-long pike, the murderous elongated steel tips gleaming dully in the poor light. Below the pyramid was stacked their heavy breast and back plates, dented and rusting in some cases, some sporting a mottled coat of a primitive paint which was chipped and scratched.

Some way off, a gibbet sported the mouldering corpse of one Ezekiel Wells. The earthly remains of an impressed comrade who had run away some weeks ago and enjoyed three days of freedom before being recaptured and summarily executed. His mouldering body swinging idly in the fitful breeze was to serve as a warning at any other would-be deserters. A huge crow was perched on one of the cadaver's shoulders watching the card players with a liverish eye.

Peering with little interest at the cards held in his hand, John allowed a sideways glance at the profile of his father, his worry and concern for his parent etching lines around his eyes. His father had for some time now been pre-occupied and deeply troubled. Whenever John asked his father what was troubling him, he was rebuffed in the embarrassed way his father always reacted with when asked about his feelings. His only remark being that he feared something was wrong at home. He noted again that his father was not really paying attention to the game but was peering to the north concern clouding his face.

Picking his way through the sprawling soldiery and piled equipment, a sergeant slithered through the mud and camp detritus towards them, his eyes under his helmet bright with malevolence.

"You can put those cards away," he sneered. "There's work to do." He stood a little way off wary of his charges. Many, it was true, had joined the army out of conviction or political bias, but now after nearly four years of fighting, too many were pressed men who would slit his throat given the chance. The card players as one dropped their cards and struggled to stand up.

"What work?" someone said, the voice flat and fearful. The Sergeant grinned with malice relishing the effect of his news.

"There's faggots to be cut and bound. There's to be an attack this afternoon." His grin became a cackle as he enjoyed the look of horror that crossed their faces. Then he stepped backwards as they gained their feet. He would not be the first man to be badly beaten for bringing unwelcome news. But as they made no move towards him, his confidence returned and hitching up his belt, he continued

"Lots have been drawn in the usual way and you, my brave boys, are some of those chosen to carry the ladders this afternoon."

There was an audible sigh of dread. Someone uttered, "God protect us." The Sergeant began to mercilessly chivvy them away, weaving behind them like an anxious sheepdog as they trudged off.

Two hours later, Martin and John stood sullenly amongst five hundred other men who stood in ranks unheeding of the rain. They knew the tactics to be employed once again this afternoon. At the very front of the attack were the ladder bearers and musketeers, each of whom carried strapped to their back a faggot of brushwood bundled tightly together and tied with hemp. These would be thrown into the ditch immediately to the front of the defences allowing the main shock force to scramble across unhindered.

Behind these were the dismounted dragoons, their once colourful clothing now ragged and faded, giving them the appearance of flamboyant tramps. Their job was to swarm over the rampart defences using the ladders if necessary and gain a foothold until the heavy pikemen arrived. Pikemen without pikes, it must be said, for they would be far too unwieldy for this day's work. Rather, they would fight with short lethal stabbing swords, or mauls and hammers or anything that could kill in a confined space.

The whole phalanx now stood some one hundred yards long in the downpour peering forward at the defences two hundred yards away. They could see from here that the ramparts were swarming with helmeted heads jostling for position for a better view. The smell of gun powder in the air and the obvious massing of troops, had given them ample warning of an attack.

A small grey-haired man with a thin weather-beaten face swore obscenely and turned to look backwards standing on tiptoe the better to see. His movement brought the inevitable rattle of wood as his apostles knocked against each other.

"Damned rain," he muttered, as he caught John's eye. "My powders so damp I doubt this thing will fire at all." He shook the cumbersome musket that he cradled upside down in his arms in an attempt to keep the flash pan dry.

John nodded sympathetically and turned to his father who held the other side of the heavy ladder.

Martin was praying, his eyes closed tightly, lips moving soundlessly as the rain ran down his face. John felt a surge of protective affection for the ageing man and he had to turn hurriedly away in case his father opened his eyes and saw his look of concern. The little musketeer unlaced his breeches and, without ceremony, urinated up the ladder

"There you are, son," he chortled, "that's for good luck today." Many around about burst into grim laughter. A fat man behind John similarly added his libation to the ladder.

"I'll wish you luck as well, mate," he grinned, "and me," added another. As the inevitable chaplain arrived, there were five or six soldiers baptising the lucky ladder. Many were laughing and even Martin had ceased praying and was smiling softly.

Pompously without preamble, the black clad chaplain raised his hand and intoned in a loud voice, "The Lord of Hosts, He knoweth and Israel shall know. If it be in rebellion or if in transgression against our Lord, save us not this day."

Martin leaned forward, thrusting his face close to the black clad figure. "Go away, sir, please. We all wish to be saved this day and will trust in God without your prompting." There was a muttered growl of agreement from many who heard.

Unperturbed, the chaplain smiled indulgently. "To die in martyrdom for a just and noble cause is a holy thing, soldier." Elbowing past John, the little grey-haired musketeer spat at the ground.

"Martyrdom and suffering are only thought of as holy by those who have not tried them, Reverend."

The chaplain took a wary step backwards. "And yet, my son, did not Christ save the world by suffering?"

"And was it worth it?" snarled Martin, losing patience now. Before the chaplain could answer, someone else behind shouted,

"Christ did not have a wife or children who depended on him, sir."

Colour suffused the chaplain's face. "You blaspheme!" he snarled. "May the good Lord in his wisdom have mercy on you."

"Think you that our Lord has anything to do with this?" shouted the little musketeer. "God is in his heaven and we are down here. God's grace and mercy will not help us."

The chaplain's face had grown stern. "You would all do well," he shouted, "To ask for our Lord God's forgiveness this day. I will pray for your souls." Kneeling in the mud he raised his face and his arms to the sky. "Oh Lord," he boomed. "Look kindly on us sinners… "

His words were drowned in a howling cacophony of noise as every cannon and mortar in the line opened up against the defences. The very ground shook as huge balls of metal and stone were hurled forward as a precursor to the attack. The air became heavy with thick acrid powder smoke that stung the eyes and choked the throat. All along the line, musketeers added to the pall as they lit the length of rope-like match that they all carried to fire their muskets with. Once lit, these would smoulder for some time. The smell of saltpetre became cloying.

Some form of chanting started away to John's left and encouraged by officers attempting to inject some fervour into their troops, spread desultorily down the line. But it was soon drowned out by the crashing of the guns and quickly degenerated into catcalls and taunts. Fists were raised and shaken at the defenders and obscenities roared. Martin, quite unmoved by the tumult, gazed around him in mute disbelief at how quickly anger and ferocity overtook mute stolid acceptance. He had seen this many times during the last year, but it still amazed him. What had, only moments ago, been a group of sane quiet men was becoming a rabid animal eager for blood. Drums to the rear began to thunder, adding to the cacophony and someone shouted that the colours were out.

The small musketeer grinned up at John who was pulling his leather gauntlets on tighter. "Done this before, son?" he shouted.

John shook his head. "Not this far forward and never with a ladder."

"Take some advice then." Out of the corner of his eye, John sensed his father turn to listen. "Don't stop for anything, you with me? Anything at all." They all ducked as a mortar exploded in the rear, a sign of incompetent gunners. Shards of red-hot metal from the shattered barrel hissed overhead and even from there they could hear the screams of the maimed crew through the din.

"Another thing," shouted the little man. "When… if you get there, do not stand under the ladder, stand well to the sides." Seeing their blank faces. "They'll throw anything they can down on the ladders; rocks, boiling water, hot oil, even sewage. I've seen it done."

Martin leaned over and extended his hand. "I'd like to shake your hand, friend, and wish you good luck." Incredibly he smiled.

"I'll accept it right gladly," said the little man as solemnly they shook. The musketeer pulled his floppy hat down low over his brow. "Not long now I'm thinking," he said and bent to light the length of match he carried by striking a flint.

Somewhere further down the line, an officer shouted at the top of his voice, "Come on then, lads, let's go!" With a yell, the whole line swung forward driven on by the thunder of the drums. The shouting increased as they neared the rearing defences.

John could see nothing but the heaving shoulders and homespun coat of the man in front of him but had no time to think too much about it as he and his father wrestled to hold the heavy cumbersome ladder aloft and not trip over their own feet. He could hear nothing now but the pounding of his own heart, so loud that he thought someone else must hear it. He and his father tried to weave as best they could, but it was not easy when every running sweating man was trying to do the same. He was not aware of how close to the ramparts they were until suddenly they reared up before him. Immediately to his front, a man fell sprawling clutching his neck which welled blood, John was just able to step over him, noting the eyes of the unfortunate wide with terror and pain.

The ditch to his front was already half-filled with the brushwood faggots and the earthen ramparts here were not high but topped with hastily thrown-up stone blocks, unmortared and falling apart. He and his father managed to lean the ladder over the ditch and wedge it against the stones. Helmeted heads peered down at them and John felt rather than heard a musket ball whip by close to his head.

A rank of musketeers appeared behind him and, at a shouted command, every one of them rammed his five foot long 'rest' into the ground, levelled their muskets atop the rests and a crashing volley hammered out. Immediately, piratical looking dragoons appeared out of the smoke and swarmed up the ladders now placed all along the defences. They clutched a variety of weapons; pistols, knives, swords, some even held second weapons in their teeth and appeared to grin wolfishly as they went up.

Standing wide-eyed chest heaving, Martin found time to peer across at his father who nodded breathlessly back at him. There was no need for words even if they could have been heard amidst the din. Martin was saying, 'so far so good,'

Some dragoons held primitive 'grenadoes' which they hurled over the top of the ramparts before following with a yell. One such missed its target and bounced back down amongst the scrambling men at the foot of a ladder. It exploded thunderously causing a musketeer's clattering apostles full of powder to explode with it. The smell of warm blood mixed with the gunpowder smoke whilst fresh screams filled the air.

A dragoon put his foot on the lowest rung of Martin's ladder and paused to wink hugely at him. As he did so, a musket ball hit his lower arm taking it off at the elbow and, with a shrill disbelieving cry, he fell writhing to the ground, screaming repeatedly mechanically. Martin, already covered with the man's blood knelt to help him, but was reprimanded by a bellowing Sergeant some yards away, "Never mind him, hold that bloody ladder."

More and more men flooded up the ladders and it appeared at first as if they were gaining a foothold. The confused melee on the top of the ramparts heaved to and fro amidst screamed invective, cries of pain, musket and pistol discharges and the clash of steel. More and more defenders were arriving by the minute and suddenly, John and Martin staring wide-eyed at the chaos, discerned that more men were now sliding back down the ladders than were going up. Casualties, some of them horribly wounded, were being thrown callously over the ramparts to fall like broken rag dolls amongst the trampled brushwood faggots in the ditch. A florid thick-set youth of about sixteen fell almost at John's feet who clearly heard the loud snap as his back was broken. The youth's dull face stared up at John, full of surprise and incomprehension, turning to sadness as he coughed hugely and died.

A section of the wall a little away from them exploded outwards, sending lumps of masonry and flotsam in all directions. A dragoon, one leg blown off below the knee, hobbled out of the smoke and raising his fist, screamed back at the Royalist line, "Stop firing, you bastards, stop firing!"

All down the line now, men were beginning to run away, some of them hobbled as best they could, those more gravely wounded crawled. Those too injured to move, screamed for help at their erstwhile comrades who ran unheeding past them.

Martin and John took their cue and turned themselves to jog as quickly as they could away from the blood-soaked ground. Behind them a cacophony of jeering and catcalls could be heard as the defenders laughed and cheered them on their way.

Martin almost tripped over the prone corpse of the little grey-haired man who had anointed their ladder. The left side of his face had been blown off and he was stone dead. The one remaining eye stared with surprise at the sky. Martin turned to point out the dead man to his son but John did not see, so intent on running and weaving was he.

Then, through the noise, dimly heard at first but growing stronger with each passing minute, could be heard the psalm chanted by the men of Parliament in times of victory.

"Babylon is fallen, is fallen, is fallen, Babylon is fallen, to rise no more." It did not stop until long after the Royalist attackers were back in their muddy trenches.

Much later, when the day had turned to night, they were once again sprawled around a meagre fire that someone had managed to light from scrounged scraps of wood and turf. Two of the card players that had been with them only hours before would never be playing cards again. A slow drizzle had set in as darkness fell and with it a damp light breeze. The rain fell into the thin gruel that they had been given and diluted even further the thin poor stuff. Still, it was almost warm and welcome.

Out in the darkness, flaming torches held high, small parties of soldiers criss-crossed no man's land searching for those who survived. The rain gave some relief to the parched throats of the dying who lay patiently, hoping to be found, or perhaps lay resigned, content to give themselves up to God.

Martin and John sat once more huddled together under the single threadbare blanket. They and their companions stared dully into the small flame, the horrors of the day keeping sleep away. John put his arm around the thin shoulders of his father and was concerned to note how much thinner his father felt during the last few weeks. More, he was concerned that once more the old man had sunken into the sullen despond that was his of late. He risked a sideways glance again at his father's profile and did not like what he saw. Behind them, ghoulishly lit by firelight, a procession of wounded; some able to walk unaided, some half-carried by companions, made their way to the small ramshackle cottage some way off where surgeons worked. The occasional scream could be heard from the sad little dwelling.

The man next to them finally fell sideways and lay snoring in the mud. John knew him to be a cobbler from Bristol, a kindly man who had a wife and five daughters somewhere. He leaned down and gently lifted the man's head onto a piece of sacking to ensure he did not drown in his sleep. Then, having satisfied himself that he could do no more, he returned his arm around his unheeding father.

Somewhere in the distance a cow lowed mournfully and he found the time to be amazed that farming life was continuing as normal elsewhere. Milking was done every morning, animals were fed, crops were planted and reaped, wives chatted to each other at markets, children went to school, merchants made deals, life went on, and all whilst he and his father were stuck in this nightmare. He glanced at his father, the old man's face in the firelight showed deep crow's feet under the eyes and two deep grooves from nose to the corners of his mouth. He looked a hundred years old.

"Pa?"

No answer

"Pa, are you okay?"

Slowly, Martin turned his head. "What did you say, son?"

These two had had for many years the traditional father-son relationship as they filled the daylight hours with work on the farm, and night times in shared companionship with Martha and Mary, the mother and daughter, as they sat and conversed in low tones around the kitchen range, or on Sundays in the parlour whilst Martin smoked his clay pipe. John had found distressingly of late that ,after a year, he could not really remember the face of his younger sister, but strangely his mother's face was ever clearer.

"I asked if you were okay, Pa."

His father snorted contemptuously. "As well as I'll ever be after a day like that. I've been sitting here thinking, what's it all for. Do they really think God sees all this?"

John retrieved his arm feeling suddenly embarrassed. "I dunno, Pa. I think we've just got to get through it and go home. As to what it's all about, that's more than we know or should ask about. Maybe old Parson Roberts will be able to tell us when we get back."

Despite himself, Martin smiled at the memory. "Parson Roberts is a good man. Christ, what would he have made of today?" He shivered and, picking up a twig at his feet, threw it into the flames. "Do you know, son, I don't think that good old man has ever left the village." He sighed. "It's given me some comfort to know that he is there to be of some aid to Martha and young Mary, if the need arises."

John nodded. "Yes, he will and so will many others back there, Pa. Be at ease a little. We will get back there, a man would drive himself mad to think otherwise." He was struggling to sound convincing despite being far from sure himself.

Martin half-smiled in the darkness and cleared his throat to hide his concern. "I know, son, I know," he repeated. He chewed his lip in a more and more frequent nervous gesture. "But when you have been married as long as your Ma and I, you develop a feeling, a sense of the other. I could never explain it the way scholars do, never at all, but I have known, felt for some time now something is wrong." He turned his head once more away from his son and the firelight to look to the north. "Something is wrong."

Chapter 6

Gloucester / Taunton, Late May 1645

Jacob's footsteps rang loudly on the wet cobblestones as he tramped through the dark, narrow Gloucester streets. It was long past the curfew and chains were thrown across every street corner to trip the unwary. Here and there fitful lamplight shone from an upstairs window, illuminating a small fragment of the street below. He jumped, dragged suddenly from his dark thoughts as a rat ran across his feet pursued by a mangy cat.

His head ached and he cursed himself for a fool to be out alone at this hour. It was dangerous to walk through a garrison town like Gloucester after dark. How many times had he heard stories of unwary troopers found dead in an alley in the cold light of dawn, their throats cut, their money, boots and clothing taken by desperate thieves eager to sell whatever they could for food or ale.

It had been a terrible day. He was not a lecherous person when compared to the casual sexual encounters of his peers in the army that he knew, but he had needed intimate contact with another human being following the events of this day and had sought solace and human comfort with an elderly, willing… whore whose kindly face he could now not recall in any detail, save for the unusual feature of one blue eye and one green. His horror had welled up inside him and he had fallen asleep against the woman before he could undress properly, some maternal instinct in the woman allowed him to sleep, time had passed too swiftly and now he was late. Inelegantly, he gagged and spat.

Neither was he a drinker and the effects of too much rot-gut ale were churning now in his stomach. He stumbled over an unseen pile of refuse and almost fell. Swearing vilely at the world in general and at himself, he leaned feebly against a house wall to gather his wits, then breathing deeply, straightened and continued on his way.

He had heard of the punishment, of course, and knew it was a widespread military practise but had never had to view it up close. He rubbed his forehead as again he heard the terrible screams and smelt the charring flesh. Suddenly it was too much and he vomited into the central drain of the street, cursing weakly as he splashed his own boots. Having voided the entire contents of his stomach he felt marginally better and stood to straighten his jacket and reseat his hat, breathing deeply.

Returning from Honeywell farm and the events of that afternoon two weeks ago, he had duly delivered his dispirited and bedraggled prisoners to the deputy advocate's office in the town. Cursorily he was told to keep himself available to give evidence if needed. So, it was with a groan of resignation he had reported once again to the cadaverous Major Wilmott and found himself temporarily seconded onto his staff and, to his disgust, given a multitude of minor tasks to attend to.

He soon found himself both hating and fearing his chilly, pedantic superior. On many occasions, he found the tall Major casting strange, unfathomable glances in his direction and he puzzled at their meaning and the reason why he was given one onerous task after another. Wilmott seemed for some reason to actively dislike Jacob, who had no idea why, and thus their infrequent conversations were always terse and brief.

"You will attend the hearing on my behalf," Wilmott had barked at Jacob this morning, "and if sentence is pronounced, you will stay to witness its execution. Is that clear?" The hard eyes had bored into Jacob who stared stonily ahead.

"Yes, sir," he intoned.

"You will then report immediately back to me. I wish to know the outcome of this little fiasco directly. Those creatures mouthing their slanderous creed are under my command and I will not have my reputation defiled."

"Very good, sir."

He had failed to carry out this order so far. His only thought, following the trial and punishment, was to get drunk as soon as possible as he stumbled away from the crowded noisome cellar where together with fourteen other 'witnesses,' he had watched the brief military trial of two troopers for sedition. He then watched as the wretches were strapped to planks and bored through the tongue with hot irons.

Wrenching his thoughts from the scene once more, he realised it had started to rain, a dull persistent whispering drizzle. Removing his hat, he gazed up at the dark sky, enjoying the cool refreshing rain on his face. He rubbed his eyes. This would not do. "Come on now," he muttered to himself. Cautiously he moved off, picking his way past a snoring drunk in a set of stocks who seemed impervious to the sewage and offal that surrounded and covered him. Again, he felt his stomach churn but managed, with a great effort, not to vomit once more. Christ and his Angels, what a day.

Twice, before he reached the house which served as the Regimental headquarters, he had to hide in shadows to avoid the unwelcome attentions of watch patrols who tramped by, their flaming torches held high. He was an officer in the Parliamentary army and thus should have escaped punishment or a summary beating for being abroad after curfew, but one never knew.

Walking into the large downstairs lounge of the headquarters, Jacob was amazed that even at this hour, there were still a few drink befuddled officers slouched over tables conversing in muted tones. Here and there a recumbent figure snored quietly. The air was thick with smoke and the smell of stale wine. Jacob stood staring around him owlishly in the dim light unsure of his duty.

A Captain glanced up from lighting his long clay pipe, "Sedgewick," he drawled, "I was unsure whether you would be back tonight."

Jacob removed his hat. "No, sir, neither was I. But the Major asked for my report as soon as I returned."

"There were some people here looking for you a little earlier. I told them I did not think you would return tonight, but they insisted on staying. They are in the back room there." The Captain jerked his head at a door on the far side of the room.

Jacob found time to be puzzled, 'who would be looking for him?' before his overriding fear of Wilmott returned.

"I must report to the Major first," he persisted. "Is he in his quarters?"

A strange questing furtive look crossed the Captain's face. "He is. Is he expecting you at this hour?"

Jacob sighed, "I imagine not." One or two heads were raised as his brother officers heard snatches of the conversation.

"Go on up," one of them sneered. "He will be pleased, I guarantee it." Jacob turned to move to the stairs.

"Sedgewick," the Captain's voice halted him.

"Yes, sir?"

The Captain held his gaze for a moment and then shrugged. "Nothing. Carry on." He turned away.

Still pondering the strange glances, Jacob climbed the stairs and tramped down the narrow corridor to the

Major's room. He tapped the door gently. There was no answer, so he tapped again louder this time.

There was an irritated exclamation from within and the door was flung open.

"Yes?" Wilmott was in shirt sleeves and stockinged feet. His riding boots flung casually against the far wall of the small room. He eyes red-rimmed from too much wine bored into Jacob.

Jacob began to stutter an apology but, at the same time, noticed over Wilmott's shoulder a young subaltern also in shirt sleeves casually lounging on the rickety four-poster bed. It was something about the attitude of the youth that aroused a looming suspicion, the languid air, the casual appearance of Wilmott.

Suddenly, with a rush of intuition and realisation, Jacob understood. The strange glances from the Major, the sneers of his brother officers and their obscure remarks during the last two weeks, the odd smothered laughter he had heard, now it all made sense. He had been aware of rumours during his young life of men who preferred the company of other men and were aroused not at all by women. He was unsure if these were just stories, as such behaviour was condemned by God. He cursed himself for a fool, how could he have been so gullible and naive? His officer was a pederast.

Far too late, he began to stammer an apology. In that second, Wilmott had noted the flash of revulsion and understanding that glittered across the far too handsome face of this young insolent puppy of a junior officer.

"Silence!" Wilmott's voice was a whiplash. "How dare you arrive at my door at this hour, drunken and dishevelled". Stepping forward, he forced Jacob backwards across the corridor until the wooden panelling of the opposite wall stopped him. He leaned forward, his long greasy hair swinging like drapes, his dark eyes liquid with dislike and malice.

"You will return here at noon tomorrow," he sneered, his yellow teeth much in evidence, "When you will give a full and faultless report of today's proceedings."

A hand gripped Jacobs throat like a vice. "Is that clear?"

Jacob, struggling for breath, was able to nod his head. Sedgwick held his gaze for a moment longer before Wilmott, turning on his heel, stalked back into his room, slamming the door behind him.

Stunned, Jacob stared at the closed door, massaging his neck. He had never seen such hatred in a man's face before and he was afraid. Suddenly, his stomach heaved once more and he stumbled down the corridor, scrambled down the stairs and throwing wide the small, mullioned window at the bottom, vomited into the alley which sided the house. He leaned weakly on the lintel whilst he regained his composure. Christ, what a day. He was sweating, his hat felt too tight.

"Jacob, are you ill?"

The concerned voice at his shoulder startled Jacob and he slowly turned. A small portly figure dressed in black took a step forward and the dim candle-light fell on the kindly, concerned old face.

"Why, Parson Roberts?" mouthed Jacob, genuine pleasure in his voice. "What do you do here?"

The elder man took hold of Jacob's arm. "I repeat, my son, are you ill?"

"No, sir, merely a surfeit of wine, I assure you." He straightened his jerkin and, taking the Parsons elbow, moved away from the window. "Come, we'll share a glass of wine, I sorely need one."

The little man restrained Jacob with a hand to his chest. "Jacob there is someone else with me."

"Oh… who?"

"Young Mary Honeywell."

The image flashed into Jacob's mind of the startlingly beautiful young woman with the silver blond hair who had been in shock when he last saw her and barely able to speak.

"Here? Good God man, you have brought her to such a place as this, are you from your wits?"

"No, my son, she has been obsessed with the idea of thanking you for her life since that terrible day. I and my wife have tried to dissuade her, but she will not have it and threatened to come alone if I did not relent. At first I thought she was raving, but I now realise having lost her father, brother and mother,she feels a debt to you and it has become of paramount importance in her young life to find and thank you."

He spread his hands in a hopeless gesture. "I have

known her to be wilful and headstrong since the day she was born, so," he sighed. "Here we are."

Seeing the deepening frown on Jacob's face, he hurriedly continued, "Is it such a terrible thing to be thanked for a beautiful woman's life, Jacob Sedgewick?"

It had been a long and eventful day and Jacob's resistance was at its limit. His shoulders sagged in surrender, "No, sir," he half-laughed. "I suppose it is not."

"Thank God, you are still here," said the Parson, as they moved across the dishevelled room to the far door. "I thought perhaps you would have left some days ago."

"No," said Jacob, glancing at the stairs. "I was... Detained."

It was a night that Jacob was to remember for the rest of his life. He went with the Parson and was introduced formerly to Mary Honeywell. The soft yellow lamplight accentuated the beauty and calm assurance of the soberly-dressed young woman who sat waiting for them. Her long blond hair the colour of wheat in the sun glowed lustrously, whilst her cool grey eyes gazed into Jacobs with startling frankness. When she spoke, her voice was low pitched and husky. Her grief was with her still, but she bore it bravely.

Over the last two weeks since that terrible day she had faced her grief, struggled with it and mastered it. All her tears were shed, there would be no more. She was grave at first, courteously thanking him for his actions that day and when it was done, visibly relaxing, as if this final task brought to an end the terrible episode that had turned her young life upside-down. She had paid her debts to the past, and now, hopefully, could look forward.

They talked of many things that night; the beautiful young woman, the soldier and the Parson. They talked of serious things and of trivial things, of war and politics and religion. As the night wore on and the sky turned pale outside the windows, the Parson fell asleep in his chair and snored softly. Their conversation became more intimate. Drawn to each other as to a refuge from the… chaos around them, the two young people told of their lives, their dreams and their hopes. It was as if meeting a kindred spirit for the first time in their lives, each was eager to confess themselves to the other. To cleanse themselves of the world's ills, to seek solace in each other, by laying open their innermost thoughts and fears. She told him of her plans to go south, despite the insanity of such a rash undertaking, to seek out her father and her brother, if they still lived, God willing. He told her of his life since the death of his father some years ago, how he had sold up the small farm where he had grown up and gone to seek his fortune as a soldier. Finally, he told her of his missing elder brother, Ethan, the last relative he had, probably long dead in the foreign wars. She saw with the eyes of one newly-acquainted with grief that this subject of his brother was most painful to him, that it was an open ever-present wound and, gently probing, she drew out his pain. Having met only hours before, it was as if they had already begun to guess at affection and love.

Slowly around them, the new day dawned and the sounds of a waking city permeated into the little room. The guttering candles were extinguished being no longer needed. They sat holding hands and enjoyed the companionable silence between them. Occasionally, they would shyly peer at one another and they would smile.

Finally, they woke the Parson who complained grumpily of aching joints as old people do. Jacob mollified the little man and insisted they have his room for the day to rest whilst he returned to his duties.

What he now knew, even if he had not fully admitted it yet to himself, was that if allowed, he would stay with Massey and, unfortunately, with Wilmott. He would stay with the army in Gloucester and endure the degradations that the Major was bound to subject him to after the events of last night. For to stay here was to remain close to Mary. He watched the pair climb the stairs to his room, the old man in black and the beautiful young woman who helped him and, as he turned to leave the building, he was smiling. For the first time in his life, Jacob Sedgewick was guessing at love.

In mid-May, General Edward Massey was ordered by the self-styled 'Committee of Both Kingdoms' at Westminster to move as soon as possible and in full strength into the West Country.

'There, to create havoc and Divers diversions that will occupy to the fullest extent those forces therein, commanded by Lord Goring.'

Massey himself, eager to do what damage he could to the Royalist cause, was ever the true professional and determined, before he left for the west country, to take by stealth or storm the formidable Royalist fortress of Evesham Town, with its important river crossing. The loss of this garrison would deal a serious blow to the King, severing, as it would, easy communications between Oxford and Worcester and thence to South Wales. He felt, in addition to its tactical advantages, it would act as a fitting epitaph to his efforts and successes in the midlands, leaving, as it would, all convoys and troop movements on their way to the King, subject to unhampered attack.

For many days, Gloucester became a hive of frantic activity as preparations were made for departure. Reinforcements arrived from London, bringing the total number under the command of Massey to around four-thousand men. Troopers, musketeers, pikemen, cavalry, gunners, smithies, cooks, engineers, physicians and members of the ever-present clergy, all preparing to march to war.

During those days of confusion, Jacob requested via Major Wilmott, permission to stay with the army of Massey and march with him into the West Country. It was a small matter amongst so many and it took only minutes for a sneering Wilmott to agree. Possibly he was already planning the demise of the hated young man whom he lusted after but realised was not for him. His eyes bleak with contempt and loathing, followed the retreating figure of Jacob as he left the brief meeting.

Ignoring the icy sarcasm of agreement to his request, Jacob was nevertheless elated as he told Parson Roberts and Mary his news, for it meant that he could keep them both close by him as they journeyed on business of their own along the same route to the south. The Parson, already in mortal fear of the journey, agreed with relief that it would be far safer for the pair to travel at the rear of the army amongst the baggage, the wives, and the inevitable whores, who trailed after any army. Safety in numbers was what the Parson thanked his God for and Mary agreed as a matter of common good sense.

It had taken all of Jacob's persuasive skills to keep her here for this long. The urgent desire to find her father and her brother stronger even that of her confessed feelings for him. Their relationship had blossomed during the last few weeks and it was now an unvoiced understanding that, when this journey was at an end, they would turn their thoughts to a more lasting arrangement of their own. The quiet assurance and simple beauty of the woman seemed to Jacob to be above the horrors and degradations of the world in which he livedand, as young men will, he had placed her on a pedestal. She was his comfort and his confessor, the balm to sooth his soul, whilst he to her was the kind of love she had never known. The love of parents and kin were magical in their own right, but never before had she known the fierce all-consuming love that she was beginning to feel for this young man with his intense eyes and ready laugh.

It was an age in which carnal love was considered a sin and sexual relations before marriage were rare. God was feared and, for such a sin, one would surely go to Hell. Nevertheless, Parson Roberts was ever watchful, fearing that the young people he had come to regard above all others would be swept away in the surge of their own desires if he were not ever vigilant. He was God's watch dog and he would not fail in his duty.

The morning of the 23rd May dawned fresh and fine. The dew on the grass just outside the city walls glinted in the early sunlight. Slowly, the huge wooden gates creaked open and a river of men, horses, wagons, and baggage streamed forth, the rising sun throwing huge, elongated shadows out behind them. The air became full of the shouts of men, the whinny of horses, the jingle of harness and the rumble and screech of wagons. Above them on the stone walls, hundreds of cheering citizens vied for a better position, elbowing and shoving each other in their eagerness to view the sight below as they squinted through the rising dust into the low sunlight. They watched the snaking column march away towards the Evesham Road, helmets glinting and banners waving tramping to the thunder of drums.

Those that remained to watch as the baggage train

and camp followers trailed out of the gates in the wake of the army could perceive, if they peered hard enough, a tall young woman in homespun grey clothes with silver blond hair escaping from her calico bonnet, matching her long stride to the smaller plumper figure of the old man in black who hurried along beside her aided by a wooden staff.

"But, sir, if you please, it will kill him, he is an old man." John's voice was shrill with concern and desperation, as he stood before the camp table his arms pinioned at his side by burly sergeants.

The middle-aged Major, who sat with two other officers behind the rickety wooden table set up in the open air beneath the huge elm tree, stared impatiently up at the man before him and tapped his fingers with irritation. These proceedings were always tedious and to hear 'appeals' annoyed him as they would inevitably lengthen the time taken. Regimental justice was being meted out this windy sunlit morning. The table at which they sat formed one side of a square, the other three sides formed by ranks of stony-faced soldiery, contingents drawn from each regiment present, here to be witnesses.

Half a mile behind them, the grey walls of Taunton reared still resolutely defying, some would say mocking, all of the costly efforts to force an entry during the last weeks.

Behind John, stood the motley group of prisoners who were to be judged this morning for a variety of crimes; theft, rape, insubordination, and in Martin Honeywell's case, desertion.

The sentence could have been the gallows but for whatever reason, possibly the opinion of the major that Honeywell was not right in the head, it had been commuted to fifty lashes. It was as this sentence was announced that his son, John, had stepped forward, in so doing, risking his own life and told all present that his father had become ill of late with the obsession that something had happened at his home and that his family were in dire straits.

Throughout it all, the prisoner in question stood unmoved, looking at the ground, his grey wispy hair fluttering in the breeze. Around the sullen prisoners stood three or four sergeants who, bored with proceedings, lounged idly on their halberds and watched with casual disinterest.

Briefly, the officers at the table conferred after hearing John's plea. "We have heard your explanation of your father's behaviour," said the Major finally. "We understand that since this unfortunate obsession gained control he has been somewhat... difficult, in fact, we feel the term deranged would not be a slander." His gaze flitted to Martin who stood unmoved seeming not to hear. "Nevertheless, discipline must be maintained in His Majesty's armies and soldiers, for whatever reason, cannot be allowed to just leave and go home. I think I speak for all when I tell you that we all have had desire at some time to be quit of this terrible place," he cleared his throat ready to pronounce sentence and raised his voice, "but we cannot have it soldier, we cannot. It is, therefore, our decision that tomorrow morning, Martin Honeywell will be stripped of his clothing save only his breeches and before the assembled regiment will run the Cantaloupe." Here he paused and gazed back up into the face of John, "And you, Jonathon Honeywell, for the heinous crime of interrupting these proceedings and speaking disrespectfully to an officer, will run it with him. Take them away and bring forward the next case."

They had been trussed like chickens, hand and feet, the night before, lying on the cold hard earth floor of the woodshed behind the inn that served as a temporary regimental headquarters

Awaking from a fitful sleep, John peered through the gloom at the recumbent figure of his father who lay a few feet away. It was almost dawn, he could tell that from the fitful light that filtered through the rickety wooden shutters.

"Pa? Pa, are you awake?

"Yes, son. I'm awake. The voice was toneless, flat. I was thinking of home."

John's heart sank. "Pa," he said as gently as he could. "You have to stop this, it's madness else." His father did not answer. "Pa, try to prepare yourself for the Cantaloupe."

"The cantaloupe." Martin snorted, contempt thickening his voice. "They are only inflicting pain and humiliation on us because I wanted to go home." With a stifled grown he sat up leaning his back against the wall. "Because I wanted to be a man again and not some frightened rabbit obeying their every ridiculous order." His voice hardened and took on some of the old tone that John remembered. In spite of himself, he smiled; this was more like the father he remembered.

"Do they think," Martin continued, "that God doesn't see all of this?"

Now it was John's turn to snort. "I don't think God has anything to do with us at the moment, Pa."

He would have spoken further but, without warning, the rickety door crashed open and they were half-carried half-shoved outside still blinking sleep from their eyes. An elderly sergeant with thinning grey hair stood waiting for them. His ears at some point had been cropped for a long-forgotten felony and it gave him the look of an evil perky elf. Although he was brisk, his tone was not unsympathetic.

"'Morning, lads," he said breezily. "All ready are we?" rubbing his hands together.

Neither Martin nor John answered and the Sergeant's face took on a pained expression. "Come now, it's not that bad, is it? You two are famous now, you know, probably half the army turning out to watch."

He signalled to the troopers to untie their hands and feet and continued in the same vein. "Take me, for instance," he said. "I've been a soldier for half my life, but I've only seen this done once before. That was under the King of the yellow coats himself, old Gustavus Adolphus, just before the battle of Nordlingen."

"Take off their clothes," he rasped at his men, "all except the breeks." Seeing that all was being done as instructed, he returned to his theme. "That Major, the one who sentenced you, he was in Saxony, I'll bet that's where he got the idea." He nodded to himself. "Yes, I'll bet that's it."

John and Martin stood rubbing twine-pinched wrists as circulation returned. John was looking around him to see if he knew any of the troopers. Martin showed no interest, his attention being on the scudding clouds that wafted across the pink dawn sky.

"Right," said the Sergeant with one final check on his prisoners. "Let's go."

Orders were rapped out and between two files of soldiers, they were marched towards open ground beyond the village, where hundreds of soldiers were standing in clumps and groups awaiting them. As they arrived, much to the consternation of the Sergeant and the small knot of officers, there was the odd shout from amongst the crowd. "Good luck, lads!" or "God save you, boys!"

At the centre of the crowd stood two rows of soldiers from the Major's own troop. The two rows were facing each other forming a narrow corridor about forty yards long. Each trooper held a cudgel, some small and thin, some thick as a man's arm. In the growing light their faces were grim. Each man would do his duty, however obnoxious he found it to be.

Martin and John were positioned at one end of the corridor and told they must make it to the other end. All was quiet now, only the sighing of the small wind disturbed the silence. The Major raised his voice to speak above the buffeting breeze.

"We are here today," he pitched his voice to reach the furthest edges of the crowd. "To witness the punishment which, until this place has fallen, will be the lot of any man who deserts our ranks for any reason whatsoever." He paused to refill his lungs. "Most of you will have heard of it, though none, I'll wager, have seen it. This then is your chance. Let it serve as a warning!" There had been angry scenes last evening at the headquarters' inn as the Colonel had voiced his displeasure at 'a foreign nonsense of a punishment being doled out to Englishmen.' However, the sentence had been allowed grudgingly to stand to avoid undermining the Major and spreading dissension amongst the lower ranks.

"Tell your comrades throughout the army what has occurred here." The Major concluded and, stepping back, nodded to the Sergeant.

Once more, there was complete silence. John could hear the whispering and sighing of the wind in the trees which stood hard by. He took one last glance up at the sky and breathed deeply.

"Now!" shouted the Sergeant and shoved both Martin and John forward.

After the first few blows on his naked back, John ceased to feel anything at all, his only thought, bent almost double and staggering, was to keep moving forward. Ignore the pain, just keep moving forward. One mistimed blow hit him cleanly on the back of his head and he fell forward, his mouth biting grass and earth. Sucking in a lungful of air, he fought to regain his feet, senses swimming. Somehow, he made it and, beneath a barrage of blows, began to move forward again. Dimly, he was aware of a torrent of noise that beat at his ears as thousands of raised voices urged him on. Excited, desperate voices that had made him their champion, their hope. Another blow struck his forehead and he went down again, blood flowing down his face, blows still hammering his back and legs.

'That's it,' he thought, 'I'm done for.' He lowered his head and closed his eyes.

A hoarse cry jerked him back to consciousness and, raising his head to look back, he saw his father was down some yards back and taking punishment. Anger like a scalding, boiling liquid welled up in John's throat and, with a yell, he got to his feet and, screaming like a maniac directly into the faces of his startled assailants, staggered back and, with difficulty, lifted the prone figure of his father over his shoulder. Years of hard unyielding work on the farm since his childhood had given him a strong body which, after months in the field with the army, was immensely powerful. Screaming his rage at the sky, he started to move forward again inch by inch, yard by yard, ever closer to the end of the corridor.

Until the day he died, John could never remember how he had made that walk. It was an effort that cost him two broken ribs, a bruised and cut scalp and two days' unconscious delirium nursed by his comrades.

Reaching the glorious open grass at the end of the corridor, finally away from the raining cudgels, he collapsed forward and felt the weight of his unconscious father roll off his shoulder. Amidst the thunderous silence as he fought the enveloping darkness, he was aware of soldiers forming a cordon around him glowering with bunched fists at the cudgel-wielding troopers who, along with their Major and his small staff, were moving away looking around them with some concern.

Rough, concerned hands lifted John and his father off the grass and began to carry them away. Dimly, as his senses began to drift away, he could hear their voices, "They tried to kill them, the bastards," sSaid one voice. "God rot them," said another. He fell into a dark pit as their voices diminished.

Somebody in the standing crowd shouted, "Hats off for the Pikemen, lads," and hundreds of floppy hats and helmets were lifted into the air. It was then that the cheering started, it grew in volume as more and more joined in and it continued for a long time as the prone figures of Martin and John were roughly but carefully carried away to be tended.

Chapter Seven

Evesham, late May 1645

General Massey to Colonel Robert Legge, Governor of Evesham. 25th May 1645

'You are hereby summoned to make a speedy surrender of the garrison with all possible arms, ammunition and provisions or upon refusal, expect such justice as fire and sword will inflict.'

Colonel Legge, Governor of Evesham to General Edward Massey. 25th May 1645

'You are hereby answered in the name of His Majesty that this garrison, which I am entrusted to keep, I will defend as long as I can with men, arms and ammunition therein, being nothing terrified at your summons.'

"You have set all as I instructed?"

The deep resonant voice of General Edward Massey could be heard by all who attended, even though some were yards away as he sat gazing at the closed and barred gates of Evesham town, quieting his fidgeting horse with a gauntleted hand. His staff and senior officers, all of whom worshipped their deep-voiced commander, nodded in unison and muttered assent. They trusted him implicitly; he had always brought them success in the past and they knew he would do so again.

Bleakly, he stared around at them, the sharp watery morning sun etching deep shadows across his face. His long straggly brown hair stirred in the fitful breeze, a movement mimicked by the feather in his hat. Absently, he pulled at the voluminous orange sash that was draped over his shoulder and across his breast-plated chest.

He was experiencing an emotion known by all commanders who must soon give an order for men to move forward and perhaps die following a plan that he himself has devised. Had he covered all eventualities? Had he foreseen everything that could happen? If he had not, would men die because of his error?

Again, he stared at the eager faces around him, the young and not so young, all awaiting his word. He hated this moment, had always hated the time when he became the loneliest man in the world and must give the order, 'Very well, let us proceed.' He took comfort from the men around him, knowing that these were veterans of a hundred fights or skirmishes. The dented helmets and battered breastplates giving ample evidence of their frequent use. There were non better in the land, that he knew, and he took comfort from the fact.

Breathing deeply, he visibly shrugged off his uncertainty and, dismounting, would lead the attack on the palisade himself. He said,

"Very well, gentlemen, let us about it. You all know your parts, I trust?" Once more, his officers muttered assent.

"Sir," the cadaverous figure of Major Jeremiah Wilmott stepped forward, his thin hunched shoulders swathed in his long greasy black hair. "Will you not reconsider? I ask this once more. Supervise the attack from here, I beg you. A musket ball is no respecter of rank and without you, we will be as a body without a head. Please do not go forward with us."

Massey stared at his second-in-command and masked his dislike of the tall, helmeted figure in front of him. He found this man overbearing, petty, cruel and vengeful, and there were other whispered rumours. Despite this, he also knew that, standing before him, was one of the finest soldiers he would ever meet; professional, ruthless and as loyal as a hound to the commander he followed and revered.

Massey gave a tetch of irritation. "Wilmott, we have been over this many times." Pulling his leather gauntlets on tighter, his brown thoughtful eyes swept the men who surrounded him. "I take it there are non here who believe I join you in this attack from a sense of schoolboy adventure?" There were two or three, 'No, Sir's' from the group. "My priority in life, at this time, is to win this… war. After too many years of blood-letting, we are close now, so close." He rubbed his eyes and settled his hat more firmly on his head. "If God wills, it will be over soon now, but first, there is work to do and that work is to take places like this." No one spoke. Again, he peered at the assembled faces. "Hard, brutal work, gentlemen, and never mind the parades and flag waving."

He turned to peer at the newly thrown-up defensive earth rampart that was before the town, topped by helmeted heads. "I lead today because this will be no May Day jig. Colonel Legge, who commands here, is a doughty and committed fighter and, if his men are like their master, this will be a victory earned in pain, blood and death."

Once more, he turned his electric gaze on to them. "You must lead your men today, sirs, lead them by example, as I must do. For be assured if you do not and we are first driven off from those ramparts, the men will not stop running until they reach the safety of Gloucester once more."

Having spoken with intensity, he allowed a smile to cross his face. "I see you understand me, but do not let my words overawe you. Do your duty to God and Parliament and, God willing, they," he jabbed a leather-clad finger at the fortifications, "will not gainsay us. God willing."

Dismissing his commanders, he watched them return to their posts amongst the troops who stood in serried ranks behind him, awaiting the order. The clumps of pikes swaying slightly in the breeze, with blue smoke from the muskets drifting amongst them. Foot soldiers only for this work, the cavalry had been sent to guard the Worcester Road to prevent reinforcements from that direction. Seeing all was ready, he nodded and spoke to himself, "Very well then." Raising his voice, he called for his bugler.

"Can you see anything, daughter?"

Parson Roberts peered anxiously up at Mary, who was perched precariously on the lowest branch of the oak tree which stood squarely in the centre of the camp, and which, as such, bore many scars where soldiers or their woman had lopped or torn off small branches for the cooking fires. Standing on the small cart beneath, Mary had just been able to reach the lowest branch and, aided by the breathless Parson, had scrabbled up on to it. The old man dutifully averting his eyes from the flash of legs and petticoats.

Peering intently forward to where the thunder of guns and the rattle of musketry boomed from the thick pall of smoke that obliterated the palisade and the town, she appeared not to have heard.

"I said, can you see anything?" he repeated. Looking down, she shook her head,

"No, only a lot of smoke and the odd powder flash." They imagined they could almost feel the percussive thump of air from the big guns.

He shook his head in exasperation. "Just as I prophesied, girl. Come down before you break your neck." She did not answer. "Mary," he called again. "For the love of God, please, come down and let an old man breathe once more."

Sighing theatrically, she glanced down at him and, with a flash of white legs and flowing skirts, she was standing beside him. Despite his age and religious calling, he was still man enough to admire the beautiful young woman who now stood before him, her calico bonnet unable to restrain the mass of blond hair that poked out from under it. Her grey eyes, usually so calm and assured were clouded with worry, her smooth brow lined.

"Please God, he is okay," she said, then like a child seeking reassurance, "Do you think he will be?"

It was the same question that she had asked a dozen times in the last hour as a child will seek reassurance. She gripped his arm with surprising strength and his answer was the same once again.

"God will look after him, I am sure, my dear." He attempted a smile, but his assurances sounded hollow even to himself. Nodding, she turned once more to squint through the smoke towards the fighting. Many women were at the edge of the camp gazing forward themselves, hands wringing their aprons with worry, unable to get closer past the camp guards. Twice Mary had attempted to go nearer the action but, each time, had been unceremoniously prodded back by the musket of a guard.

Wounded were being helped or carried back to the camp now with alarming regularity, blood trails marking their passage; women were wailing and children screaming. The injuries she saw made her agony worse and she thought she would go mad. She pictured Jacob with such wounds and turning, sobbed into the Parson's shoulder. It was thus for the duration of the fight, watching and worrying, as men died for Evesham Town.

To Jacob it seemed like hours that he and the men around him had been struggling and scrabbling up this blood-spattered earthen bank. The shouting and screaming of men, the thunder of the guns and the clash of metal on metal, like some demented blacksmith's shop, was deafening. He was covered in a fine film of dust from the recently-constructed earthwork and around him in the thick smoke, men peered owlishly at each other attempting to tell friend from foe. Once Jacob had almost forced his way through the rough planking palisade atop the bank, but a glancing blow from a heavy musket stock had starred his vision and, in seconds, he found himself dazed and vomiting once more at the bottom.

Forcing himself to stand on trembling legs, he started to climb once more. Under foot, the bank was littered with the debris of battle. Discarded weapons or pieces of armour, occasionally a body tripped the unwary. Attackers alive or dead crashed down through those climbing, sending them rolling back down that awful slope. Cries of anger, frustration and pain were almost, but not quite, drowned out by the bellow of guns. Those who did reach the top found themselves involved in ferocious hand-to-hand fighting with no quarter given or expected. Massey had been correct; Colonel Legge and his men were doughty fighters. Outnumbered by many to one, they still doggedly defended the palisade with unyielding courage. A breach had been opened and it was here that the fighting was fiercest. Massey himself had been hurled to the foot of the bank and a blood-stained bandage around his head bore witness to Wilmott's remark that a musket ball is no respecter of rank.

To his men, he seemed like some paladin of old, appearing everywhere, urging them on, bellowing imprecations if they faltered, blood running unchecked down his face. His breastplate was half torn away, his sword glutinous with blood.

Looking up, his senses reeling once more from a musket barrel smashed across his face, Jacob found that it was Massey's strong arm that hauled him to his feet. The intensity of the gaze that raked over him seemed to restore his strength. "Come, Jacob," said the elder man. "At them again, lad, it's nearly done." Then he was gone back into the smoke.

Amidst his terror, Jacob found time to marvel that the great man should remember his name at such a time and in such a place. Shaking his head to clear it, he once again began to clamber back up the bloodied slope.

Some yards away, the incident had been witnessed by someone else. Wilmott was as bloodied as his master.

His helmet gone, blood matting his long greasy hair. A scar from a blade still oozing blood into his eyes. He had watched the man he worshipped give help to that insolent whelp, Sedgewick, and his dislike of the young man burst into flame anew. His body trembled with anger as he watched the young slim figure move away up the slope. It was time this was settled and where better than in this confusion. Drawing his pistol, he plodded after him.

Every bone in Jacob's body ached, his head throbbed and he endured spells of dizziness. He seemed to move in slow motion, what was going on around him seemed far away as if it were viewed through the wrong end of a telescope. In his dreamlike state, he only knew that he had to reach the top once more, even though this hill went on for ever. A soldier he knew ran past him shouting something about cavalry from the rear, but he did not understand so just kept trudging forward. His boots slipping and sliding on the muddied, bloodstained grass and earth.

Just below him, Wilmott, his hearing and senses intact, became aware of the excitement at the top of the mound above him. He gathered that a breach had been forced through the palisade and it seemed that at the same time the Parliamentary cavalry had appeared at the rear of the defenders. "Perfect," he thought and smirked, "Now is the time, my young sir."

He levelled his pistol, unnoticed in the tumult, and fired at the insolent young whelp's back.

Jacob felt no pain at first, only a tremendous hammer blow across his shoulders and the earthen bank came up to hit him in the face. He slewed his head sideways and saw boots, hundreds of boots, running past him up the bank. "This is it," he thought, "I'm dead." Then a terrible, searing pain exploded across his left shoulder. He arched his back and screamed. Then he fainted.

As night fell a terrific storm erupted over the town. Lightening seared across the dark sky illuminating in its electric glare the corpse-strewn bank. As the rain began in heavy relentless drops, a myriad of small craters appeared in the softearth. In seconds, the rain became a torrential downpour. Its clear cool water washing the blood from upturned lifeless faces that stared unblinking at the sky, leaving marble figures washed clean of pain and horror. Statues that had begun the day as men, with cares and troubles, who now had none.

Mary and Parson Roberts huddled under the wagon, their low voices muffled by the rain pounding on the wooden boards above their heads. Around them, campfires were hissing as the rainfall cascaded into them. The meagre warmth and comfort that they supplied to those huddled around them extinguished in an instant. No one moved, the figures around the now-blackened fires, both men and women, sat stolidly, unmoving, knowing that there was nowhere to run to.

The desultory singing that had been heard from a

fire some way off ceased abruptly, the singers unwilling to do battle with the elemental force that now buffeted them. They considered they had fought enough for one day.

A groan from behind Mary turned her head and she gazed down through red-rimmed eyes at the fever-flushed and semi-delirious Jacob, the man she now loved with all her heart. She reached out and tried to comfort the writhing figure and tucked the two threadbare blankets that they possessed more closely around him. "The fever is getting worse," she said, "What can we do?" Her voice was shrill, desperate. She felt helpless.

"We must pray, Mary," replied the old man, resting his hand on her shoulder. "Pray to the Good Lord by whose bounty we live for our fellow traveller, Jacob."

Unusually, she shrugged the hand away, "I'm that sorry, Parson, but I'm really not in a praying mood." Her sentence was interrupted by another tremendous crash of thunder, almost it seemed just above their heads. Her shoulders sagged and she managed, "I'm sorry, sir, you do not deserve that. It's just that, there must be something that I can do. I feel as if I am sitting watching him die." She sobbed and rubbed an arm across her eyes. "He's burning up. If the fever does not break, he'll die."

Leaning down, she removed the piece of cloth from Jacob's forehead and, holding it out into the rain, to replenish its coolness replaced it tenderly on the fever-burned forehead.

With a whisper like bats wings, the Parson removed his black jacket and placed it on top of the blanket. "Perhaps it will do no harm to give our Good Lord a helping hand," he said.

Despite her anguish, Mary found time to smile at the inherent goodness of this old Parson, who had left his wife and village for her sake alone. She realised far better than he imagined, what courage it had taken to do that. He had not left his village in twenty years and now, purely because of his concern for her and his horror at what had happened to her mother, he had come out into the world and the war.

Gently, she leaned over and kissed the old man's head, causing him to blush like a schoolboy.

Jacob gave a shrill scream and sat up, his eyes wild and staring, sweat running in rivers down his face. Holding his hands in front of him, he began to struggle with some unknown assailant, his fever a living thing. Mary wrapped her arms around him and held him to her as she would a child, her voice soft and soothing. He started and looked wildly around and then, as her presence calmed him, allowed her to lay him down once more, his teeth chattering.

The Parson's voice was low, almost drowned out by the relentless downpour. "We need more blankets," he said uselessly.

"There are none," said Mary flatly. "I've begged and borrowed all I could but there are many men tonight who need blankets."

The old man nodded in the dark. "The surgeon said it would be thus. The wound is clean, the ball passed completely through his body, breaking no bones mercifully, but he's lost a lot of blood. Praise God, he is young and strong."

Mary spoke briskly as if she had arrived at a decision that had been difficult. "If we are to save him, I know what must be done. Help me strip these wet clothes from him." She worked quickly in the dark.

"But, my child," said the old man, "Will he not be colder still if we do that?"

"No, he won't ," she said, a determined edge to her voice, her face set and defiant. "Help me, please." She was attempting to untie Jacob's breeches.

The old Parson's face set in disproval. "Mary, it is not seemly for you to see a man in his nakedness."

"Oh, foll de roll, father, I have an elder brother and have worked on a farm all of my life, think you I do not know what is under here?"

"But, my daughter," began the old man, but was stopped as Mary rounded on him, her voice high with anger and anxiety, "Will you help me?" she shouted.

Mutely, he knelt forward and removed Jacob's boots.

Thunder crashed again and jagged lightening streaked the blackness. Somewhere out in the dark, a trooper on guard was struck, the lightening killing him instantly. His blackened scorched body fell unnoticed, hissing and smoking in the downpour. A tree at the edge of the camp was likewise struck, and it toppled unceremoniously onto the wagon beneath killing the men, women, and children who were huddled underneath it.

Jacob lay now completely naked save for the dirty bandage around his shoulder, blood still seeping through the bindings from the ugly wound beneath, although, mercifully, in much less quantity than earlier. Mary and the Parson piled the blanket and jacket on top of the shivering body once more. Mary sat up and, to the old man's horror, began methodically to undo the fastenings of her skirts.

"Mary, what do you do?" The old man's voice was querulous with foreknowledge.

She stopped and peered at him almost pleading. "The warmth of my body will keep him alive, father. Please do not stop me. It's his death else and I will NOT let him die!"

He was angry now. "You would not dare," he spat. "Think what your mother would say, your father, think of our good Lord and his teachings."

She leaned forward to untie the points of her bodice which ran down her back. "My mother was a practical woman, she would understand. My father may be dead for all I know. But, be that as it may, I am going to do this."

Stripping off the last garments, she clambered under the coverings, wrapping herself around the shivering man. His skin was on fire. She spoke gently into his ear and sensed that his shivering lessened as the warmth of her young body did its work.

She turned and peered up at the old man who was quietly praying to himself above her. "Sir, will you marry us?"

He raised his face and gazed down at her. "Marry you, my child? Here? Now?"

"Yes," she said. And half-smiled in the darkness. "It may save my soul." A long silence followed as the rain continued to pound the wagon above.

"Yes, my child. Yes I will." It was the voice of an old, old man.

They prised the ring from Jacob's little finger, she remembered him saying that his father had given it to him many years ago. It would do.

As the rain and thunder roared above them, the Parson sonorously went through the ritual phrases. Mary made the traditional responses and, when it came to Jacob's turn, she whispered and cajoled into his ear until he said, 'I do,' or so she would ever convince herself. She leaned forward and gently kissed the mouth of her delirious husband.

Thus were Jacob and Mary married.

General Massey sat working industriously by the light of a single flickering candle. The crashing of the storm outside the closed shutters of this small room interrupted him not at all, so great was his weariness and concentration. He was near to dropping but knew he must finish this report before allowing himself a few hours precious sleep.

He had accepted the surrender from Colonel Legge himself. After his cavalry had forced entry into the small town from another small gate, the defenders of the earthworks had found they were fighting to the front and in their rear, had realised further resistance was futile and been ordered to ground their arms to avoid further useless bloodshed. Since then, many duties had demanded Massey's attention, but now he was almost spent.

He lifted his head from the letter he was writing, stood and stretched, feeling the muscles in his shoulders and neck crack. The small room was panelled to the ceiling giving it a small claustrophobic air, which suddenly oppressed him. Striding to the casement, he flung wide the small, mullioned window, then the shutters. The hiss of heavy rain swept in with the cold draught and he relished the blast on his face.

He knuckled his tired eyes and called over his shoulder. Almost immediately, the door from the corridor opened and a hefty trooper, his dress immaculate even after such a day, stepped in.

"Sir?"

Massey spoke without turning, his already deep voice guttural with fatigue.

"See if you can find me a glass of wine, soldier, and a hunk of cheese would be most welcome."

"Yes, sir."

"Oh, and, trooper, bring me some more candles, I have a little yet to do."

"Sir." The door closed and footsteps faded down the corridor.

He stood for long minutes gazing at the dark sky, and the rain-lashed rooftops of Evesham. His thoughts were hazy with weariness and he knew he would not be efficient tomorrow if he did not rest soon, but he must finish. How... many more such nights as this must be endured? How many more must die? This realm he loved had been torn apart in the last years. Civil war, that 'child of hell,' was the most heinous of conflicts, as a nation turned in on itself and mauled its own people. There was also ,of course, the ever-present complication of religion to muddy the waters. Maybe at some point in the future, men would be able to live without their Gods, but that time was not yet. The cataclysmic wars on the continent were driven by it, witches were still tried and burnt in their thousands. This abomination was not so prevalent in England, but it happened. What was to be the future when the final victory was achieved? He knew now that his side would win, was supremely confident of it, but what then? He was not sure he liked to think on it and shrugged the thought aside with an effort.

He closed the window with regret and returned once more to the small desk that had been placed near the window and sitting, he once more picked up his quill pen. The letter was to Speaker Lenthall at the House of Commons, London.

'Evesham 27th May 1645.' He began, the scratching of his quill sounding loudly in the relative quiet, now that the window was once more closed.

'Evesham was yesterday morning assaulted by storm and took, in which we took the Governor Colonel Robert Legge, Colonel Foster, Colonel Bellingham, Major Tressillian, thirteen Captains. sixteen Lieutenants, and other officers and soldiers to the number of five hundred and forty-five.'

Outside the chimes of a nearby church-tower struck three a.m. The last rumbles of thunder sounded in the distance as the storm wore itself out and faded away.

'The assault was hot, and the defence not to be disparaged. I desire that the Government of the place be settled by Parliament with all speed, to enable me to march to the west where Parliament has ordered me.'

It was a crystal clear, sunlit morning, typical of the morning after a storm, as Parson Roberts crawled out from under the wagon. Groaning and creaking, he stood up feeling much older than his years. The damp clothes on his back steamed slightly in the morning air.

The early sunlight was strong with the watery brilliance that follows such a storm. The grass underfoot, although soaked, was green and lush, moving softly in the small breeze. The sky was a uniform deep blue, no cloud marred its brilliance. Everything was sharp and clear like an oil painting that has not yet quite dried.

The old man straightened his dowdy clothes then rubbed his hands together and began pounding his thighs to dispel the cramps. Although it was still early, the camp around him was full of bustle and noise. Soldiers strolled by in clumps or stood talking in groups probably about yesterday's fight. Somewhere a child was crying, somewhere else a woman was singing a lively tune as she tended a small fire. The usual smells of the camp drifted on the breeze; smoke, cooking, unwashed bodies and sewage. It had become so normal to Roberts that he now scarcely noticed. Now and then a single musket boomed from somewhere, but the Parson knew it was only soldiers cleaning their musket barrels which had become damp with rain or dew during the night. In the distance, someone was playing some sort of flute, the notes pleasant. Following his age-old ritual, he knelt and, clasping his hands together, thanked God for the new day, then standing slowly once more, renewed the rubbing and pounding of his thighs. He was too old for this, far too old, but what could he do? He had a duty to poor dead Martha to look after her daughter.

The events of last night suddenly occurred to him and he bent to peer under the wagon to assure himself he had not been dreaming. Jacob and Mary lay snuggled together under their blanket, like two children, their hair entwined on the old sack that served as a pillow. Jacob's breathing was slow and measured, it looked as if the fever had burnt itself out. They looked like two small children lying there and the Parson felt a fresh rush of affection for them both. Ruefully he wondered what Jacob's reaction would be when he learned that he was now married.

"How is he?"

Startled, Roberts turned and peered up at the vulture-like head of Wilmott who sat on his horse behind him. Roberts had not heard the horse approach, so intent had been his inspection of the young couple beneath him. The expression on the Major's face was inscrutable, his long black hair as usual hung lank, framing his shrewish face. Although they had not met before, the old Parson found his immediate impression of this enemy of Jacob to be unfavourable.

Straightening, he folded his arms in an unwitting defensive gesture.

"He'll live," he said, "Thanks mainly to the ministrations of that remarkable young woman."

Wilmott smirked and leaned forward to stroke the neck of his fidgeting horse with a gauntleted hand. "Ministrations of a highly desirable nature it would seem. No doubt she thought to distract him from his injuries."

The Parson bristled like a dog. "How dare you, sir, your remark is unbecoming an officer."

The smirk disappeared from Wilmott's face and he leaned down over the little man

"Unbecoming, is it, sir? What do I see before me but an officer of this army lying in the arms of a naked strumpet for all to view." His teeth were bared in a snarl and the malice in his words startled the Parson who unconsciously took a step back, banging his shoulder against the wagon.

"Have a care, sir," he retorted, pumping a confidence he did not feel into his voice. "'Tis slanderous lies you are speaking. I tell you, before this act was enabled, they were married. I performed the ritual myself."

Wilmott showed true surprise in his face but quickly recovered and sat back in his saddle. He laughed, an ugly sound in the morning air. "Well, well, so our young gallant has himself a wife. We must be careful we do not make the young wife a widow *too* soon, is that not correct, Parson?" Leaning down, he gently punched the old man in the chest, heeled his horse and rode off.

The Parson watched him go, concern etched deeply across his old face. He feared that man the more now having met him. Rarely had he seen such malice and malevolence so loosely held in check. What was it that he hated so about young Jacob? Hurriedly, he shrugged these thoughts aside, he had more immediate matters to worry about, but he made a mental note to keep a watchful eye on his young friend whenever that man was about.

"I don't trust that man." Mary's voice came from under the wagon. Roberts bent down and peered into the open and troubled grey eyes of the young woman.

"You heard?" he asked.

"Yes, I heard it all. He makes me shiver." Moving slowly, so as not to wake the sleeping Jacob, she donned her clothing and stood up from under the wagon, shaking out her skirts and arranging her calico cap.

"I share your dislike, daughter," agreed Roberts, but in truth, there is not much that we can do, save be ever watchful." He turned to gaze after the disappearing rider.

Mary gave a mew of concern and chewed her thumbnail.

"Anyway," said the Parson more brightly. "We know that nothing can befall Jacob whilst he is in this condition and in our care and Massey and his men will probably be long gone before he is well enough to resume his duties."

Mary's face brightened a little. "Yes, of course, you are right," she said. "I had not thought of that."

As she further straightened her clothing, she began to consider more practical matters, such as what were they to eat today, when a voice behind her made her jump. Turning, she gazed at the grizzled figure of an ageing musketeer who had strolled up to them both unheard. His unshaven chin bristled with greying hairs and the scars on his face denoted an old soldier of long standing. Mary surmised he was a professional who had been in the small English standing army long before this war started.

One of his eyes was partially-closed and sported a huge bruise, which gave him a war-worn look. He seemed furtive and, more than once, glanced around to check he was not being watched.

"How is the young sir?" he enquired, his voice accented with a west country burr.

"He will recover, God willing, sir," answered the Parson, moving up beside Mary. "Thank you for your concern."

Once again, the soldier peered around him contemplating his next words. "If anyone asks," he said, his voice low, "I never said anything, right?"

Startled, they both nodded.

"During the fight yesterday, when all was smoke and noise, I saw it." He coughed, still unsure of going on, then decided. "I saw the Major Wilmott draw his pistol and shoot our young lad there in the back. I saw it plain as day, I tell ee."

Mary's mouth opened like a fish. "What?" she managed. "What did you say?"

"You heard me, young maid," said the musketeer, not unkindly. "And now I must leave. If our darling knows I saw what I have just told you, I'll be a dead un before the sun goes down. Good day to you both." Hoisting his musket across his shoulder, he strode away his wooden powder apostles rattling and was lost almost immediately amongst the sprawling soldiers and smoking campfires.

Mary and the Parson stood there dumbstruck. Shock rendering them speechless. Finally, Mary managed to splutter, "Why? Why would he do that?"

Roberts removed his hat and rubbed his thinning white hair contemplatively, "I do not know, my daughter. But the danger to Jacob is far greater than I imagined."

"Can't we tell someone?" began Mary, but her sentence was cut short by the agitated old man. "Tell whom? And tell what? That some musketeer, who you will never find again, told us that a trusted officer in the army of Parliament and of General Massey shot one of his own officers in the back?" He gave a derisive half-laugh, "Think you anyone would believe us? Do you?"

"No," she said and sobbed quietly into her hands.

"They would whip us out of the camp for sedition, my daughter. No! we must keep this to ourselves and be ever vigilant."

Roberts turned and gazed into the distance at the battered bank and palisade, beyond it the half-timbered houses and honey-coloured abbey, all basking in the morning sunshine. Smoke still drifted lazily over the town, only the glint of sunshine off helmeted heads atop the town walls betrayed the presence of soldiers.

"Ever vigilant," he repeated to himself.

Chapter Eight

Dieppe, France, 1645

Ethan tilted back his head and drained the crude stoneware mug of the last drops of the sour wine. He grimaced in disgust at the bitter taste and reflected that he should be used to the taste now after four, or was it five, such mugs in the last hour? He was aware that it was poor fare, but any wine after so long without was a miracle.

He stretched out his cramped legs and signalled to the slatternly serving wench to bring him another. He was sitting in the open courtyard that fronted the dowdy harbour side-tavern in the little port of Dieppe. Everyone that could be, was outside as the stifling heat grew worse. There was going to be a storm and the sooner the better. The yellowing sky was the colour of an old bruise and huge thunder clouds were mushrooming up to the heavens in the near distance.

He was watching the people around him with some fascination. They were going about their lives with no thought of danger, the war was a long way off and had, it appeared, hardly affected the good folk of this slovenly little port. They went about their business with a rough good humour. Sailors and fishermen getting drunk, whores plying their trade and hucksters selling a variety of shabby artefacts to any who would buy. Merchants were discussing business as they strolled by or sat at tables deep in conversation. A rat catcher picked his way through the crowd, around his neck were draped twenty bloody, furry little corpses. A man with no legs pushed a small makeshift trolly along the cobbles begging disconsolately for a few coins.

No one had approached Ethan as he sat quietly sipping his drink, the air of quiet menace that surrounded him discouraged any attempt at casual conversation. His monosyllabic requests for wine had elicited gossip from the serving woman to the regular customers that the stranger spoke in some guttural accent unknown to her. She earned extra money by taking whomever was interested up to her room for a 'quick one,' as she called it, but having tried twice to entice the forbidding stranger, she had given up in the face of stony rebuff.

Ethan removed his hat and, producing a piece of cloth from somewhere beneath his jerkin, mopped his brow and wiped the inside rim. It was an action he had repeated often since arriving at this dowdy little inn. The cloying heat was oppressive. The rain, when it came, would be heavy, cool and welcome.

He was annoyed. The visitor he was expecting was long overdue and he decided to drink one more mug of rot gut before leaving. The serving wench flounced over to him, her chin held high, to register to this chilly man her disinterest. She was offended by his curt refusal of her offer of company, she fancied herself choosy about her favours, even for money and took his disinterest as an insult. Nevertheless, he was obviously a soldier from the wars and that usually meant money, also she had peered sharply at the inanimate face and decided that, once, long ago before the hair started to discolour and without the hideous scar, the man had been handsome.

Standing beside him and looking down at the cool grey eyes, she decided to try once more. She leaned against him as she bent to refill his mug from the jug that she carried, making sure to press her thigh against his arm. He could feel the warmth of her body through the coarse material of her skirt.

"Will there be anything else, monsieur?" she pouted down at him.

He looked her over slowly, noting the heavily wine-stained skirts and the unwashed bodice loosely tied at the top displaying an ample greasy cleavage. Her unkempt brown hair was inexpertly fashioned into ringlets mimicking the fashion of the great ladies and hung in clumps upon her shoulders. He could smell the animal muskiness of her body and was mildly aroused despite his aversion.

"No," he said briskly, and it was some moments before she realised the conversation was ended. With a toss of her head, she flounced off again.

Ethan drank deeply from his refilled mug and gazed about him once more. The light was now almost gone and a tavern worker moved amongst the drinkers lighting the lanterns that hung from the whitewashed courtyard walls. Irritably, Ethan scratched under his shirt and realised that some of the fleas that inhabited the shabby little room he had rented in the nearby garret, preferred his company to that of his scruffy bed. He could feel the sweat running down his back, his homespun shirt hot in the sticky air.

A small thickset man, with dirty blond hair and a huge beard, entered the small courtyard and gazed around him, obviously seeking someone. The large coral earring in one ear danced jauntily to the movement of his head. Ethan straightened and raised a hand in greeting. The man pirouetted through the crowd, slumped down opposite Ethan and bellowed for wine. He grinned through a ruin of broken and blackened teeth.

"Sorry I'm late, friend, something came up, you know how it is." Casually, he rubbed his hand up the thigh of the serving wench who had appeared promptly to pour him some wine. She gave a mock squeal of outrage, grinned down at him and moved off.

The sailor laughed, licked his lips as he watched her go and winked hugely over at Ethan. He was somewhat disconcerted by the expressionless icy stare from the grey eyes opposite and, to cover his discomfort, coughed and took a swig of his wine.

"So," he said, placing his mug down in front of him.

"You wish passage to England, yes?"

Ethan gave a brief nod.

"You're not in any trouble, are you, I want no truck with the authorities?" The thick burr in his speech betrayed his Devonshire origin.

Ethan shook his head. "No." He sipped his wine, his eyes never leaving the sailor's face.

"What sort of a fool accent is that?" thought the bearded man. He was a little disappointed, a man on the run was apt to pay more for his passage. But, having assessed the man in front of him, correctly guessed this was not someone to mess with. Seeing no trace of compromise or even friendliness in the man, the sailor decided on bravado. He tucked his chin into his beard and belched loudly.

"Well, my friend, I sail for Dartmouth on the early morning tide. If you want to come, let's talk money." He named his price.

Ethan stared back his face emotionless. The seaman held his gaze for some moments and then looked away. This silent menacing Englishman made him uneasy.

"That is probably double what I was expecting to pay," said Ethan steadily.

"The times are hard, one makes money when one can," reasoned the sailor, his earring swayed jauntily against his tanned neck. "You can wait for the next boat." He shrugged. "It's all the same to me." This scarred emaciated figure with the harsh voice scared him, but he considered he was safe enough in this crowded little courtyard.

Ethan eyed the man coldly and considered his options. The price was extortionate but he had money. He could wait for another English vessel certainly, but this oaf was leaving on the morrow and, having been in Dieppe some days, he was loath to wait further.

He nodded agreement. "Very well. I'll come aboard after midnight."

The seaman, grinned with relief, explained where his boat was moored and, without ceremony, held out his hand for his fee. His expression changed when he looked at the coins placed in his palm and he looked up enquiringly at Ethan.

"Half-now and half when we get there," said Ethan flatly, his tone negating any argument.

The sailor swore long and low, but pocketed the coins quickly, swilled down the contents of his mug, stood and shouldered his way out of the inn.

Ethan sighed and stretched out his legs again. He was almost home. Christ, he was tired, weary beyond the telling. He had been dreaming again so had slept fitfully for the last two nights. Thoughts and pictures of the last years flashed through his mind and a smiling tender face appeared in front of him *"No, not now, keep those thoughts away, Christus. No more. No."*

He gave an unconscious mew of concern then looked around him to see if anyone had heard, but no one appeared to have noticed. Conversation and noise carried on unabated. He rubbed his eyes until his vision starred and he finished his wine with a gulp.

His journey across Europe had emphasised to him what this endless war had done. It was a little better in northern France but before that, he had travelled for days and days through a wilderness of devastated land. Germany was the worst. Ruined villages, corpses mouldering in roadside ditches, charred fields, plundered towns, destroyed and burnt churches, plague, all instigated by a religious intolerance that was endemic and drove the fighting. He had seen the evidence also of cannibalism; discarded human bones obviously picked clean by frantic starving desperate human beings. He remembered the priest he had killed and the image of that smiling self-righteous face disgusted him even now.

With an effort, he thrust the thoughts aside and raised his eyes to find the serving wench watching him with interest, she came over to his table and raised her eyebrow. It was an enquiry, but both knew not for wine. He peered at her again and his vision blurred and her face became a much more beautiful face, with tender caring eyes and long lustrous dark hair. *'Come, my love, take some rest, you are tired, lay with me. Come, my sweet.'* He winced as he heard her voice once again, a voice now long gone. He shook his head slightly and the face of the serving wench came back into focus.

"You say you have a room here?" he said.

"Yes, my fine sir, you could take another drink away from this noise."

"Very well," said Ethan curtly and standing,

followed her across the courtyard and up a set of rickety stairs to a tiny unkempt dormer room directly beneath the roof. His fatigue was a living thing and he sat on the bed to avoid falling over. The woman stooped at a small table and lit a candle. The wobbling small flame looked like a bright eye in the gloom.

He made no move towards her and she noted his resolve was fading. She began to remove his jacket.

"I will massage your shoulders if you wish, my lord?" she said smoothly, "you look spent." He acknowledged somewhere in his tired mind her professional and automatic responses.

He meekly allowed her to remove his jerkin and then his shirt, as she ran the fingers of her other hand through his hair. Then, stepping back and seeing his body in the candle glow for the first time she froze, appalled at what she saw.

From neck to hips and down both arms were a riot of scars and gashes. More than she had ever seen on one man. Some had been little more than deep scratches and had healed, leaving crusted scar tissue, some had obviously been deep wounds, evidenced by the silky-smooth cicatrice of renewed skin. In two or three places were the puckered and shrivelled wounds left by a musket ball.

He looked up at the sound of her indrawn breath and realised what she was seeing. "Are you shocked?" he asked and gave a harsh embarrassed chuckle, there was no humour in the sound. She did not answer but continued to stare and was surprised to see a tear run slowly down his cheek. It was dawning on her just how damaged this man was.

"No, monsieur, that is, yes, a little." There was real concern in her voice now; the concern of one tired and worn-out human being for another. She took a tentative step forward and laid a gentle hand on his shoulder. "You have seen much death, I think."

He nodded imperceptibly, peered up at her face and then looked away. "Yes," he said almost to himself. "Much death." He rubbed his eyes irritably and then, as if some puppeteer had cut the strings that controlled him, he abruptly lay back on the dishevelled sheets and was almost instantly asleep.

She stared at him for long moments, this wreck of a man illuminated as he was by the single candle, his breathing deep and rhythmic. Then, for whatever the reason, which she could not explain to herself, she covered him with the single blanket and sat quietly down on the rickety chair next to the bed to watch over him whilst he slept.

It was some hours later that Ethan, feeling slightly better for the few hours of sleep, made his way through the silent streets of the little port towards the harbour. The heat was oppressive still, the storm had not yet broken. A river of sweat still ran unchecked beneath his clothing and under his hat, his hair was damp and matted. He noticed these inconveniences not at all but concentrated his mind on the dark corners and deep shadows before him. His inbred caution automatic, the result of ten years in the wars. It was second nature not to take anything for granted. It was a premise that had kept him alive this far.

Arriving at the jetty, he paused in the shadow of a small warehouse. He felt the meagre comfort of the minimal breeze blowing off the sea. The sound of waves lapping against the mole out there in the darkness was somehow refreshing.

Carefully, he scanned the length of the quay. Like jetties everywhere, it was a litter of piled lobster pots, barrels, cases and upturned small boats. Coils of thick rope lay like huge snakes ready to trip the unwary. A drunk lay snoring in a pool of his own vomit, the empty stone jug still clutched in his hand. The vessel that he sought lay at the end of the quay, rocking gently at its moorings.

The first flicker of lightning illuminated the scene with its electric glare and, as he moved forward, the first heavy drops of rain began to fall. By the time he reached the gangplank, the downpour was torrential, water bouncing high off the cobbles. With a thunderous roar, the first peel of thunder sounded, seemingly directly above the little port and the flashing lightening became almost constant. The air was heavy with static.

Ethan stood absolutely motionless at the top of the gangplank and surveyed the wet, cluttered deck below him. He was once more the professional soldier in control, doing what he knew best, marking each possible hiding place, every danger. The unfortunate incident at the inn when he had showed weakness had been shoved to the back of his mind and, in time, he may even convince himself that it had never happened. He felt strangely refreshed, renewed and his tired mind revelled in the violence of the storm. His battered body felt rejuvenated by the coolness that the breaking storm bought with it, banishing the cloying heat of the last hours.

He could hear the waves just outside the harbour that were being driven by the rising wind to crash against the stone jetties. Beyond that mole out there in the darkness lay England, his home, with whatever he may find there and nothing now would prevent him from completing his journey.

His immediate distrust of the seaman that he had met at the inn dictated that he boarded this shabby little craft prepared for whatever may come. Hoisting his saddle bags higher on to his shoulder, he strode down the bouncing gangplank.

Crouched behind an upturned barrel on the deck, the scruffy Captain of the shabby little craft waited anxiously clutching his knife. He was soaked through and feebly cursed himself for this plan in a steady stream. One of his more disreputable men was hidden near the gangplank, a huge brutish oaf who was useless as a sailor but hired by the Captain for just such eventualities as this.

There was money on the stranger and times were

hard.

"Be careful," had been his final instructions to his henchman. "Mind your skill with this one. He's an evil-looking bastard and could be useful." They had done this many times before but hiding there in the rain, drenched and shivering, the Captain could not get the stranger's face from his mind. The cold expressionless gaze that betrayed no emotion and those terrible soulless eyes. Again, he shivered and wished he had not started this.

Hearing the approaching footsteps, he peered over the top of the barrel and, illuminated by the constantly flickering lightning flashes, saw his partner rear up as the stranger alighted on to the deck. There was a brief struggle and then a terrible gurgling scream. The huge crewman fell to his knees clutching a throat open to the world as great gouts of blood cascaded down his jacket front.

Rising swiftly, the seaman forced his heavy legs forward to aid his partner but, turning quickly to face him, the stranger crouched low and levelling a pistol that had appeared from nowhere, whistled shrilly through his teeth to stop the rush. Skidding to a halt, the seaman raised his arms letting his own knife fall with a clatter to the deck through opened fingers.

Somewhere in the darkness, the dying man gave a wet whimper and choked to death noisily. The sailor knew the stranger would fire, the whole meaning of his existence was to fire, he would not hesitate. He closed his eyes and waited.

In a few quick strides, Ethan moved forward and crashed the barrel of his pistol barrel across the bridge of the seaman's nose breaking the gristle. The seaman cried out in pain and shock and fell to the slippery deck, blood streaming down his face. Crouching over the terrified figure, Ethan grabbed the front of his jacket and held a huge razor-sharp knife against his throat.

"Be grateful that I recognised you, my friend," the voice was granite, "Or you would be choking on your own bile like your friend there." Gazing up at the terrifying figure above, silhouetted as it was against the constant lightning, the sailor knew that he was indeed lucky to be still alive. A worm of unease moved in his belly as he wondered why.

"I need you to take me to England as agreed," Ethan's voice was hard and flat. He glanced briefly at the corpse that lay in the rain a few feet away "You have other crew?" The Captain nodded weakly. "Down below, asleep or probably awake by now but too scared to come on deck."

Ethan released his grip on the man and stood. The knife blade disappeared and he stepped back, moving the pistol from one hand to the other. "Honour our agreement and you will live. But should there be any more… problems and your end will be messy." He gave a low humourless laugh, his teeth gleaming in the fitful light. The sailor stared up at the figure above him and grunted an assent. No there would be no more problems.

He watched Ethan walk off to the hatch that led below-deck, then rolled over on to his side and was weakly sick. For the first and only time in his life, he prayed to a God that he did not really believe in to save him from this terrible man.

Chapter Nine

Dartmouth, late May 1645

Ethan leaned idly on the sun-blistered gunwale at the
bow of the shabby little lugger and watched England
approach. His feelings were in turmoil. Was he pleased
to be arriving home once more? What was home? So
much had happened, so much. If he met the man that he
had been ten years ago walking down the quay towards
him, would he recognise himself? If it was possible for
him to smile, he came close, but the smile did not quite
reach his ice-grey eyes. They showed no emotion, like a
doll's eyes. The scorching sun that beat down
relentlessly on to his thick clothing brought with it a
pleasing warmth. As ever, under his homespun shirt, a
river of sweat coursed down his spine. He took pleasure
from the sensation. His worn and battered doublet and
hat lay in a heap at his feet, on the gently lifting wooden
planked deck. Absently, he moved his toes inside his
heavy thigh-length cavalry boots and felt the hot leather
against his flesh.

It had been a cold, rai- lashed day when he had last
looked on these shores a lifetime ago and he had not

been interested in looking back as the land of his birth receded. His new life beckoned and excitement and apprehension bubbled in his brain. That was before he had learned the truth about the 'foreign wars.' Before he set off to inexorably tramp the long road that had led him to the person he was now. Grimly, he acknowledged the realisation that, no, he would not recognise himself if he met the young, innocent, Ethan Sedgewick. The years inbetween had changed and marked him forever. Too much horror and death, and... other things. In later years, the act of staying alive was all that mattered. To eat, to breathe, to survive and kill or be killed... to forget.

The voyage had been uneventful. The dowdy and frightened Captain of this unkempt little craft had retired to his cabin the moment they had left the French port and, apart from the young boy who took him his meals, had not again been seen by anyone. The rest of the crew, wary of the distant and forbidding character who had joined them, kept their distance without being unfriendly and quietly went about their business. The tall gaunt figure standing for much of the time at the bows staring ahead, ceased to be of interest. He had shared a flea-infested cabin for the last two days with the stocky, bald bosun who, having assessed his guest, kept himself to himself. Occasional stilted conversations had, however, enabled Sedgewick to glean snippets of information about events in the land he had so long ago forsaken.

"The King is finished," the bosun had breezily stated during one such exchange. "But he won't lie down and the poor buggers who follow him still are dying for nothing."

"Dying for nothing… " Sedgwick had given a harsh half-laugh. "Maybe they always did? Which bunch of idiots do you favour?"

The bosun scratched inside his shirt and cursed the fleas. "Me?" he said. "Leave me out of it. I spend little enough time on land anyway. Give me a heaving sea and a fresh breeze and you can keep all your politics and generals." He leaned forward and lowered his voice as if afraid that someone may hear." I'll tell you, my friend, down here in the southwest, we have a general of King Charlie, name of Grenville, all fire and brimstone and defending the family honour. Big landowner in these parts. Famous amongst the nobs and well-thought-of by the King himself. Know what the common people think of him, those with any sense anyway? A dangerous idiot who gets people killed."

This was a long speech for the sailor and he looked suddenly embarrassed by his outburst. "Oh well," he said and gave a half laugh. "What do I know, I'm just an old sailor. No wife, no children and only a few good memories to take with me to my maker when the time comes. I've had some good mates in my time, most of them now dead, most of me teeth gone. I find solace now in a jug whenever I can. We cannot run away from ourselves and the choices we have made in life, can we?

Just got to live with it."

"Or maybe run away from it, our lives, our memories, ourselves?" mused Ethan, almost to himself.

The bosun gave him a searching look and decided to risk a question. "Was it that way with you?" Sedgwick stared moodily at his feet and ran grimy fingers through his hair. "Who knows?"

Standing alone now at the bow in the sunshine he searched his soul for the answer. Perhaps he would find out when he reached home if home still existed. Perhaps his brother or his father would know. Perhaps.

The coastline on his right shimmered in the mid-day heat and he felt the deck lift under his feet in the swell, the sails above him flapped and orders were shouted as the little vessel altered course. Squinting as the sun bounced off the sea, he saw the entrance to the river Dart open up before them. The gusty wind bouncing from the tree-covered hills on either headland, whilst the turbulent cross-currents as the river met the sea rocked them.

The soft burr of the bosun's voice startled him. "Got your answers ready?" The bosun was coiling a rope purposefully as part of readying the craft for docking.

"Answers?" Sedgwick ,gathering his jacket, hat and cloak, looked blank. "You'll be questioned when you go ashore."

"Why?"

The bosun looked incredulous. "Great God, man, there's a war on. This," he gestured with his outstretched arm at the small town of Dartmouth that basked in the sun on the slopes before them like an old cat, "is a Royalist stronghold and one of their main ports. Do you think an armed and obvious soldier coming ashore will not attract any attention?"

Sedgewick was shocked despite himself. The thought that he was leaving a war-torn and devastated landscape behind him had overridden any thoughts that he was, in fact, arriving at another war-torn land.

He shrugged and his face set into the traditional blank mask. "I'll tell them I am returning from the foreign wars and have no interest in their little domestic matter."

The bosun stared at this frightening man for a long moment, then turned away, shaking his head. "Well, good luck to you." He could see trouble ahead for this man. It was a bad time to be turning up anywhere without good reason, he had heard the rumours, as had everyone else ,of the expected Parliamentary drive into the west country led by Lord Fairfax himself to 'clear that benighted land of malignants.' If the common folk had heard such tales, it was probably true. 'Oh well,' he stalked off with his rolling sailor's gait. He would not get involved.

The squat, fat-bellied little vessel was entering the mouth of the Dart now, under the lowering menace of the small Tudor castles on either bank. Had the shabby little craft not been flying the appropriate signals it would already have been challenged or blown to pieces by the huge cannons protruding from the crenelated walls. He could see the sun glinting from helmets as the garrison interrupted their mid-day meal to peer down at his craft.

Sedgwick squinted down at the heaving sea, watching his elongated shadow leap from crest to crest. The bosun had told him that there was a huge chain down there on the riverbed stretched between the forts. If the anchorage were threatened, it could be raised, effectively blocking the river entrance. He squinted forward at the port itself bathed in the bright sunshine, its narrow, cobbled streets climbing steeply away from the quayside and flanked by a third fort, the maw of its guns visible even at this distance. The soldier in him responded to the formidable defences of this little port.

Three or four warships rode at anchor in midstream, men moving around on their decks and smoke billowed up from busy cooking galleys below decks. Fatter, slower merchant hoys were tied up along the quay which was alive with people. Just ahead, a fishing smack was returning to port, a host of moaning seagulls hovering and swooping above it.

Sedgewick breathed in deeply and raised his head to look at the sky. He had made it, he was home. A country he had thought never to see again. Unbidden fleeting glimpses of the horrors he had left behind flashed before his eyes. The death and disease. The fear and the blood. Some of the faces he had left behind; MacDonald his friend lying in the mud half of Europe away, and… others. Hurriedly, he forced those thoughts from his mind and returned his gaze to the approaching quay.

They were nudging into the jetty now which the Bosun had told him was called Bayard's Cove. He could see it was swarming with people. Sailors and fishermen loading or unloading cargos of all sorts. Merchants and clerks busy with their tallies. Hawkers selling a range of products, whores in their red scarves and soldiers. Soldiers everywhere. They lounged against buildings watching and chatting or shouldered their way rudely through the crowds.

Sedgewick watched it all from his place on the deck, his face expressionless, then abruptly, he turned and went below to his cabin for the last time to retrieve the rest of his belongings.

Surprisingly, he was neither stopped nor questioned in any way as he strode down the bouncing gangplank and stepped onto the earth of England. Perhaps it was because he moved without pause or hesitation away from the cobbled, crowded quay and, with long purposeful steps, headed for the start of what was obviously the main street, its black and white half-timbered buildings crowding and jostling each other. He surmised, rightly, that it was only a lack of purpose or direction that drew the attention of the lounging troopers. He had spoken to no one as he left the vessel, merely a cursory nod to the bosun, who, busy with his duties, raised a cursory hand in farewell.

The further he walked along the noisome, crowded little street, the slower his progress became. Manners were non-existent, with men and women shouting obscenities at each other or merely shoving through the smelly throng without thought. Above the cacophony of noise, shopkeepers vied with each other for attention as they bawled their wares. Being a seaport, fish was much in evidence, laid out on fly-blown slabs or in wicker baskets. Lobsters and crabs, still alive, were prodded and poked mercilessly by prospective buyers.

Underfoot, the cobbles in places were slippery with discarded rotting fish carcasses. Beggars with legs or arms missing squatted in the filth crying for alms.

Having no idea where he was headed for the present, Sedgewick hoisted his saddlebags over his shoulder and allowed himself to be drawn along by the crowds. He was taking some pleasure in hearing the English language spoken or shouted all around him. For many years, he had conversed in either poor French,German, or the pigeon patois of the multi-national camps. He feared the time he must first open his mouth for he was aware that, after so many years, his guttural voice would sound foreign to west country ears.

A thin hand grabbed his sleeve forcing him to stop and turn. He looked down into the world- eary eyes of a girl in her early teens whose russet and stained hood proclaimed her trade. "Got some money, soldier?"

Sedgewick stared down at her, his face a granite mask. Under his scrutiny she shuffled her feet uncertainly and stroked his hand.

"Won't cost you much," she smiled a gap-toothed smile.

"Get away from me," Sedgwick's voice was low so that few might hear his voice. "Not interested."

Startled by the unexpected vehemence of his words and the strange deep guttural voice, she took a step back, "You're a foreigner," she shouted, "You aren't no Englishman, that's for sure!"

Heads were turning, interest was being stirred. Sedgewick had feared just this, so turning, he shoved roughly through the crowd and walked quickly away.

Behind, he could hear the shrill voice of the girl shouting, she had seen a Frenchie Papist.

He emerged from the crowded street into what was obviously the town square and, for safety, edged deeper and deeper into the crowd until he felt comparatively safe and anonymous. It was only then that he looked around him and noticed that the crowd was stationary. Heads were craning forward as people strained to see what was happening in the centre of the square. It was obvious that some spectacle of interest was about to begin.

He looked at the lanky red-haired youth next to him who was attempting to lift his female companion to give her a better view.

"What's this?" said Sedgwick, wisely keeping his choice of words short and to the point.

If the youth noticed anything peculiar with the voice

of the forbidding looking stranger next to him, he was prudent not to remark on it.

"Nothing much," he said, with a shake of his head, "A whipping, is all."

Seeing the interest of his listener fading fast he attempted to add colour to his story. "Only twenty lashes. Her ad a baby last week and her aren't married neither." He chuckled mirthlessly. "Sommat to watch."

Sedgewick was a little shocked. Immured to violence of every sort where he had come from, he had not expected such barbarity in England.

"Harsh," he said.

"Well," began the youth, warming to his task as informer, "It's always been the law and you and I know it, but it's only recent like that the magistrates have insisted on the full penalty of them that's sinned afore God. Me, I think it's to curb the licentiousness of them troopers."

A roar from the crowd prevented Sedgwick answering, the entertainment was beginning. He could see over much of the crowd and peered at the rough platform that stood at the centre of the square. On it had been placed a wooden tripod which stood out clearly against the frieze of black and white buildings behind it. In front of the dais, lounged a dozen or more troopers. Their casual attitude evidencing that they felt they were at little threat.

Sedgwick doubted if their cumbersome muskets were even loaded.

At the top of the tripod had been secured a large metal hook. As he watched, a leather-aproned workman climbed the steps to the platform, tested the hook by hanging briefly from it, then to scattered applause, bowed theatrically to the crowd and moved away.

Briefly, Sedgwick glanced about him and was repelled by the holiday-like atmosphere. Hucksters were moving amongst the gathering selling sweetmeats and bread.

Disinterested and mildly disgusted, he was about to force his way back out through the crowd when, with an animal growl of expectation, the crowd moved forward as one.

Climbing the steps on to the dais, came the self-important little group headed by the magistrate and two constables. Then followed two burly troopers holding between them the diminutive figure of a petite, obviously terrified, young woman. She looked to be in her early twenties and was being held up off the ground by the grinning soldiers.

With little ceremony, they hoisted the woman up and looped the manacles on her wrists across the hook, forcing her to stand on tiptoe with her back to the crowd. One of the troopers casually stepped forward and, grabbing the collar of her gown and bodice, ripped them down exposing her back. The crowd sighed like an animal and moved a little further forward in anticipation.

The magistrate, a pompous little man, stepped forward and silencing the crowd with a raised hand stertorously read out the charge and the punishment.

Deep in the crowd, Sedgewick was fighting to control himself. He was sweating profusely. His hands clenching and unclenching as he fought to control his trembling body. He knew he must stop this or die in the attempt.

"Christ that woman looked like, NO! Don't let those thoughts in. Keep them deep and dark where they belong. But she looks like, NO! Force them back down.

Christus, Christus. He must stop this. They'd pay, Christus, they'd pay. He'd send them to hell. Christus and his Angels."

As the magistrate finished his impromptu little speech, Sedgwick dropped his saddle bags and began roughly to force his way to the front of the crowd.

To the people who were there that day, it would be a talking point for many months and a memory for a lifetime.

The portly little magistrate moved to the edge of the dais and signalled to one of the constables, who casually, as the crowd cheered, took out a small twin-thonged whip from its calico bag and deftly administered the first stroke. The metal tipped twin-leather thongs hissed through the air and bit deeply into the soft white flesh of the woman's exposed back. Welts appeared, oozing blood.

The woman opened her mouth and stared wild-eyed at the sky, her facial muscles stretched in agony, but no sound came, the shock was too great. It was only as the writing leather seared her back for the third time that a shrill unbelieving shriek of animal pain and terror rent the air, the sound almost drowned by the jeers of the crowd.

Then, from nowhere, there was another figure on the platform, a tall gaunt figure with battered travel-worn clothes and a scarred face. With unbelievable speed before the constables or troopers could react, he was in amongst them; kicking, gouging, punching and clubbing. In seconds, a trooper and both constables were down. One clutching testicles mushed to a pulp by a viscously slammed boot, one clubbed senseless with the butt of a pistol and the third jerking and writhing on the floor, his fingers trying to stem the flow of blood from an eyeball gouged from its socket by clawing fingers with incredible strength.

As the crowd watched stunned, the magistrate turned to run, but he was much too slow. Before he went two paces the tall thin man was on him, spinning him around and crashing his forehead into the shocked and screaming face, crushing the nose and breaking off three of the front teeth cleanly at the gum. Mercifully, that was all the little man remembered as he fainted with pain and with fright. But the crowd watched in horror as, shouting in a strange high-pitched yell of triumph, his attacker knelt over him, drew a huge knife and sawed off one of his ears. Standing, the terrifying figure stood and, still shouting in some strange guttural language, hurled the hideous object into their midst. It landed amongst a crowd scattering in panic. Trampling each other in a desperate desire to get away.

Turning, the man moved towards the manacled woman who was still hanging from the hook, but he never reached her. Finally recovering from the surprise and speed of the attack which had stunned them into immobility, the troopers below the front of the dais swarmed up on to it and engulfed the tall, shouting man.

There were eight of them but, nevertheless, it took some minutes and several blows from heavy musket stocks before he was finally down on the floor, bloody, bruised and unconscious at last.

Standing over him with heaving chests, black eyes, broken teeth, and bloody noses, the trembling troopers looked wide-eyed at one another, at the carnage around them and, finally, at the senseless figure at their feet.

One of them swore obscenely as the others, still fighting for breath, nodded agreement soundlessly.

Captain Andrew Thornton, a meticulously-dressed Devon-bred gentleman of thirty years of age, sat at the bare wooden table in the dimly-lit room that in more peaceful times had been a store-room and cellar. Plaster peeled from the walls and damp patches covered the ceiling. It was hot and fetid, the only light coming from a number of candles which flickered in the gloom. There were no windows, this room was below-ground.

Before him, the battered figure, naked to the waist was trussed to the wooden chair which held him upright.

The sweat-soaked torso was streaked with blood and heavily-bruised. The scarred body looking too thin and emaciated to possess the enormous strength they knew it in fact did. Thornton looked down at the paper sheet in front of him and shook his head in exasperation. After almost an entire day of constant beating and questioning, they did not even know the prisoner's name. Again, he shook his head, they were getting nowhere and he would undoubtedly be blamed for any lack of progress. He peered at the man in front of him, listening to the laboured breathing and watched the blood dribble down the chin onto the chest.

If he could not be made to talk before they hanged him, there would be hell to pay. The magistrate, though alive and slowly recovering, did not take kindly to having his face smashed and losing an ear. It had looked for some hours as if he might die from loss of blood or shock but had rallied and was a very angry man indeed. His pride severely wounded as well as his body. The girl had, unfortunately, died from shock of both the scourging and questioning without revealing any details of this man, her obvious accomplice. Thus, he could not continue much longer with the 'interrogation' in case this man died before they could publicly hang him for his crimes and thereby assuage, to some extent, the angry citizenry.

Thornton looked up from his papers and signalled to one of the three other men in the room, who stood in the shadows, all stripped to the waist and all sweating from the heat and their exertion. At his nod, one of the three, a small squat, bald man with small piggy eyes, stepped forward and lifting a wooden pail, threw the contents with great force into the face of the prisoner. Ethan Sedgewick groaned as he returned to consciousness and raised his head. One eye was completely closed and a deep purple colour, his lips were split and swollen but, despite this, Thornton noted with anger and amazement the stare of defiance was still there.

Ethan spoke through his swollen mouth, the deep guttural, strangely accented voice gasped out, "still alive." His head sank forward again.

Thornton leaped to his feet and leaned forward on his knuckles. "Listen!" he bellowed. "If I have to kill you I will, be in no doubt, before God, I swear this."

Looking into the shadows, he noticed his men smirking at his anger, which irritated him still further. With an effort he regained control, took a deep breath, and sat down once more.

"Let's start again," he began talking as to a backward child. "What is your name and why are you here?"

He waited for almost a minute before he realised with a growing sense of futility there would be no answer.

"Was his honour, the magistrate, the intended and planned target of your assault?"

Peering once more into the battered face, he realised

with a start that his questions were not being heard, the single visible eye in the battered face was staring intently at the candle flame on the desk, the mind far away.

Leaping to his feet, he bellowed, "Listen to me!" but he got no further. The door behind him opened and a tall authoritative figure with short iron-grey hair framing a hard, angular face strode in. Thornton and his three henchmen all immediately stood to attention.

Major Tobias Bulmer stared around the room, taking in the sordid scene at a glance. "Sit down, Andrew," the voice was deep and resonant. "I have just returned and have been appraised of the events of yesterday."

Removing his gauntlets, he walked to the table and picked up the sheaf of paper on which should have been written the list of questions and the prisoner's answers. He was visibly startled when he saw that the page was blank. He looked up sharply at the younger man, "Nothing?"

"No, sir."

"After so long?"

Thornton's face was rigid. He could not look at his Major. There was an uneasy silence as intelligent eyes appraised him. "I see."

Casually Bulmer turned and glanced at the prisoner, he seemed about to turn away, when recognising something, he stiffened and leant closer, peering into the battered face. His intense scrutiny lasted for perhaps a minute before he straightened and sat easily on the edge of the table. His eyes were troubled but enlightened and he sighed.

"And is it well with you, Ethan?" he said not unkindly.

The soldiers in the room all gazed in surprise at their major and then swivelled to the prisoner who was raising his head. The two men stared at each other before incredibly, the prisoner nodded his head slightly and spoke.

"I'm alive, Tobias, still alive, and for all I know, that's all there is."

The Major nodded and leaned forward a little, "how long have you been home, my friend?"

"I'm not home."

"In England then."

"I landed yesterday."

The Major leaned back and rubbed his hand across his eyes. He shook his head slightly and, turning to Thornton, who still sat with a mystified expression on his face, said,

"This woman, she was small with long dark hair, yes?"

Thornton stared up at his Major. "Why, yes, sir, she was."

Sighing again, the Major nodded to himself and turned once more to look at the figure bound to the chair. "Oh, Ethan," he said, his voice low and intense. "Will it never be finished?"

Sedgwick said nothing but, from the corner of one battered eye, a tear emerged and rolled down the bruised face.

The Major stood, his attitude suddenly brisk and rapped out, "Take this man back to the cells and see that he is fed and given some water." The three men emerged from the shadows, untied the prisoner and hustled him out. As the door slammed to behind them, Thornton stood indignantly.

"But, sir, the report."

The Major waved him back into his seat ."It's all right, Andrew, I know this man, we can now complete your report, as I am now satisfied that this attack was in no way political and that no one hired him."

"Forgive me, sir, but how can you know?" The younger man's pride was bruised.

Slowly Bulmer moved over and sat heavily in the recently-vacated prisoner's chair and removed his broad-brimmed hat, which he laid carelessly on the floor.

"I knew him some years ago," he began. "We were in the Swedish army of King Gustavus Adolphus together, fighting the Protestant cause with the zeal of young men. Both of us with the rank of Captain. We became firm friends, shared interests and our careers in front of us." He paused and nodded at Thornton. "Much as you are now, Andrew." Mollified Thornton smiled back.

"Anyway, to continue," said Bulmer. "When I met

him, he was freshly married to a little French girl whose beauty would fetch your heart out of your mouth, I promise you." He raised his hands to give expression to his words. "She was so fragile... so delicate, you understand me? You were always afraid she might break." His eyes peered at the guttering candle remembering. "There was a tiny daughter also, maybe two years old, I'm not sure. Together they looked like one of those little porcelain statues of the Madonna and child. Ethan... " He stopped and nodded his head at the closed door. "That's his name by the way, Ethan Sedgwick. Captain Ethan Sedgwick adored them. He had tried often enough to send her home to his family farm back here somewhere, but she would have none of it. Insisted on following the army around like some camp follower, never mind the squalor and the filth." He stopped again and looked at Thornton.

"You've never fought in the foreign wars, have you, Andrew?"

"No, sir."

"Well, let me tell you those camps are a special kind of hell and for a woman and child like her... my God, she must have loved him." There was a lengthy silence again as Bulmer became lost in his thoughts.

Thornton cleared his throat. "So may I ask what happened, sir?" He was intrigued now despite himself.

Abruptly, Bulmer stood and began to pace the room. "Yes, yes, where was I? We were marching under Torstensson, my Christ, that man was an evil one, we'd slaughtered the Saxon army at Schweidnitz and were marching into Moravia." He was pacing restlessly now, the dredged-up memories affecting him. "The army was burning and pillaging, all under orders, you understand, that's the way things are done out there. They favour scorched earth to deny your enemy sustenance. I remember some of the troops found a monastery and fired it.

They even dug up the cadavers of the dead abbots for the rings on their fingers. Some of my lads had alter cloths on as cloaks, some of them even had the mummified fingers of the corpses in their hat bands." He stopped. "My God!" he said with feeling. "Christ, shield us."

"It was about noon one day when a runner came up to inform us that a large band of Croats was attacking the baggage train at the rear of the army. You have to remember, Andrew, those huge armies are strung out for miles on the march."

He stopped and looked at Thornton. "I suppose you know what I am about to say?"

Thornton had been shocked by the story and shocked that his commanding officer was telling him this. He gave a cough to cover his embarrassment. "I suspect so, sir, Sedgewick's wife and daughter were killed?"

"No." Bulmer shook his head. "If that were the case, I believe he could bear it, but it was not like that. By the time we reached the baggage train, the Croats had done their worst and were starting to retreat." Uncharacteristically, he gagged and spat on the floor. "Croats, vermin, scum, animals, they were used as light cavalry and foragers by the other side, lived on booty. They had taken many of the women with them and we followed after. Sedgewick was like a madman shouting, screaming all the time, I don't think he even knew we were there. Eventually, we caught up with some of them and, without waiting for the rest of us, he charged straight in, he was crazy like a maniac. I couldn't reach him until some more of our lads came up, but we found him surrounded by about a dozen he had killed, and they told me afterwards, and I have seen evidence today, that he had taken almost twenty sword or dagger thrusts before he went down."

"But... but he should be dead," expostulated Thornton, "No one could survive that."

"He did," said Bulmer. "For days we thought every breath would be his last, but he kept breathing, and gradually got stronger. I think it was hate that kept him alive and a desperate hope."

There was a silence, Bulmer was deep in his own thoughts far away in Moravia. "So, his wife was killed then?" queried Thornton.

Bulmer sighed and picked up his hat from the floor. "We never found her. We found the child though or rather her corpse. They had tried to rape her and she had died from what they were doing. As I said, she was about two."

"Dear God, preserve us," breathed Thornton, "and he's never recovered from it?"

"No," said Bulmer. "Physically, he recovered slowly but ever after that he was a changed man, vicious, a killer, given to mood swings, a cruel pitiless husk of a man. The husk of that man."

"So, the woman in the square in his mind was his wife?"

Bulmer placed his hat on his head preparing to leave. "No, Andrew, I don't think it's as simple as that. I think he knew what he was doing every second."

"But he must have known that would lead him to a rope. I cannot believe he would disregard that."

"Of course not," said Bulmer, moving towards the door. "He wants to die, that's really what he has been seeking these last years, to go out like a soldier." He paused his hand on the door latch and turned one last time to look at Thornton.

"Well, he'll get his wish now. But tell me this, Andrew, how can we kill a man that's already dead?"

He trudged off down the hall.

Chapter Ten

Evesham / Dartmouth, June 1645

The rotting rat's corpse was almost in two pieces, the pathetic furry little body torn and mangled beyond recognition by the two mangy mongrel dogs that fought over it. A small crowd had gathered around them to watch the meagre entertainment. Despite their troubles, there was little the average Englishman liked more than a dog fight.

It was crowded once again in the narrow streets of Evesham, the curfew having been lifted some days before. It was two weeks since the town had so bloodily changed masters and, as ever, the common folk had accepted the changing fortunes of war with resignation and resumed their humdrum existence. As long as their domestic lives were not dramatically altered, they would always take up the reins of normal life quickly. There had been the usual spate of arrests as neighbours, eager to settle old grudges, had informed on neighbours accusing them of blatant Royalist sympathies and allegiances. Most were briefly questioned and released. Only occasionally had the gallows in the main square been employed.

Many troops now resided inside the walls of the town, forcefully billeted on loudly complaining householders. In some cases, an entire house was taken over and the unfortunate occupants, grumbling loudly, although not too loudly, forced to move in temporarily with friends or relatives. They grudgingly acknowledged that it would only be until the army moved out again that the town could return to its sleepy existence.

Innkeepers and shop owners barely able to supress smug grins listened sympathetically to the moans of their customers and neighbours, whilst secretly relishing their blossoming profits. Off-duty troopers, with money in their purses and little to do in their meagre leisure hours, were good for business, although it was wise not to say so out loud, especially to a friend whose house had been commandeered.

It was with some difficulty that Mary, loaded with recently-purchased vegetables, hurried down the crowded street. The overhanging half-timbered houses and shops blocking out much of the fitful daylight made these narrow noisome streets claustrophobic and difficult to traverse. No one, it seemed, was inclined to make way for the young woman and she was forced to shove her way through a group of distracted townsfolk. So intent was she on this task that she almost fell headlong over the fighting dogs. There was a shout of annoyance from the crowd whose sport she had temporarily spoiled. She did not stop to apologise and, anyway, had not gone ten yards further before the snarling and yapping combatants resumed their squabble behind her.

She arrived at the three-storey house where the room she shared with Jacob and Parson Roberts was perched on the topmost floor and, with the energy of youth, ran up the narrow creaking staircase. A single swede came loose from her arms and, bouncing all the way back down the stairs, rolled seemingly with a mind of its own into the cobbled street and out of sight. She tutted with irritation but ran on. Her news was too urgent to stop for a lost vegetable.

Shoulder-charging the small unlatched wooden door, she almost fell into the attic room.

Jacob, his arm and shoulder heavily bandaged, sat as usual in the only upright chair gazing out of the small, mullioned dormer window. The Parson was sitting on the bed in deep concentration writing a letter to his wife. He did not know yet how he would send it but was confident he would find a way. Both men looked up in surprise as she almost fell into the room, her cheeks flushed with exertion and excitement.

"What's the matter?" Jacob's face was pale and the etched lines under his eyes showed recent suffering. His shoulder was healing well now, aided by his youth and fitness. If the young do not die of injury or illness, they recover quickly. But his wound still ached and only slowly was his strength returning. His weakness a constant irritant to him.

"News," she gasped. "Tomorrow the… "

The Parson interrupted her as he strode up to relieve her of the vegetables, "Gently, Mary, gently," he smiled. "Whatever your news, it will wait whilst you regain your breath." She nodded and began to take deep breaths whilst the two men exchanged concerned looks.

"I'm sorry," she began finally. "But I've just heard the news that's abroad in the market-place. Some troopers were full of it."

Jacob jumped up, wincing with pain at the sudden movement. "How many times have I told you not to go near the soldiers especially when you are alone!"

"Oh, fiddle, Jacob," although annoyed at his tone, she found time to be gratified that he worried about her. "I am a married woman not a child.". She smiled as she saw the colour rush to his cheeks as it always did at the mention of their marriage.

"Anyway," she continued. "They say that General Massey has had his instructions from Parliament in London and is making ready to move, probably tomorrow or the next day." She stood looking at them, her hands on her hips, proud of her role as amateur spy.

Jacob sat down again, his face troubled. The Parson said nothing but blew out his cheeks in consternation, his eyes flicking from one to the other.

"I have not been notified," said Jacob almost to himself. "They mean to leave me here."

"But what else would you expect, my son?" queried

the Parson. "You are a badly-injured man, for all they or you know, you may never be fit to fight again." He realised, even as he spoke, that this was the wrong thing to say.

Jacob's head jerked up. "Of course I'll fight again. That is a ridiculous thing to say!" he said hotly, before he checked himself. "I'm sorry," he began meekly and let out a long breath, "your pardon."

The Parson smiled and nodded to show that it was all right and he need not concern himself.

Jacob stood awkwardly and gazed once more out of the window deep in thought. Finally, he said,

"Could one of you perhaps take a message for me to Major Wilmott?"

Mary moved up behind him and laid a hand on his shoulder, "You cannot mean to go with them, my sweet?" she said, concern thick in her voice "Your wound is not yet near-healed; you'll struggle to sit your horse."

He put his arm around her waist and smiled down into her troubled eyes. "Yes," he said. "I'm going. I've got to go."

"But why?" with an effort, she did not raise her voice. Tears started in her eyes and she pulled away from him. "You'll kill yourself." She turned to the Parson.

"What was it that Major Wilmott said about not making me a widow too soon? I do not think he will need to bother overmuch, my husband will do the job for him."

The Parson rubbed his hands through his sparse white hair. "Mary is correct, you know, Jacob," he volunteered. "After what we told you of that musketeer's comments, you must realise that, if the fighting does not kill you, he will surely try again, do not doubt it."

Jacob looked from one to the other and shook his head sadly, "I do not doubt it, my friend. I think I know why he hates me so, but that is between he and I and that must not stop me from my duty."

Mary's control broke. "But why must you go?" she wailed, grabbing his hand and holding it to her cheek. "I don't understand."

Jacob struggled vainly to find the words to adequately describe how he felt. "Because," he began lamely. "Because I believe that Massey is a great man. Because, until recently, I did not greatly care about this war, it was just my vocation to be a soldier." His eyes gentled as he looked at his beautiful new wife. "Now I do care and I believe, with just a little more effort, it is all but won and we can live our lives in peace. And, if men such as I stay away because of a small hole in my shoulder, then we would not be able to look at ourselves in the mirror ever again." It was a long speech for him and, despite this, he knew he had failed to convince them. He had viewed in his mind's eye many times since the fight, the face of Massey leaning down to help him up, the gentle intense brown eyes boring into him and the voice, "Come, Jacob, it's almost done now."

He rubbed his hand across his eyes and lowered himself back down on to his chair. He looked up at the Parson. "Do you understand, sir?"

Reluctantly, the old man nodded his head, he had perceived the depth of passion and belief in the younger man's words.

"Yes, Jacob, I think I do. I am an old man and have seen much more of life than you two. This war is an abomination and an afront to our God. The sooner it ends the better. BUT, have a care for yourself, Jacob. Your shoulder is nowhere near healed."

"Well, I don't understand," sobbed Mary. "I don't understand any of it. I hate this war. I hate Massey and all like him. My mother has gone, my father and brother are God-only-knows-where, if they still live, and now my husband is going off again." Her voice became shrill with anger and foreboding, "and for what? Can you tell me, either of you?" She turned away from them and buried her face in her hands. "I tell you, Jacob," she sobbed. "If you go and get yourself killed, I am afraid, despite my love for you, I will hate you for it."

Jacob took a tentative step towards her, "Mary."

"No," she said, "I mean it."

They had reached an impasse. No one spoke for some minutes. Each deep in their own thoughts.

Mary turned at last, wiping her eyes on her apron. "If I really cannot persuade you to stay," she said, "I have one condition."

Jacob half-smiled, "Which is what, my love?"

"That the Parson and I come with you."

He opened his mouth to protest but she stalled him with a raised hand. "If you do not agree to this, Jacob, I swear before God, that I will follow you anyway. Far better that I am with the women of the army than tramping the roadways of England alone."

He could sense the steely resolve in her voice and acknowledged her depth of feeling and marvelled at her courage.

"Who knows," she continued, "I may find my father and brother." She stared defiantly from one man to the other, daring them to gainsay her. Her skirts rustled as she took a step towards the old Parson, "Will you come with me, Parson?"

The Parson breathed out slowly, aware that he was in an impossible position. He had known this young woman from the day she had been born and she had always been wilful and headstrong. That she meant every word she had spoken, he doubted not at all. He had also become fond of this brave young... man who had entered their lives so dramatically and now realised he felt true affection for this young couple attempting to make sense of the madness that surrounded them as they began their lives together. There was a darker reason for his reluctance to leave this young woman. To agree to go with them would mean hardship and physical effort which might be beyond him, he had no doubt, but he could also admit to an excitement to life of late that had

213

been missing for many years now. He made his decision.

He stood and held Mary's face between his hands. "Yes, my child, God help me, but I will go with you." The look of relief and gratitude that she gave him made his heart lurch. Despite his lifelong calling to God, he was also a man and could acknowledge true beauty when he saw it.

Mary turned to look at Jacob, her expression triumphant. Their gazes locked for long moments each striving to bludgeon the other to their will. Suddenly Jacob relented and, tipping back his head, laughed aloud. It was a sound they had not heard for an age.

"God save me, Parson, but look what you have married me to!"

He held out his hand to Mary. "Very well sweetheart. I agree." The tension vanished and they were all laughing.

"Well, well. Such merriment and at this early hour too, it cannot be wine."

The sneering, nasal voice cut through the laughter like a whiplash. Standing in the open door was the tall cadaverous figure of Wilmott, he had arrived unheard despite the creaking staircase. His head bent forward to avoid the low lintel and he stepped lightly into the room. He was fully dressed for duty. Thigh-length boots, buff coat, helmet and sash all immaculately turned out. He looked exactly what, in fact, he was; a horse soldier par excellence. His height dominated the room and an aura of business-like efficiency exuded from him together with the smell of leather polish and gun oil.

"What, no explanations?" he queried. "Am I entered into a room of mutes?"

Jacob was first to recover. "It was nothing, sir," he managed, "A joke between friends. You would find no humour in it."

"Indeed?" The cruel lazy eyes swept all three of them. "Well, then," he said, removing his helmet releasing a cascade of greasy black hair. "To business, Lieutenant Sedgewick, I am here to inform you that my General has received his orders from Parliament and that he, his officers and men are leaving this place on the morrow to march into the west country as we are bid. I am come to see if you, as an officer under my command, will be ready at first light, fully armed and accoutred for war to attend on me?"

Jacob stiffened and, wincing with pain, began to remove his bandages. "I will be ready, sir."

Wilmott stared at the young man and slowly replaced his helmet. "Good," he intoned. "Until first light tomorrow then. I bid you good day."

Turning abruptly, he ducked his head once more, stalked out through the door and stumped off down the stairs.

"Well said, Jacob," into the silence, a weak smile crossing his face. "That settles that."

Mary and the Parson did not return his smile.

Later that night, Jacob and Mary lay abed, comfortable in the warmth from each other's bodies.

They did not wish to disturb the old Parson who, out of consideration to the newly married couple, slept on a makeshift truckle in the other room. The so-called 'bedroom' that they were in was, in truth, little more than a large cupboard, but in these challenging times it served its purpose.

As yet the 'new' marriage had not been consummated. Partly due to Jacob's injuries but also partly due to their natural reticence and embarrassment resulting from the unusual circumstance of their marriage. There had been little or no wooing or courtship and, in truth, they did not know each other very well at all. Growing love between them was helped by a genuine affection and liking for each other. God willing, they would have many years ahead to develop their relationship but that was for the future. For now, they took pleasure in each other's company and, on a more practicable level, warmth from each other's bodies.

Mary lay comfortably on the straw-filled mattress, her head in the crook of Jacob's arm. She lay as still as she could, unwilling to disturb her husband's injured shoulder. He had fallen into a fitful sleep some time past, but she knew he must be up early and tomorrow would be a difficult day for them all.

Outside the small, mullioned window, a dog howled mournfully, the only sound in a dark and silent Evesham. A little earlier, a patrol had tramped by and she had watched the light from their flaming torches process across the raftered ceiling above them. She heard a brief bout of laughter from one of the small rooms below them in this shabby little garret but then silence again.

How her life had changed in these last few short weeks. He mother dead, remembrance of this still brought with it an almost physical wince of pain, her new husband and her possibly forlorn quest to find her father and brother. It had all happened with a suddenness almost incomprehensible to a farmer's daughter who had only rarely left the family home in her young life. It was a time when personal freedoms, especially for women, were governed by a strict set of rules as to the way one behaved. Mary was a rarity in her village in that she could both read and write, courtesy of her father's friendship with the kindly little Parson in the next room. She was both comely and intelligent and, but for this war, would long since have been married off to some local young man who had, as her father would term it, 'prospects or land.'

Jacob stirred next to her and she laid her hand on his chest. The bandages across his shoulder would need changing before he left and she made a mental note to tie them differently.

"Are you awake?" His muffled voice startled her; she had presumed him deep in slumber.

"Yes," she murmured. "Does your shoulder hurt you, sweet?"

"Aches a little," said Jacob. "Throbs in the night. I

don't notice it in the daylight." He shifted position slightly with a grunt. "What keeps you awake, it must be almost dawn?"

"Oh, nothing and everything," she answered as lightly as she could. The silence stretched on and she felt she must elaborate. "Do you ever think about this awful war and how it all started, how we all arrived where we are now?"

She felt his chest rise as he silently chuckled. "Serious questions for so early in the day, wife of mine." Saying that phrase gave him a thrill of pleasure; 'wife of mine,' he could hardly believe it!

She raised herself on one elbow and peered down at his face in the gloom. "No, Jacob, I mean it. What happened? We continue with our lives as best as we can, we lose people, things change always it seems for the worst and we never ask why?"

Sensing the deep concern in her voice, he decided against the flippant answer that had sprung to mind and frowned to construct another. "In truth, I don't know. I've thought about it often. Perhaps it's not a question for the likes of us. Its more than we know. All we can do is say our prayers and hope we do the right thing in the eyes of God and get through this." It was a long speech for him and he realised that it clarified his mind a little.

"When I was younger, I was aware, as was everyone, of the excesses of our King. Father used to tell us some evenings as we all sat in front of the fire, news that he had heard talked of at the market or in the street.

I can still see him now resting in his rocking chair, his long clay pipe in his mouth, rumbling on about taxes that were always increasing, life was ever harder and there were stories of waste at court."

Mary nodded. "Pa never used to tell us anything. I heard him in long discussions with the Parson and others of his friends many times, but if I ever asked him about things, he would chuck my chin in the way he always did and say, "nothing for you to worry your pretty head about, little maid."" She smiled at the memory.

Jacob shifted position slightly again and hissed as he stretched his wound. He sighed and looked up at the beautiful face above him framed as it was by long hanging silver gilt hair. 'My wife,' he thought again and smiled, 'God above, my wife.' He reached up with his uninjured arm and touched her face. She took his hand and kissed his fingers.

"How did you come to be in the army?" she asked, remembering to keep her voice low. "I've never thought to ask?" She could hear the gentle rumble of the little Parson's snores in the next room.

"After Ethan left, we just carried on as best we could," said Jacob slowly, "although with him gone it was hard for the two of us and father not well, to do the work of three. But we had no choice, times were hard for everyone.

Then when he died, I had a choice to make. The country was full of urgent gossip at the time. Pym and Hampden railing at the King for misgovernment.

Strafford advocating that an Irish army be brought over to subdue the people of the country. Can you imagine that?" He dropped his hand from her face and placed it behind his head. "Then the King went into parliament with armed men, armed men! To arrest the five members who opposed him. That was it for me. My mind was decided as to who had the right of it, so not long afterward when the time came, I leased the farm to a neighbour for a peppercorn rent and joined the army to fight for Parliament."

Outside another patrol went by, muttering and laughing at some comment. Together they watched as, once more, the torchlight moved across the ceiling. Each glad of the interruption to gather their thoughts. For each of them it was a new experience in their young lives to share intimate thoughts in the darkest hours of the night with someone lying next to you. They each found it both comforting and, in some way, disconcerting. Mary realised that God-willing this would be the way of it for the rest of her life. Every small snippet of knowledge she could gain about this man, her husband, was of intense interest.

Overwhelming in its importance. She sucked in each morsel and stored it away amongst the memories of her life.

"Did I do right, my love?" His low-voiced question startled her; it was the first time he had used this term of endearment. She smiled into the darkness and felt the warmth of belonging and love wrap itself around her.

She leaned down and lightly kissed his forehead.

"Yes, my love," she whispered, mimicking his words. "You did right and now we must try to sleep a little more before the morning." She snuggled down into the crook of his arm once more, careful not to jar his shoulder, revelling in the warmth and strength of his body. Lightly, she laid her arm across his chest. 'He is mine,' she thought and smiled even more broadly, 'my husband.'

Presently they both slept.

In the next room, the little Parson was not sleeping either. Dimly, he was aware of muted voices from the other side of the thin plastered wall, but he paid them no heed. He was very troubled.

The last few weeks had descended on him with the suddenness of a summer storm which always starts with an unexpected thunderclap from behind the dark clouds as they threaten the afternoon sun.

He was worried beyond telling for his ageing wife, Bridget. They had not been apart for more than the odd night during the whole of their long married life. She was always called upon in their village to attend a woman in an awkward labour or to ease someone's suffering as they passed away during the dark hours of the night. These small temporary absences he accepted without demure, it was good that she was respected and needed by the simple folk of the village. His spiritual care, such as it was, augmented by her earthlier comforts.

He had hardly ever left the little collection of cottages and small farms that he called home. His own little Norman church was his solace and his comfort and he spent many hours within its safe homely walls, both praying and meditating on life. Now, because of his loyalty and care for the daughter of his friend, Martin Honeywell, he had ventured out into a world he neither understood nor liked. What had happened to his fellow countrymen? Why did they fight and kill each other? He had asked his God many times but received no answer.

He and Bridget had wanted a family of their own many years ago when they first married, but three miscarriages had put paid to that dream and, amidst comforting a grieving and distraught young wife, he had to acknowledge that, for a reason unknown to him, his God did not want children to divert him from his path of spiritual guardianship. He had accepted his lot but was quite sure that Bridget never had. But somehow, they had stayed together and made a success of their lives, hadn't they? They served a useful purpose and lived a fruitful existence, albeit alone. He had to believe that, how else would a man continue? But now, the companion of his life, his helpmeet and strength was alone back there in the little Herefordshire village and who knew what perils may threaten her. This war had not touched their cosy little existence much at all until that dreadful night when Martin and his son, John, were taken by a gang of ruffians that had appeared out of the dark.

He could find no way of discovering if his Bridget was still in health. That the villagers who surrounded her would keep an eye out for her he had no doubt, but was that enough? He hoped so. She, in turn, must be so anxious for news of him. Try as he might, he had as yet been unable to find any way of sending a letter to her. Jacob had hinted that he would attempt to arrange for a military messenger to divert and pass by the village to deliver a missive but, thus far, had not found the opportunity.

He was an old man now and his body during the last few days was beginning to tell him about it. The arthritis in his knees and hands was painful and daily he could feel his old body's strength ebbing as he demanded more from it than in many a year.

He levered himself on to his side and stared at the flaking plaster of the wall. Where would this end? Would they find his old friend, Martin, or would they discover that both he and John had perished in some pointless skirmish during the last year? He sighed hugely and tried to calm his mind. He needed sleep; he and Mary must be ready to resume their march to the south tomorrow in the wake of the army. Mary would not entertain the idea of leaving her new husband now, nor would she give up the desire to find her father and brother and 'slink back home,' as she termed it. The train of wives, prostitutes and hangers-on would straggle along amongst the dust of the military supply wagons, eating the dust of the foot soldiers and cavalry ahead of them. It was the same whenever armed regiments moved in any war, that much he knew, but he had never imagined in his wildest dreams that he would ever be part of such a rag- tag band.

'The Lord is my shepherd,' he intoned in a low voice to himself, the well-known oft-repeated words a calming balm and a comfort to him. 'I shall not want. He maketh me to lie down in green pastures, he leadeth me beside still waters, he restoreth my soul. He leadeth me in the paths of righteousness for his name's sake. Yea though I walk through the valley of the shadow of death I shall fear no evil for thou art with me.' Before he had finished the Psalm, he was asleep once more.

Dartmouth:

Someone was roughly shaking him by the shoulders, trying to wake him. He did not want to wake, he wanted to stay where he was where it was warm and safe. He fought to stay there, deep down in his dreams, but it was a losing battle. Slowly, like a diver coming up from a deep pool, he surfaced to the real world, away from the loving embrace of a wife long-dead, from the delicate touch of a child's hands on his face.

The pain in his body erupted as his senses returned, and he groaned as his battered body and bruised face registered, as did the damp stone-flagged floor on which he lay, trussed hand and foot. He growled an obscenity, expecting a blow or a kick in return, but none came.

"Ethan," a voice from the past stirred his memory and he remembered last night. Experimentally,, he opened one swollen eye and gazed up at the face above him dimly illuminated by the flaring torch held aloft. Again, he was shaken and, again, the insistent voice, "Ethan, come now up."

Bulmer, that was it, Tobias Bulmer, a name from the past had turned up into that dreadful cellar and halted the beating. He came fully awake and sat up slowly. His whole body was damp from the moss-covered flagstones. He shook his head to clear his vision.

"I'm going to cut your bonds, Ethan," said Bulmer. "Don't try anything. Your word on it?" Ethan nodded dumbly.

The pain as the blood flow returned to his hands and legs was excruciating but he made no sound. He leaned back against the damp cellar wall and massaged his thighs waiting for what would come next.

Bulmer straightened and loomed above him, concern on his face. "Can you stand?"

Sedgewick nodded. "Let's find out," he grated, and with an effort and a groan, stood on shaky legs. He leaned against the wall so as not to fall back down again, but every minute brought fresh feeling and pain to his legs and body. He breathed deeply feeling slightly better despite the fetid air and looked at his old colleague in arms, a long questing look.

Bulmer was obviously fighting an internal battle with himself as to what to do. His loyalties were being tested here and he had come down to this dank, dark cellar not really sure of what he would do.

"Ethan," he said at last, "I'm going to let you go."

It was the last thing that Ethan had expected to hear and he peered suspiciously at the grey-haired major in front of him.

"Let me go?" he croaked. "Why?"

Bulmer lowered the flaring torch and glanced over his shoulder to ensure they were still alone. "Let's say, I owe you," he said. "You remember that fight on the bridge over the Elbe? Those Spanish pikemen? You saved my life that day and lost blood doing it, my friend." He reached forward and gripped Ethan's shoulder. "But I pay my debts only once, you understand me?" His eyes had grown hard. "For what you did, I should have you flogged through the streets and hanged before the jeering mob and, be in no doubt, should you fall into my hands again, that is exactly what I must do."

Ethan levered himself up off the wall, finally standing unaided. He looked at Bulmer and nodded, "I understand... thank you."

"Get far away from here," said Bulmer, not unkindly. "I know what you've been through. It's enough. Go home, if it's still there, be a farmer and try to forget."

"Forget?" said Ethan. "Is that what you said?" He gave a stifled sob. "I will never forget. Never." With a physical effort, he collected himself. "The devil rules the world, Tobias. To survive is all, there is no redemption, only the will to endure." He rubbed grubby hands through his hair and stared into the dark, his catechism stated, his demons riding him once more.

For long moments Bulmer stared at the broken figure in front of him, briefly remembering the man he had known. It was a strange thing for his old friend to have said and delivered in that eery monotone, as if someone else had taken over his speech, it had set the hairs on the back of his neck on end.

Perhaps the wise men would know why he had changed character in an instant, perhaps not. He shrugged the thought aside and became brisk once more. Stepping forward, he shook Ethan's hand. Then, as if this simple act finally discharged his debt, he stepped back and became the professional soldier once more.

"So, the guard at this door has gone. Turn left, up two flights of stairs and through the door into the alley. There you will find my saddled horse. The trooper guarding it is unconscious with a large bump on his head, that I will attribute to you. Ride north, always north."

Ethan was still a little dazed but, even so, began to move forward. Halting him briefly, Bulmer gave him his retrieved saddlebag and weapons. "God go with you, Ethan," he said and gave a sketchy half-mocking salute. "I hope you find some peace, my friend."

Ethan moved away into the darkness. "God does not know me," he grated out of the gloom and was gone.

Interlude

Naseby, Northamptonshire. 14th June 1645

The Parliamentary army had been on the march since three o clock in the morning, long before the grey of dawn began to lighten the sky. Now, hours later, like some huge uncoiling snake, it was marshalling into battle array, to the incessant, urgent beat of a hundred drums and the shouts of officers. The milky light of a chill dawn illuminated the pinched, drawn features of fourteen thousand faces, as men marched and manouvered through bitter, drifting rain, under a lowering, pewter-coloured sky. Drummer boys blew on cold numbed fingers and dried slippery drumsticks on their jackets. The soldiers with heavy pikes fourteen feet in length or heavy, clumsy muskets to handle, could not afford such luxury, so their skinned knuckles showed white through cold blued skin.

Each man's view of the world was restricted to the neck and head gear of the man to his front and had been since the first faint suggestion of light, that now seemed hours ago. Tired by the endless march through the wet darkness, stiff with cold, most had ceased to notice the constant rolling orders of the drums and merely followed where the man in front of them led. On the wind above the drum's demanding beat, could be heard the constant barrage of obscenities and invective from the sergeants and officers as they laboured like so many sheepdogs to position the ranks of sullen, wet men into line of battle. Laying about them brutally with their insignia of rank, the halberd or half- pike.

Surveying the scene from the crest of the slope on which the army was forming, sat a tall, immaculately-dressed man on a bay horse. The fine tawny orange silk sash slung voluminously over his left shoulder and across his breastplate of fine steel denoted someone of high rank. His long shoulder-length black hair, thick and curly when dry, hung lank and dripping now despite the protection of his broad-brimmed hat. The thin, almost ferrety face, held brooding eyes that gazed with worry at the forming army. Absently, he pulled at his sparse moustache, made thinner by this constant habit.

Thomas Fairfax, his Excellency the Lord General of the Parliamentary Armies, was uneasy. As nervous as the greenest recruit in his army this bleak June morning. The regiments forming up below him had never fought together as a unit before but had been selected piecemeal from the various armies of Parliament in England. The 'New Model' army, or as followers of the King unflatteringly called it, the 'New Noddle' had yet to prove its metal. Unfortunately, the army it was about to meet was not one to be indecisive or haphazard with.

Although, if his scouts were to be believed, outnumbered by two to one, the grizzled veterans of the main Royalist army, especially with Prince Rupert and the King himself present, were without doubt the finest fighting force in the land.

Fairfax's horse shied as he involuntarily jerked at the bit. "This battle," he mused grimly. "This one decides it all. Praise God for small mercies, at least Goring is not with them."

Below him, the army was making final adjustments to its positions as it stood almost a half a mile in length along its front. Before it, the ground sloped away gently to open scrubland, which continued for some half a mile until rising again up an identical slope. It was as if God himself had fashioned an ideal fighting ground.

The formation was standard according to current military doctrine. Cavalry on either flank. Thousands of stern, sober men sitting on fidgeting, nervous horses. Steam from fresh dung rising in clouds between the buff-coated and leather-clad ranks in the drizzle. Between these 'wings' were marshalled the infantry. Huge forests of standing pikes, swaying slightly in the sullen breeze, edged on either side with musketeers. These regiments were arranged in the popular Swedish fashion, purposely left gaps in the front line covered by regiments to their rear. A huge chequer board of ten thousand men. Ten thousand faces, expectant, nervous, bored, or resigned, all peering through the rain from under a roof of helmets. Their wives, children, doxies and goods left half a mile to the rear, where they crouched around the baggage wagons near to the barred and shuttered village of Naseby.

Fairfax's saddle creaked as he turned to survey the staff officers who sat their horses in a bedraggled but gaily-coloured group behind him. Their grey faces, like his were taut with tension. A wry smile curled the corners of his mouth.

"Well, gentlemen, not too cold, I trust"?

The ironic question brought a response of laughter as the tension cracked momentarily. He fed it with a further light remark, knowing from experience the value of light conversation at such a time. He did not want officers ruined by nerves on such a day as this was likely to be.

The jingle of harness and the thump of hooves turned heads, as his second-in-command, Lieutenant General Oliver Cromwel,l arrived with his aides, fresh from surveying the dispositions of his beloved Eastern Association cavalry on the right flank. Cromwell heeled his horse to Fairfax's side as his aides took station with the rest behind him. His face, under the triple barred helmet, was flushed with excitement, the eyes glittering and feverish. The warts on his face stood out proudly as if they too were excited. He removed his helmet and ran his fingers through his thinning sandy-coloured hair. His voice, when he spoke, was deep and, as he was used to speaking in the commons, pitched to carry.

"Well, Thomas, so the day has come at last."

Fairfax nodded. "Indeed it has, Oliver. Indeed it has. Let us hope that we do not regret we forced it, until the end of our days." He stood in his stirrups to survey the army from one end to the other.

Cromwell snorted, his look derisive.

"You surely do not doubt we have the beating of them? They are overmatched by two to one?" He stared flatly at Fairfax, his belief in what he was about to say absolute. "And God is with us this day, Thomas, as we smite down the sinful."

Fairfax stared back, striving to probe the smaller man's mind, but gave up in the face of the bland self-righteous expression.

"Yes," he said, lowering his voice so that only Cromwell could hear, "we outnumber them, but too many of our regiments are untried, many are casualty replacements. Garrison duty is not like the lightning of battle."

Cromwell smiled and rested his hand on his superior's arm. "Nevertheless, Thomas, we shall, with God's help, prevail. I feel it calmly and surely."

Fairfax smiled back. "As to that, Oliver, I trust you are correct."

Their conversation was halted, as with squealing wheels, the great guns of the artillery train were trundled past, manhandled by sweating, swearing gun teams, struggling in the knee-high slippery grass. Fairfax drew some slight comfort at the sight of these menacing, efficient dealers of death. The cloying sulphur-like aroma of gunpowder and wadding filled the air, and he wrinkled his nose. When he could be heard, Cromwell spoke again,

"You cannot doubt the competence of those men when faced with Prince Rupert's whoreson rabble?" He pointed to the massed ranks of his own cavalry. The dour men of Lincolnshire and East Anglia, whose reputation for iron discipline and professionalism had been hard-won in many a battle.

Fairfax shook his head, spraying raindrops. "No, Oliver, I do not. I think much today will rest on those gentlemen. It is of the infantry that I worry. Would to God they were more experienced. The men they face today have proven metal."

Cromwell made to interrupt but was silenced by Fairfax's upraised hand, "and be not scathing of their horse, sr. Any body of men led by Prince Rupert, or Marmaduke Langdale are no whoreson rabble, but stout-hearted men who have faced steel before."

He would have said more but their conversation was halted by exclamations from the men behind them.

"My Lord, look." Gloved hands thrust forward, fingers pointing through the rain. Not half a mile away on the far slope, the Royalist army, its gay colours muted by mist and distance was emerging from the trees and forming up in similar battle-formation. Cromwell raised his face to the sky,

"Praise be to God. They are going to fight." There was a chorus of Amens.

Fairfax turned his horse to face the assembled group. "Gentlemen, you all have your orders. I think the time has come for you to take up your positions. Good luck and God be with you this day".

As if nature herself wished to set the scene, the rain stopped abruptly. The wind strengthened, tearing the clouds to ragged tatters, allowing a weak, watery sun to break through. A patchwork of light and shade that raced across the ground between the armies. Steam could be seen rising from horses and men alike as the air became warmer. The parliamentary standards were unfurled to flap and crack wetly on the breeze, whilst the inevitable chaplains roamed through the ranks intoning prayers. Their words were greeted with reverence or indifference by the standing, waiting men, who craned their necks to peer anxiously forward to where they could hear, above the religious utterings, the ominous rumble of the enemy drums. This was the worst time of all, when men were forced to stand and watch death in all its garish colours take up position just half a mile away. The air became thick with the stench of sewage, a smell well-known to the older soldiers, as men answered the call of nature for the last time. Smoke from the freshly-lit match of the musketeers and gunners drifted silently overhead. Slowly, as the minutes passed, all sound died away until there was only the sighing of the wind as thousands of men stood and peered at each other.

From his vantage point above the Royalist army, Charles Stuart, King of England, stared silently, intently forward. His huge eyes troubled, but his outward countenance calm. It was only by a supreme effort and long practice that he was maintaining this charade. Inwardly, he was in tumult. His staff around him were jittery, nerves and tension manifesting themselves with tell-tale finger tapping or tuneless low humming. The horses themselves trembled, sensing the disquiet of their riders.

Rupert was positioned with his cavalry on the right wing of the Royalist army. It was expressly against his advice that they fought today and, finally, after strong confrontational words with his uncle, he had stormed off, his words about ill-conceived time and place still ringing in Charles's ears.

The King knew that today was a gamble, but it was a gamble he had convinced himself he was justified in taking. His army he knew was strong and well-drilled. True, it was smaller than the one it faced, but what it lacked in numbers it made up for in experience. He also knew he might never again have such a force under his command.

He shifted his position in his saddle slightly, easing the pressure on his spine. Like those around him, he had been on horseback for most of the night. Bowing his head, as he had done many times this morning, he prayed once again to his God for victory. His muttered plea done, he raised his eyes to peer intently at the army massed against him in serried ranks, not so far away. Squinting, he tried to identify individual figures standing apart from the main body and almost imagined he could see a man named Fairfax staring back.

Men standing in the parliamentary ranks heard trumpets sound shrilly and immediately heads craned to see what was happening. It appeared on their left, a cloud had drifted across the sun, casting a huge shadow that raced across the ground towards them. But this shadow screamed and howled and was accompanied by the rolling thunder of hooves.

Rupert and two thousand cavalry hurled themselves across the dividing gap in an awesome, terrifying, gut-wrenching charge. Swords held aloft glinting and winking in the weak sunlight. It was both beautiful and horrifying to see and was immediately followed on the right as Marmaduke Langdale's horsemen threw themselves forward.

Fairfax, his quickly drying hair fluttering in the fitful breeze, watched them come unperturbed, his staff murmuring around him. With grim satisfaction, he saw his own cavalry wings, the right under Cromwell, the left under the command of one of parliament's brightest rising stars, the young and chilly, Henry Ireton, move forward to meet the attacks.

Theirs was not the magnificent but undisciplined charge of the royalist horse, rather they jogged forward, knee-to-knee in dense formations. They looked what they were, solid, dependable and professional. Beneath him, his horse shied sideways as the big guns on both sides opened fire with a ground-shaking roar. The air was suddenly filled with the sounds of battle. The crunch and thunder of cannon, serried musket fire, the screams of horses in pain and the animal roar of thousands of men eager to fight yet held back.

The infantry on both sides swung forward with a yell, the pikes dipping, casting long shadows on the grass, their murderous long steel points seeking bellies and breasts to tear and gouge. Slowly, the distance between the armies narrowed. Fairfax and the King sat and watched like chess players, and each silently prayed to the same God for victory.

Events on the wings differed greatly. Rupert's men smashed through the roundhead horse in five furious minutes but, once again, making his habitual mistake, Rupert allowed them to career on blindly towards Naseby, chasing the fleeing stragglers of Ireton's broken cavalry, leaving behind them a wreckage of maimed, squealing horses and slashed men writhing on the ground already soaked with fresh blood.

At the other end of the field, Langdale's dour Yorkshiremen crashed into the equally dour men of Cromwell's Eastern Association, bounced off and were promptly routed without ceremony. Here Cromwell's inborn genius for battlefield quick-thinking showed through. Not for his men, the wild hallowing pursuit of a fleeing enemy, rather under his iron control the whole wing, halted, regrouped and swung left to crash into the now exposed flank of the furiously fighting Royalist infantry.

Charles Stuart leaned forward anxiously in his saddle, his fists balled and his knuckles shining whitely with tension. Down there in the centre of the field the incredible was happening. Outnumbered two-to-one the superb Royalist foot were nonetheless rolling back the vastly larger Parliamentary centre. As he watched, aware of the murmurs of excitement behind him, the incredible was happening. Before his eyes, the whole confused mass of screaming, yelling, struggling humanity was moving away from him. He closed his eyes and raised his face to the sky where the wind whipped clouds still raced.

"Dear God, who is with us this day," he whispered, "By your mercy, dear Father, let it happen, please let it happen."

The slaughter and carnage in the holocaust that was the centre of the battle was terrible. The vicious pikes wielded by men who knew their trade, were scything down bodies in droves. Blood founted high, as swords slashed and hacked, hissing through flesh and jarring on bone. Musketeers unable now to fire in the hand-to-hand fighting, reversed their heavy weapons and laid about them with skull-crushing gusto.

The noise was terrific. The screamed obscenities, the snatches of chanted Psalm, mingling with the cries, and shrieks of the maimed, and the dying. The ground underfoot was soggy with blood,and men's feet became entangled with jerking, twitching bodies or the snake-like clutch of purple, glutinous intestines. The clang of metal on metal was constant, like some demented blacksmith's forge. Sporadically-fired musket or pistol balls whistled and whispered around men's heads. Father stumbled over son, brother over brother in this relentless butcher's shop. No two men remembered it alike. To some it was minutes, to some hours before it became obvious that the Parliamentary army was inching remorselessly, grudgingly backwards, rage giving way to near-panic. Those at the rear of the army, seeing what was happening and unable to do anything to help, hacked at the ground in useless, impotent anger. Those at the front fought with a remorseless intent, like savages, as the latent ferocity of Englishmen overtook them. Their torsos and arms blood-soaked, eyes rolling with terror and excitement as they struggled to stay on their feet, trampling on their own dead and dying.

Almost unnoticed at first amidst the chaos, the inexorable advance of the Royalist army slowed and stopped. Sweating, weary men, fighting for their lives in the bitter melee became dimly aware of the tall shapes of horsemen at the edge of their vision. Those foolish enough to turn and look, paid for the mistake with the swift painful darkness of sudden death, as a pike head, or sword edge found their defenceless bodies. Amidst the din, a new sound could be heard, the high-pitched scream of frantic horses. Pikes ripped through their bellies and they danced on their own hanging entrails, their unnoticing riders hacking viciously about them with razor sharp swords. Somewhere a pike severed a horse's jugular, spraying thick dark blood for yards around, somewhere else a sword stroke severed a horse's foreleg and the beast fell shrieking and squealing to the ground, its flaying hooves doing terrible execution amongst those close to it.

Slowly the fury began to slacken and it became apparent that the Royalist host was now itself moving backwards. In ones and twos and then tens and twenties, they moved back, giving ground grudgingly inch by inch, walking and finally running away, until the whole Royalist foot were in full route, pikes and swords flung to the ground, only one thought remaining as they ran for their lives, to escape, hands held high above their heads for protection. So they ran, dodging and ducking, pursued savagely and unmercifully by the roundhead horse, because cavalry gives no quarter.

Fairfax, watching the drama below him, let out his breath with a hiss as he sat back in his saddle, the tension evaporating. From his position, he had clearly seen what had happened. Whilst Rupert and his cavalry swept off the field and away in their unstoppable charge, the scattered parliamentary horse had been reformed, by a shouting, hustling Ireton. Then, emulating his mentor Cromwell, he smashed them straight into the exposed and vulnerable flank of the struggling Royalist infantry.

Fighting fiercely and with a stubborn pride, even these superb fighting men had to give ground as they found themselves attacked by cavalry from both flanks, as well as fighting to their front. Now with their inevitable route, the battle was over.

"Now," thought Fairfax, "The King must surely admit it is over, only a mad man would continue."

He leaned forward, absently patting his restive mount's neck. "How long has it been?" he mused. "Three years, four years?" He smiled grimly, allowing himself to hope that, God willing, he would soon return to some sort of normal life with his wife and children. Bursts of shouting from below broke his train of thought. "No," he said to himself. "The killing is not yet over".

Across the valley, seeing what was happening below him, the King was half-crazed with impotent anger. Jerking his horse savagely around, he surveyed the remnants of Langdale's horse to his left and, turning his head, screamed to his staff officers and personal bodyguard, his composure for once in tatters.

"With me, my Lords. If we gather yon gallant Yorkshire gentlemen, one brave charge can yet save the day."

He swayed forward in his saddle against his horse's neck when the beast did not move. The hand that held the bridle staying the horse belonged to the grizzled Earl of Carnwath, a lifelong servant of the house of Stuart.

Leaning from his own mount he gazed up at his monarch, fear and compassion working his face.

"Will you ride upon your death, sir?"

For long seconds the two men glared at each other, the King and his faithful subject, whilst all around held their breath. It was the eyes of the king that dropped, his steel-clad shoulders slumped and he bowed his head.

"Aye," he said, his voice flat and empty. "You are right, of course, my friend. My very dear friend."

Tears rushed to the bluff old earl's eyes, as they did to many about. He turned to look at the carnage below.

Dead and dying lay thick in the trampled grass, their blood soaking into the soil of England. Maimed and dying horses limped aimlessly across the field whilst here and there small groups of royalist foot still with fight left in them stood in clumps surrounded by jeering, cat-calling roundhead infantry, still eager to do murder.

"This is a sad day for the realm indeed," he said almost to himself, then made a business of coughing to hide his emotion. The King sat with his head still bowed, his reins slack in his hands. Carnwath leaned over again and took them from the loose grip of his monarch, then followed by the rest of the group, led his King away through the trees.

The savagery of the roundhead cavalry became legend that day as they relentlessly pursued the fleeing royalist infantry. Catching them in the open in ones and twos, they slashed and hacked without mercy, at the men who sobbed with fear and frustration as they ran. Many were not given the grace of a sword, but merely ridden down under trampling hooves, the riders laughing and joking that it was not worth the trouble of swinging tired sword arms when the horses could do the work for them.

They killed them in fields and woods, in ditches and in barns, or outbuildings where they had crawled for safety. Local villagers, who had strayed too close to get a better view of the battle, were likewise butchered where they stood, by over-exited cavalrymen, be they men, women, or children.

They found the baggage park of the Royalist army sometime during the riot and their commander, Oliver Cromwell, the staunch disciplinarian, turned a blind eye as over two hundred women were hacked to death where they stood. Those that survived the first onslaught suffered multiple rapes before having their noses slit as whores.

Cromwell was later to write of the battle, 'Naseby was a great battle of which I had a great assurance, and God did it.'

Chapter Eleven

Somerset, June 1645

On June 18th four days after the great battle at Naseby, George Goring wrote to the Prince of Wales that he had been appraised that General Massey, with a substantial force at his command, was heading down into the west country. He also advised that he must soon be forced to lift the siege of Taunton, as he put it, 'Out of Hunger.'

Just over a week later, Massey and his force met up with the much larger force of Fairfax and Cromwell, fresh from their victory at Naseby. The Dorsetshire village of Blandford was the rendezvous point and, from there, the joint force moved south to confront the forces of the King still active in the west country. This was important work for, as everyone knew, the three south western counties had long been a major source of manpower and raw materials for the Royalists. Goring knew he could do little to stop them but was determined to do whatever he could for his royal master.

The constant jolting constantly sent lightning bolts of pain searing through Jacob's shoulder and on down through the whole of the left side of his body. The crusty skin that had formed over the half-healed ugly wound in his shoulder had cracked with the incessant punishment and was weeping puss under his clothing. He could feel his homespun shirt sticking to the scar and the weight of his buff coat was causing it to rub painfully, adding to his discomfort.

His face under his broad-brimmed hat was pale and drawn, his lips pressed together in a thin line as he gritted his teeth against the intense throbbing agony wracking his body. Tears started in his eyes as his horse stumbled in a rut.

Dust was everywhere, covering men and horses, thrown up by the hooves of the thirty-strong patrol as they jog-trotted over the earthen track baked hard by the recent hot weather. It covered Jacob and his fellow soldiers from head to foot in a white film, giving the impression to a pair of farm labourers who watched them go by from their hiding place behind a bush that a troop of ghosts had ridden past two-by-two.

Shouts of command were kept low. This was a reconnaissance patrol out on its own, exposed and vulnerable, advancing into enemy territory. Five miles behind them, the main Parliamentary army toiled and sweated through the midday heat moving ever deeper into Somerset. Their slow progress dictated by the heavy guns and wagons that accompanied them. They were seeking to locate river crossing points over the Parrett and the Yeo as Goring's troops had destroyed many of the bridges, but they were well aware that somewhere up ahead were units of Goring's cavalry still eager to fight and anxious to pinpoint for their leader the position of the Parliament men.

Two or three ranks ahead of him ,Jacob could see the lanky frame and greasy hair of the man he now hated and feared above all. Since leaving Evesham Town three weeks ago, every disagreeable, and hazardous task had been assigned to him by Major Wilmott. Initially maintaining that this was due to petty spite and antagonism, Jacob now nevertheless realised that Wilmott desired his death. In the evening, unless he was on duty, he had the meagre comfort of Parson Roberts and Mary watching his back, but out on a patrol such as this, he was well aware that he was very much on his own.

His wound showed a stubborn refusal to heal and daily strenuous wear and tear were, if anything, making it worse. His pride would allow no one, least of all Major Wilmott, to learn in what discomfort and pain he was and it was only in the depths of night that his wife heard the odd involuntary groan. He suffered from an intermittent feve, and occasionally tossed in light delirium, but still, he would not report sick, knowing far better than his companions that this would place him in increased danger.

Deep in his disconsolate thoughts, he failed to hear the command to halt or see the upraised fist signal and his horse crashed into the trooper in front of him drawing a string of curses. Sheepishly apologising to the snarled rebuke from the sergeant, he dismounted as did the rest of the troop. He gingerly stretched out his arm easing the stiffness and pain a little in his inflamed shoulder.

Glancing up at the sun, he judged it was past noon, which meant they had been riding for around three hours. The narrow track they were now on was wide enough only to allow two horses abreast and flanked on both sides by low banks topped with brambles and scrub.

'A terrible place for cavalry to be caught unawares,' he mused.

The troop rested whilst a low conversation took place at the front of the column. Jacob sat on the grass bank holding the reins of his horse which nibbled disinterestedly at the short grass. Low conversation and muted laughter hung in the sultry air that was heavy with the buzzing of insects.

His thoughts turned to Mary his new wife and he smiled. She had become the single most important thing in his life and he loved her with a passion. They had found a mutual comfort in each other's company and, occasionally, laughter amidst this chaos. Sitting here on this god-forsaken grass bank he could feel her gentle touch on his face, feel her breath on his cheek. Her calm soothing voice whispering in his ear, things that he would never dare tell another living soul. He gave an involuntary mew of desire and his smile broadened as he blushed despite himself.

His eyelids came slowly down and he began to

doze, the dull pain in his shoulder beginning to abate with the lack of movement, but he was nudged awake by the trooper next to him, offering a water flask.

"Drink, sir?"

Murmuring his thanks, he drank deeply. The water was warm and tasted of leather but very welcome. His throat was dry and he realised he still had a fever. He chatted desultorily with the trooper next to him until the order to remount came down the line. With dull resignation, he climbed into his creaking, hot saddle and, with a start, became aware of Wilmott standing at his stirrup.

"How is the shoulder, Sedgewick?" The smiling cadaverous face oozed malice. "It mends well, thank you, sir."

"Excellent, then you will take a turn leading the van, if you will." He stalked away.

The trooper alongside looked at him sympathetically and nodded his commiserations as Jacob heeled his horse forward. He was being given the most dangerous position in the patrol, some yards in front of the troop, it was inevitably the position which brought the first casualty in any ambush. He walked his horse to the front of the column, past the lines of waiting men, past the bugler and the standard bearer, both of whom gave him smirking looks.

He briefly glanced up at the banner, of necessity much smaller than those followed by foot soldiers, its gold braiding and tassels hanging limply in the lifeless air.

Slowly, he moved forward away from the safety of his comrades then turned and gazed at the twin rows of men headed by the tall figure of Wilmott sitting his horse expectantly. He nodded.

"March on," came the command from Wilmott and the jolting and the pain began again.

It was two hours later that it happened. The scenery had changed dramatically and the countryside was now open and rolling with clumps of trees topping sharp little hills so typical of Somerset. The sun, a yellow ball in a cloudless azure sky, beat mercilessly down on them and broiled them in their leather and buff coats. Metal helmets scorched the foreheads of those who wore them.

Topping a small rise, Jacob jerked his horse to a halt, his cry a surprised howl. Moving towards him, not two hundred yards away were horsemen, enemy horsemen. Not in twos or any formation at all but spread out in a mob, chatting idly. Their horses were being given a breather, their flanks slick and white with sweat. It was obvious they had been riding hard. All of this Jacob noticed in a second. From somewhere in the crowd, a percussive shot rang out and a ball whirred past his head, so close he felt the crack of its passing.

Stung into action, he wheeled his horse and waved at the troop coming up behind him. Wilmott, ever the true professional, had already acted. The bugle rang out and his men fanned left and right drawing their razor-sharp sabres as they came on at a dead run.

Jacob rammed his spurs hard into his excited mount and heard it scream as it turned on its haunches and launched into a full gallop. He thought briefly, 'I'll be the first in,' but he need not have worried, the guardian angels at his back in seconds were all around him screaming and shouting obscenities, eager for blood.

Horses screamed as glinting murderous blades bit deeply into their bodies. Fleetingly, he remembered the instructions of his first commander after he joined the army. 'The first thing you have to be concerned about is not to chop the ears off your mount as you lay about you. I've seen it done, believe me.' Gripping the hilt of his sword tighter, he prayed for composure. Men shouted and swore, metal clanged on metal and pistols erupted, their roar thunderously loud at such close quarters. The warm air was filled with the smell of smoke and warm blood.

Struggling with his terrified horse and desperately parrying a rain of wicked blows from a red-haired man dressed in blue, Jacob felt a bone jarring blow to his upper thigh. A white-hot pain erupted down his leg and he screamed with the shock of it. Glancing down, he saw a nasty gash open in his leg, like a mouth opening. Clearly, he saw the glint of bone through the red blood. He screamed again and, looking around, caught a glimpse of Wilmott booting his horse away from him through the melee, his sabre red with blood.

Seeing his opportunity, the red-haired man aimed a vicious blow at Jacob's unprotected head but, at the last moment, the man's horse shied to one side and the blade hissed inches past Jacob's nose and buried itself fully twelve inches into his horse's neck. Blood founted high in the air and the horse began to fall, its terrified squealing shrill above the battle's noise. Jacob flung himself clear at the last moment, anxious not to be trapped under the animal,and then he knew only the churning hooves around his head and the shouts from above, before darkness engulfed him.

He came around to find a burly blood-spattered trooper tugging him out from under the still-warm corpse of a man dressed in blue. The dead man's eyes were open, still glaring their hatred.

"There you go, mate," said the warm west country accent. "You've taken a chop in the leg, but I think you'll be all right." He tilted back his head and yelled for the surgeon.

"He's dead," someone yelled back. There was a chorus of hoots and catcalls.

Jacob raised his head painfully and saw the prisoners, those that had survived the fighting standing in a mutinous group surrounded by wooden-faced guards. Around them, lying like discarded toys in the afternoon sunlight, were dead and dying horses and the smaller bodies of men. Troopers were already busy laying the dead in rows. One row for Parliament men, one for Royalists, separated even in death. A shot rang out as a trooper finished off his severely-injured mount.

"Did we win?" muttered Jacob, through clenched

teeth, his leg in painful competition with his shoulder. The bound wound under his jerkin had opened again with the effort of the fight, he could feel the blood running down his body.

"Of course, we did, sir," grinned the trooper busily cutting away the blood-soaked breeches from Jacob's fresh wound. "Although to be truthful, there were not many to go around." He laughed good-humouredly like a man pleased with himself after a successful day's work. He was inexpertly tying a tourniquet around Jacob's upper thigh. Sitting back on his haunches, he surveyed his work, "There," he said, "That should hold you until we get back to camp."

"Is Major Wilmott still alive," Jacob's voice sounded weak from loss of blood.

"That he is, sir," said the trooper cheerily. "He's hotfooted it back to his Lordship to report this." He peered over his shoulder at the glum group of gaily-dressed prisoners. "They'll want to question this lot as soon as possible I'll warrant."

"Question or torture?" queried Jacob, his vision was dimming.

"Well, now, that's up to them. Me, I'd tell us everything and never mind being a hero." He laughed at his own philosophy. "Wouldn't you?"

"I… don't know," managed Jacob and fainted again.

He was swimming in a milky warm sea, comforting and

foggy and, in the distance, he could hear voices. Slowly, the voices became one, a voice he recognised. Mary. He opened his eyes with an effort, his vision was blurred, forcing him to blink several times to focus his gaze. He peered up at the raftered ceiling above him and, as he did so, the pain returned drawing an involuntary hiss. The pain was a persistent dull ache that started in his thigh and spread upwards through his groin and lower belly and up to his shoulder. He tried to move, but the effort increased his discomfort and beads of sweat broke out on his face.

Gently but firmly her hands rested on his shoulders. "Stay still, my sweet," she soothed and then, looking over her shoulder, she said to someone else, "He's awake."

She leaned down and kissed his forehead. "Lie still," she crooned. "You were wounded in the fight but the surgeon says you should be fine, you have lost a lot of blood." She gently stroked the sweat-slicked hair away from his eyes. "You've been unconscious since they brought you in." The concern and worry had etched new lines around her eyes, he noted.

"How long have I been here?" he managed. "Two days," she answered.

He found the energy to be incredulous. "Two days?" It seemed to him only a matter of minutes since he was lying on the grass with a trooper binding his leg.

The bed creaked as he craned his neck to look down at the rough blankets that covered him. He could feel that his thigh was heavily bandaged. He began to raise himself once more, but Mary pressed him back firmly. "I told you to lie still," she said, her tone brooking no argument. "Not only has your shoulder wound opened up again, but you now have a nasty gash on your thigh to show us how brave you are."

He sighed deeply and let his thoughts cloud and drift. Darkness enveloped him and he slept once more.

Waking again sometime later, he called out her name and she was there at his side immediately, her face above him, her hand seeking his.

"Be still, my sweet," she soothed again. "You are safe now."

His anxiety was a living thing. "It was Wilmott," he blurted. "He chopped me from behind in the fight. It was him."

Again, she stroked his forehead and uttered low calming words. Slowly he quietened. She glanced once more at the other person whom Jacob could not see beckoning him forward. The concerned face of Parson Roberts came into view, peering over Mary's shoulder.

"We know, my son," he said, "One of the troopers who got you up to this room told us, we know everything." He leaned forward and gently patted Jacob's good shoulder. "Take ease, you are amongst friends here."

Something occurred to Jacob even in his befuddled state. "Here?" he questioned "Where is here?"

"We have taken a room at this small inn, my son.

We are in the town of Yeovil and the army is all around us."

Jacob turned his head and peered at the mullioned window, noting the setting sun beyond the trees in the distance.

"He will not rest until I am dead," he said flatly. "I know it now."

"Aye," agreed the Parson, his voice low within the thin plastered walls of this small room. "You speak true. I fear the man is crazed. I have seen his look before on men who care nothing for rules or convention and think the world exists for them alone." He shook his head at the wickedness of the world.

"He will not get another chance," intoned Mary, her voice harsh, and defiant. "Seeing Jacob's questioning look she continued. Your Colonel and a powerful force including Major Wilmott have gone for the time-being. They are moving towards Taunton on the orders of the Lord Fairfax. The streets are alive with the talk, is that not right, Parson?" Mary rose and smoothed the sweating brow of Jacob. "I think they are saying there will be an action," said the little Parson. He sighed hugely and, looking around, sat down on the small rickety wooden stool behind him. He was so weary of all of this and longed to get back to his own hearth. He took out a piece of calico from under his shirt and wiped his neck.

Mary stood and smoothed down her skirts and, to hide her concern, began to move around the room in a business-like manner picking up small items and placing them on the window-sill.

"We are leaving, my love, as soon as you are fit enough to travel. I'll hear no argument this time, so save your breath." She held her small, determined hand in front of her to prevent any rejoinder from her young husband. He gazed at the stern-faced beautiful young woman he now loved beyond anything he could have dreamed of and managed to smile at her tone, before passing out again.

The next day, sitting back against the crude headboard, his heavily-bandaged shoulder feeling a little better for the lack of movement in the last few days, he watched Mary as she swept the small room for lack of something better to do.

His eyes were set deep with dark shadows beneath them, causing him to look as if he had aged many years during the last week.

"What of your father and brother," he said, broaching a subject that he had avoided until now. It had occurred to him that by leaving the area and heading back north with him, she was abandoning the search for them. "Have you given up the idea of finding them?"

She swallowed noisily and looked down at her hands. Small capable hands clutching the broom tightly as she fought her emotions. For some days she had wrestled with her conscience. Her dear father and her big brother may not be far from here at this very moment, that she knew, but where? Her father did not know of ma's death. It had seemed the only thing left to do after the horrible events at the farm, to find them, to run to them and seek comfort with them. To be hugged by her dad, she had dreamt of it. But that was before all this had happened. She had to believe that God had a plan and this was the path he had ordained for her.

"If God decrees," she began, "They will survive this wicked war, whether I seek them out or not." She straightened and leaned the broom against the wall, peering at her husband. "Is that not right?" She was close to tears; in fact one had escaped her long lashes and was running down her cheek and onto the floor.

The Parson, who had been sitting quietly in the corner of the room, gazed at her with concern 'She is close to breaking,' he thought. 'This brave young woman has had much to bear and now has been forced to choose between her husband and seeking others dear to her. What strength she must possess. How I wish I could make it all well for her. For both these admirable young people.'

Jacob was watching the emotions play on the face of his young wife and it was the vision he carried with him into unconsciousness once more as his meagre strength failed him.

"He's gone again," said Mary and, moving across to the bed, fidgeted with the bedclothes until she considered Jacob to be more comfortable.

The Parson, resting his hands on his knees to ease his aching limbs, creaked to his feet. He crossed to Mary and laid a hand on her shoulder.

"Come, my daughter," he said. "You are much spent. Lie next to your husband and take some rest yourself. He is over the fever now and you will be of little use if you make yourself ill."

His words carried the power of common sense, so reluctantly, she allowed the old man to help her to climb onto the bed and lie down next to Jacob. She was almost instantly asleep. The Parson stood looking down at them both, deep concern etching lines into his kindly old face. They looked like two children lying there, this young couple who were trying so hard to make sense of a world gone mad.

He crossed the room quietly and, gently closing the door behind him, plodded down the rickety stairs. 'A walk before nightfall,' he thought. 'The air would do him good, and he needed to gather his thoughts somehow.' Apart from the young couple in the room he had just left whom he now so much admired, he was worried about his own wife whom he had left back in his village. The village he had but rarely left during the whole of his life. He missed her and longed to see her once again. He longed to sit in his favourite chair in front of his own fire, to smell bread baking, to feel safe. He wandered distractedly down the street as the light faded. He was weary, so weary.

It was cool and dark in the small unkempt disused church. He happened on it by accident in his wanderings, tucked way down a side street between and flanked by grander buildings on either side. It squatted comfortably like an old cat on a cushion before a fire. Without hesitation, he had entered, taking comfort from the familiar musty smell of the interior with the faint aroma of old candle wax. He needed to commune with his God, to seek sustenance from the Lord Almighty.

A single candle burned on the alter, its wobbling flame throwing a meagre light through the semi-darkness. The sounds of the street outside were immediately muted and he felt the familiar sense of peace and calm seep into his being.

He had half-expected to be greeted by the sound and smell of horses as he entered. Too many old churches these days were being utilised as stables by soldiers from both sides in their wickedness. The rise of Presbyterianism had rendered many old churches redundant. Roberts was well aware, even from the relative obscurity of his small village, that sects such as the Covenanters or the Quakers, Calvinists or Puritans, all vied for superiority in the Churches of England, and the old religion of Catholicism still stubbornly lingered. After four years of civil war, men's values had changed or become ever more confused.

But, thankfully, all was quiet and untouched in this shabby little building. Clearly, someone still cared enough to come daily to light a candle.

Breathing in the serenity deeply, he removed his hat and muttered a silent prayer before meandering with conscious pleasure towards the distant alter, his footsteps almost silent on the stone-flagged floor. He desperately needed to find strength from his God. He noted the old medieval wall paintings of cavorting figures on the walls, fitfully illuminated as they were by the candle flame. Many were painted in the time of the great plague, many from long before that painted by the ancients, that he knew. Most had been overpainted with whitewash in later years, but a few remained.

Not until he almost fell over him, did he notice the figure prostrated on the single step before the alter. The figure was dressed almost entirely in dark clothes and had been almost invisible in the gloom. The Parson uttered a startled cry and stepped hurriedly back, intending to move quietly away and leave the fellow to his devotions.

But the stifled sound had alerted the figure on the floor, who swiftly sprang to his feet and towered over Roberts. Unconsciously, he noticed how quick and cat-like were the stranger's movements, how menacing his stance. Even more alarming, he noticed in the dim light the dull gleam of naked steel.

"Don't move, priest," a strangely accented voice rasped out. The man's face was deep in shadow, but Roberts could see feral eyes glaring at him.

"Do not be alarmed, my son," began Roberts, his hands held in front of him in apology. "I did not realise anyone else was here, if I have intruded, I apologise."

For long seconds there was silence, as the Parson had the uncomfortable sensation that he was being closely scrutinised. Irritably, he scratched his forehead as if to ward off the penetrating gaze. With a quick light step, the tall man stepped forward and his face came into the light. Fear flared anew as the Parson peered into a gaunt-ravaged face with sunken piercing eyes, one of which was given a sinister leer by the ugly scar which ran from hairline to chin.

The stranger put away the huge knife. "No, it is I who should apologise, I did not hear anyone come in, you startled me." It was almost an accusation.

Robert's voice wavered a little with relief as he spoke. "It is a house of God, my son, all are welcome, I should have been more observant."

A strange mocking look moved across the stranger's scarred face. "House of God? Indeed? I sought only peace and quiet."

Dismissing the conversation, the tall man retraced his steps to the alter and picked up his cloak and hat. Roberts followed after him. "Are you perhaps from foreign parts, my son? I detect strange humours in your speech."

The trace of a smile flickered in the stranger's face, "I was born and raised in England, father, but of late I have been... elsewhere."

"Ah," said Roberts, nodding. "The foreign wars perhaps? How long were you there?"

"A lifetime." The answer was curt signalling that this particular topic of conversation was at an end.

Perceptive as ever, both by nature and by calling,

the Parson was increasingly aware of a terrible sadness emanating from this man. The compassion that was an integral part of his being overcame his fear.

"My son," he began, "I am a man of God, as you can see." He ignored the mocking look from the tall man. "I think there is much you wish to talk of, to unburden your soul, to ease the torment."

"No, you are wrong." Ethan Sedgwick began to move past the little man towards the door. "There is no God, it's only a fable. There never was."

The Parson risked placing his hand on Ethan's arm. "My son," he soothed. "Everyone of us needs help at some time, everyone." He realised that he included himself in this. His words seemed to penetrate some hidden place and the tall man stopped, his shoulders sagging. He seemed to be considering his reply.

"Perhaps you are right." There was a dull resignation in the harsh voice. He laughed harshly. "There is much I need to tell someone, here at the end of things, why not you?" He turned and laid down his cloak and hat once more. The little parson leaned down and sat heavily on the cold stone. He watched the stranger sit down beside him.

"Tell me," he soothed.

The telling took over an hour. The incongruous couple, the old, kindly almost innocent Parson and the war-ravaged, broken soldier of fortune. As the sky darkened outside, they sat side-by-side against the alter on the cold stone floor. Outside, the sun dipped below the horison and the first stars appeared, winking in the twilight. Inside, the drone of Ethan's voice was the only sound, save for the occasional gently coaxing remark from the Parson. Above them in the gloom, could be discerned a garish wall painting of the dance of death as lost souls were driven into hell by demons fitfully illuminated by the single wavering candle flame. Finally, it was told and Ethan, for the first time in many years, found something akin to peace of mind for a brief moment at least. He felt purged.

Roberts was nodding to himself meditatively. What he had heard had profoundly shocked him. The horrors of this war that he had witnessed since leaving his village had disturbed him profoundly, but the tales that this man had recounted, what he had seen and done, the ferocity, the scale and barbarity, the sheer horror, would stay with the little man for the rest of his life. That this man should admit to atheism after such a life did not surprise him, and it was with a jolt that he realised he was condoning blasphemy. His own mind was now in turmoil.

"Truly a tragic tale, my son," he managed. "Such horrors, I had no idea." He drew his hand across his eyes as if to wipe away the images. "But, see here, you must not blame yourself for the deaths of your wife and daughter, that way lies madness." Ethan looked up at the rafters above their heads.

"The death of the little maid was my fault and no one else's. Nothing you can say will alter my mind," he sighed. "As for my wife, I do not even know if she is dead." A sob escaped him. "She may still be out there." The anguish in his voice was palpable.

Reaching out, Roberts touched the younger man's shoulder. "That can never be, my son, be comforted for small mercies, she is dead, God rest her soul." Ethan leapt to his feet, his face a mask of hatred, his teeth bared. "Be comforted?" he snarled, "I'll tell you, priest, after that day I killed and killed to be comforted. It did not matter whom or why. Everyone I killed were the ones who took her. I killed men and women with relish." He took a few paces away and then turned and shouted at the alter, "God, damn you!"

The Parson felt a worm of fear squirm in his stomach. Only now was he realising how damaged this man was, how quickly his moods changed, how murderous he could become in an instant. He peered up at Ethan, his voice low,

"Why did you come home, my son?"

Ethan calmed a little and shrugged his shoulders. "Do you know I have asked myself that question so many times recently. I don't know, it seemed the thing to do. Suddenly I had had enough, it was time to go." He sat down once more, the impotent explosion of rage for the moment spent.

"I may have a brother who still lives, I know not. I thought to find out. To bring to an end, somehow, this nightmare, to complete the circle. My father must be long dead, but Jacob may live yet." He shrugged again,

"Who knows?" He gave an embarrassed half-laugh. "What he will think of what I have become, I dare not imagine, when a killer, a heathen scarecrow, turns up proclaiming that, like the prodigal son, he has returned." He gave a self-mocking chuckle.

Roberts had not heard the last words spoken. There was a roaring in his ears. Snatches of recent conversations. Jacob talking of his elder brother, Ethan, dead in the foreign wars. Jacob in delirium screaming for Ethan. He closed his eyes.

"Oh God, thy ways are wondrous." Roberts turned to look Ethan full in the face. "My son," he queried, his voice betraying excitement, "Is your name perchance Ethan Sedgewick?"

The tall man started and peered keenly at Roberts. "How would you know that, old man"? The Parson gripped Ethan's shoulder with a force that belied his age. "A miracle!" he expostulated. "A miracle. My son, God sent you here today, truly he did!"

"A miracle?" Ethan laughed aloud. "Really, Priest? You speak like a fool."

With more assurance in his voice than he felt in the presence of this troubled man, Roberts continued calmly, "Listen my son, I am here with a young army officer and his new young wife. They are fine young people and I am sore worried for them, they are in mortal danger."

"What has this to do with me?" began Ethan, but he was silenced by the upraised hand of Roberts. "The young officer is named Jacob Sedgewick." The silence stretched on whilst a myriad of emotions played over Ethan's face.

Roberts hurried on, anxious now to be heard. "His new wife has much to bear at present and both are near the point of exhaustion. I am an old man and can only do so much to protect them from the evil one who threatens them."

Finally, Ethan had found his voice and he reached over and drew Roberts close by grabbing the top of his jacket. His eyes bored into the older man's. "You will not tell him you have met me," he snarled. "You understand me, priest, you must not."

"But why, my son, why? It will be as a tonic for him."

"A tonic?" sneered Ethan. "Look at me, do I look like someone to be proud of? A lunatic, a tramp?"

"A very troubled man," said Roberts softly. "But not a man who cannot find religion and goodness of some sort again if he wishes. God is always forgiving, all knowing, why not speak with him?"

"Religion? God?" snarled Ethan, his mood changing once again. "Priest, I've butchered them all; Protestants, Catholics, Muslims, Lutherans, Calvinists and laughed whilst I did it, so don't speak of religion to me. Where I've returned from, millions have died and millions more will die in the name of religion.

Nations and lands have been devastated for religion." His voice had become harsh and cracked once more. He smashed his fist into the stone pillar next to him and incuriously watched as blood flowed across his knuckles.

Startled once more by the changes of mood, Roberts acknowledged that this man was close to insanity. "I repeat," said Ethan, "you must not tell him of me, not yet. I must think." He released his grip on Roberts and slouched back against the steps.

"Very well," acquiesced the old man. "It shall be as you wish.

"Now," said Ethan softly, another complete and lightening quick change of character. "Tell me who is this 'evil one' putting my brother at risk?"

Chapter Twelve

Somerset, June 1645

"What in the name of God was that?"

John gazed at his father noting how thin and unkempt he looked, as if he had aged ten years in as many days and he again found himself wondering how he could protect the older man in these desperate times. Both were tall for the times and well-built because of farm life. But Martin's clothes were beginning to hang off him as if from a clothes hanger.

"I don't know, Pa," he said, wiping the sweat from his sooty face, "and I don't think we should be in a hurry to find out." Once more, the high-pitched scream was heard clearly in the air above the noise and confusion all around them.

One of the thatched cottages was ablaze now and burning fiercely, smoke and cinders clogged the already humid sun-dried summer air and the heat from the fires was intense. Orange sheets of flame clawed impatiently at the brilliant blue afternoon sky. A tree that stood too close to the burning cottage had also burst into flames; its new growth of leaves curling quickly in the searing heat. 'That tree had probably stood unharmed next to the cottage it sheltered for centuries,' mused John, 'now within an hour of us arriving, it is gone.' He shook his head awkwardly, his heavy morion-style helmet hampering his movement.

All the food they had found in the village and most of the furniture now stood in piles in the centre of the village green. Uncaring troopers were searching through the piles, casually smashing anything that was not of use.

A youth who had dared to protest was being held by two troopers against one of the walls that still stood whilst a third systematically beat him. The youth had lost consciousness some minutes ago. Casually, the troopers let him fall and turned to survey the scene, muttering and laughing amongst themselves.

Goring's troops, aided and abetted by a mob of 'clubmen,' were out foraging. John and Martin part of the unwilling army detachment delegated to go with them. It was an increasingly regular occurrence of late, as the army began to disintegrate. Discipline was lax and riotous behaviour, drunkenness and atrocity were commonplace. Goring's drinking, ever a stain on his character, was worsening daily as he reluctantly faced the prospect of ultimate Parliamentary victory, and the behaviour of his army was a reflection of their commander. Still capable of flashes of military genius, the alcoholic General was nevertheless seeking solace in the bottle.

This small Somerset hamlet, like many of late, was

paying the price for frustration and bitterness amongst the Royalist troops. Those that still believed in the cause saw their hopes and personal ambitions drifting away like smoke in a breeze. Many others, like John and Martin, dragged from their homes and forced to follow the Royalist drum, allowed themselves a desperate flicker of hope as they dared to believe that it could be almost over.

The villagers, decent people with names like Martha and Thomas, with trades like blacksmith or carpenter, stood in clumps and watched their homes and possessions ransacked before their eyes. None, save the youth now unconscious and slumped on the ground, had dared to resist. The drunken lecherous soldiery that had descended on them in the middle of a drowsing spring day would beat or even kill without qualm, that they knew, and they reasoned, with the homespun common sense of country folk, that they could always rebuild their houses.

An animal-like scream rent the air again, coming from one of the few cottages as yet untouched. Only the door ripped off its hinges and hanging askew gave evidence of violent attention. Martin could restrain himself no longer and, throwing down his pike, began to move towards the door. John, caught by surprise as he looked the other way, hurried to catch up with his father and he arrived at Martin's side as they entered the building, ducking their heads to get through the low door.

Two soldiers, chuckling and swearing, were holding down a struggling girl in her early teens, whilst a third, his breeches around his knees, was busy between her legs. His pale fleshy buttocks heaving below his leather jerkin. The girl's face was expressionless with shock, save for when she screamed periodically as if it was expected.

"Come on in, lads," said one of the men, "plenty here for all, just be patient." He chuckled again enjoying himself. He grinned up at them showing a ruin of blackened and missing teeth. "Lovely job," he said and smacked his lips.

Martin's face set hard in an expression that John knew well. "You scum!" he roared. "You filthy whoreson bastards." Stepping forward he viciously kicked white buttocks between the legs and, grabbing a booted foot, dragged the man off the girl. The soldier gave a shrill almost girlish scream and clutched ineffectually at the pulped ruin between his legs. His cries sank into a low moan and he rocked back and forth on the hard dusty floor.

"Here now," said the gap-toothed trooper, rising, "There ain't no need for that, mate, just wait your turn, no need for that." His speech was slurred by drink and his face was flushed red.

Martin grabbed the front of the man's shirt and pulled him forward until their faces were inches apart. "I don't want a turn, you rancid drunken sot!" he shouted, his spittle showering gap tooth's face. "That's an English woman down there." His anger was a palpable thing, cowering the other man. "You are in England, you animal. Had you forgotten?"

Amazingly gap tooth looked genuinely puzzled. He was obviously one of the group of clubmen or dispossessed, landless vagabonds who now banded together to form what were little more than rapacious criminals, being recruited by the Royalist command in their desperate need for more recruits.

"It's a woman, ain't it? If you get a chance you takes it." He gave a mirthless chuckle, "so the world turns, mate."

Martin could restrain himself no longer and his forehead smashed into the bland self-righteous face, breaking the nose with a crack. Stepping back, Martin slammed a leather gauntleted fist into the now bloody face and threw the man against the wall as if he were an old sack. Waving a flapping hand to fend off any further attack, the man slid down to the floor where he lay semi-conscious, his nose and mouth leaking blood.

The third man took an ineffectual step forward. "Leave us be, mate," he began in a whining voice, "There's no need for this."

All the anger and frustration of the last months were now surfacing, as Martin began to lose control. "You foul scum!" he roared, turning to the third man. "You dog's turd, you bastard. I ought to kill you right now." Clumsily, he drew his short broad-bladed sword, standard issue for pikemen from his belt. "England is well rid of the likes of you."

He took a step forward before the anxious voice of John broke through the fog of his rage. "Pa!" John's voice was shrill and cracked with urgency. "Leave him be, Pa. He's not worth it."

Slowly, Martin remembered where he was and his anger dissipated. He turned to look at his son. "It makes you like him, Pa. No difference."

Slowly, Martin slid the sword back into his belt and fought to regain his composure. "Aye, you're right," he said and turned to the now cowering figure of the third man. "Bless your luck that my son is here," he snarled, "Or as God is my witness, I would have killed you."

He crouched down to the prostrate young woman. "Come on, lass," he said, as gently as he could, "let's get you back to your family." He shoved the thought of his own daughter, Mary, from his mind, to go there would bring back the white-hot anger of a few moments ago. He lifted the girl easily, but instead of thanking him, she began screaming again her eyes wild. He ducked out through the door again and stood the girl on to her feet. A small elderly woman ran forward her face working with rage.

"Leave her be, you swine!" she screamed. "If my husband were alive, he'd kill you for what you've done." She snatched at the girl's arm and, before turning away, spat full into Martin's face.

John stepped hurriedly forward blocking any further attack on his father. "No, missus," he began,

"You've got it wrong."

Martin laid a restraining arm on his shoulder preventing him from hurrying after the retreating woman. "Leave it, John," he said. "We're soldiers, that's all she sees, it will do no good." He gazed around in despair at the burning cottage "And can you blame her? Great God in heaven, this could be our village, our home going up in flames." He finished with a smothered sob and rubbed a gloved hand across his soot-grimed face. "The Lord bless and keep Martha and Mary in these insane times." He was sinking into the semi-trance that John had witnessed many times during the last weeks and knew that his troubled father was thinking of home and his increasing obsession that something was wrong.

Rousing himself with an effort, Martin looked around him and spoke in a muffled voice, "How much longer?"

John, glad of an opportunity to divert his father, placed his gauntleted hand on the older man's shoulder and tried to sound reassuring, "Not much longer, Pa,I reckon, although the sergeant said last night, he suspects we will have to fight a battle afore it's finished."

Martin's head jerked up. "How so?"

John removed his helmet and ran his hand through his sweat-soaked hair. "He thinks that we're the last Royalist army left and our laddo, Goring's, the only commander worth anything who has a command of any size. He said they *had* to come for us, said it was obvious." He frowned, trying to remember if he had repeated correctly. "King Charles got a thumping somewhere up north and The Lord Fairfax is on his way down to these parts and Cromwell is with him." He gazed at his father, waiting for a reaction. After a few moments, he realised none was forthcoming. "Anyway, that's what he said."

Around them, the party was making ready to leave. Men were gathering into groups to form up. Whatever 'booty' was going with them was being loaded onto a small wagon brought along for just this purpose.

Shouts of command and the jingle of harness, turned everyone's head as, followed by a troop of immaculately turned-out cavalry, Goring himself rode into the village. Halting in a cloud of dust, Goring stepped down from his mount and limped to a nearby cattle trough, where he unceremoniously removed his feathered hat and immersed his head into the murky water. Standing up straight once more, he shook his head of long brown soaking hair like a dog spraying droplets all around. Carefully replacing his hat, he looked around him and called for the officer in charge.

The officer, clearly somewhat non-plussed at the arrival of so senior a personage, sauntered forward and engaged in a muttered conversation with his General. The only sound that Martin and John could hear now as they stood watching, was the roar and crackle of the flames and the sighing of the fitful wind. No shouts or laughter now from the troops, all were cowed by this latest arrival.

"Something is up," muttered John under his breath. Martin nodded, not taking his eyes from the scene. This was the first time he had been so near to the figure of Goring and now this close, he believed all the tales that he had heard. The features were thickening despite his relative youth, but Martin acknowledged that once the face must have been handsome. Unexpectedly, Goring looked up and for a few seconds, Martin felt the electric gaze pass over him. The effect was almost physical and he found himself unable to look away, but Goring, seeming to find little of interest, returned his gaze to his companion.

Behind them, the roof of the cottage collapsed in a shower of sparks and flames, but Goring appeared unmoved and merely glanced over his shoulder.

The old woman who had struck Martin, suddenly appeared at his side and began to remonstrate in a highly-outraged voice, her arms gesticulating wildly. Two troopers stepped forward and grabbed her spindly arms to remove her, but were stayed at a sign from Goring who was listening to her tirade.

John and Martin watched as she pointed in their direction and her outraged voice became more agitated. They could not hear her words because of the roar of the flames.

Feeling distinctly uneasy, they watched as, at a sign, four more troopers dismounted and followed their limping commander as he made his way across to the two pikemen.

"You, sir, are a disgrace." The cultured voice cracked with authority. Goring was planted foursquare in front of Martin, his face inches from the older man. This close, his breath reeked of drink, although his gaze was clear. Unconsciously, Martin noted the nose turning blue and pitted from the misuse of alcohol.

He managed a stumbled reply, "My Lord, it was not what the old crone thinks."

If he was surprised that a mere pikeman should answer him back, Goring did not show it, "Not what she thinks?" he echoed. "Did you not rape her granddaughter?" His whole stance was threatening.

For the first and only time, John spoke up. "Sir, if you please, it was not so."

Goring's expression as yet another pikeman spoke was of total surprise as if his horse had spoken. "Hold your tongue, you insolent yokel," he rasped. "Speak when you are spoken to."

One of the troopers moved up beside John and stared at him belligerently.

"Now, once again, soldier," he rasped. "Do you deny the charge brought by this woman?"

Martin removed his helmet and noticed a tremor of surprise on the General's face when his grey hair cascaded out. "Yes, my Lord, I do, most strenuously." In quick, concise sentences, Martin told the story of what had happened, being careful to maintain eye contact with the man in front of him.

Goring held his gaze in a grip of iron, but his

features slowly relaxed as the story was told. He had commanded men for most of his adult life and could recognise the truth when it was spoken. He turned and nodded to one of the troopers who stood behind him. Swiftly, the man crossed over to the hanging door of the cottage, stepped inside and almost immediately reappeared, nodding to his commander.

Goring let out a long breath and removed his hat. "Your name?" he drawled. "Martin Honeywell, sir."

"Well, Master Honeywell, it would seem that I owe you an apology."

"Not necessary, my Lord."

Whatever reply Goring had expected, this was not it. Anger flashed across his face, to be immediately controlled.

"Do you play the insolent with me, Honeywell? Be very careful or I will have you flogged."

Martin lowered his gaze to his boots. "My Lord."

Goring seemed to assess the man in front of him before speaking. "You are a good and honest soldier, Martin Honeywell. I could do with many more of your like in my ranks. I am glad that you are with us."

Martin could not tell if this was sarcasm, but he suspected not. For a reason that he would never understand, he felt he had to speak further even though it meant danger.

"I did not join, my Lord, I was pressed." He was about to say 'along with my son here' but, at the last moment, decided to leave John out of it. "And I must tell you that had I been given the choice I would be hefting my pike for the Parliament."

Those all around stiffened and there was a general hissing of indrawn breath. Only Goring had been staring at his boots as he shuffled the dust at his feet, but his head came up at that, eyes narrowed to mere slits which stared at the older man.

"Of a truth, Honeywell," he said, his voice so low that only Martin could hear. "You are a brave man. Either that or a fool." He replaced his hat and, when he spoke, there was amusement in his voice. "But somehow I think not a fool." Briefly, he nodded to Martin. "Good luck to you," then abruptly, he turned and limped back to his horse followed by his troopers.

Quickly, he gave instructions to the foraging party officer, then mounting, he rode out of the village in a flurry of jingling harness and dust. As they trotted past Martin and John he glanced down, nodded and was gone. The troopers following him peered down with grudging respect at Martin, one even risked a grin.

John let out his breath and his shoulders sagged. "Pa," he half-laughed. "Christ, I thought you'd hanged us then."

Martin was trembling and wide-eyed. "I think," he said, trying to keep his voice steady, "It has been a long time since that man believed his cause could win this war. His sadness and desperation surround him like a cloak. I could feel it. God help him."

John did not get the chance to reply as a rough shove

sent him sprawling forward.

"Move you two," shouted the small balding sergeant. "It's back to camp for us all and quick as you like. We're lifting the siege." He cackled mirthlessly. "Taunton will be glad to see us go and there's a fight in the wind."

Seeing their looks of dread and dislike, he scowled at them and rasped, "So, lads, you will be given another chance to die for old Charlie." Thinking this a huge joke, he strode off in short jerky steps, his high, yelping laugh echoing around him.

Chapter Thirteen

Somerset, July 1645

The water in the cracked bowl was icy cold and brought a gasp from Wilmott as he vigorously sluiced his face. Repeatedly, he plunged his hands and hurled water on to his face, chest and back then, taking up a cloth, began to dry himself.

The water had momentarily removed the headache; a result of too much wine last night, and he felt better. His mouth tasted foul, his tongue seemed to be far too big and his teeth felt furry. He gagged and spat into the bowl absently, watching the globule spin and dissipate. His preparations for the day complete, he turned away.

He wore knee-length breeches only at present, having just risen from his bed. His white legs and spatulate hammer-toed feet betraying the onset of varicose veins. The result he knew of too many years in the saddle. Limply, he cursed and glanced towards the rumpled bed where only recently a younger slimmer body than his had lain with him. He had kicked the youth out just before dawn broke. He was a Major so could do what he wanted, couldn't he? But he knew in his heart of hearts that he could most definitely not. He was careful in his choices, but one never knew what damage could be done to his career if his preferences should become common knowledge. Certainly, he would be kicked out of the army and that was everything for him. What was he thinking last night? Again, he swore as he acknowledged the weakness of his meagre willpower to deny his baser cravings. His rank in the armies of Parliament gave him power, men feared him and he liked that. He was putting it all at risk every time this happened, it was an age when sodomy was viewed as an offence against God and could be punishable by death. It infuriated him that he was so weak, so unable to restrain himself.

Irritably, he crossed the room to his clothes piled onto a stool, swore obscenely and loudly to no one in particular and began to dress.

***

Outside in the street, a trooper stood guard at the front door of this requisitioned non-descript half-timbered building that held a good many of the officers of the army. He had been standing here since well before midnight. He was cold and hungry and he needed the latrine. 'Where the hell was his replacement?' He could smell cooked food on the breeze from somewhere nearby as soldiers from the army that was all around him, both in commandeered houses and tents, prepared breakfast.

Soldiers and citizens were about now and the small street was becoming more crowded with every passing minute. A troop of cavalry clattered by, harness jingling. He knew one or two of them and they nodded companionably. He mouthed an obscenity back and heard them laugh as they trotted off down the street.

The standard that flapped ineffectually above him proclaimed that General Massey himself was quartered in this building and so a sentry was needed but, God's arse, this was dreary work. In the hours that he had been here, only two people had gone in or out. He stifled a yawn with his gauntleted hand and scratched his backside acknowledging once again that he needed to visit the latrine pits. He could not decide which need was the most urgent, food or latrine. Then, as he had done a hundred times during the last hour, he craned his neck to look down the street for his replacement. 'Where the hell was he?'

A voice from just behind him made him jump, he had not heard anyone approach. A tall, angular figure was standing close to him. The sentry risked a quick glance and did not like what he saw. The face was drawn and gaunt with a huge disfiguring scar. The greying sandy hair was cut short and the grey eyes were glacial. The voice, when the man spoke was heavily accented and guttural, like a foreigner.

"I said," repeated the man with obvious impatience, "Is this where I might find Major Wilmott?"

"Who wants to know?" The sentry's courage was returning after this man's unnerving arrival and 'what sort of fool accent was that?' he thought.

"Never mind who wants to know, soldier." The man's voice cracked with authority, "and stand to attention when an officer speaks to you."

'God's arse,' thought the sentry, using his favourite expletive, 'Trust me.' He eyed the tattered clothes of this menacing stranger, 'and what sort of officer wears clothes like that?'

The man was speaking again and, frantically, he gathered his wits to listen and understand what was being said.

"Now, for the final time, soldier, is this the building in which can be found Major Wilmott?"

"Yes, sir. It is." The sentry peered straight ahead, not risking another glance. He leaned back and shoved the rickety wooden door open, continuing to stare straight across the street. "Up the stairs, sir, second door down."

"Thank you." As silently as he had come the officer was gone, taking the stairs two at a time.

The sentry let his body sag with relief and wiped his brow dramatically. 'Where the hell was his replacement?'

Wilmott, now in his calico shirt and leather breeches, was sitting on the small stool pulling on his boots when there was a loud peremptory knock at his door. He frowned and continued with his task, whomever it was could wait, he was a Major and a Major who had a headache. He glanced over his shoulder at the bed and was annoyed again at himself.

Another louder knock shook the rickety wooden door. Swearing savagely, he stood and, crossing the small room in a few long strides, almost tore the door from its hinges as he wrenched it open.

"What?" he snarled.

A tall, gaunt, shabby figure was standing there, head bent forward to avoid the low corridor ceiling. The man's clothes looked travel-worn and threadbare.

Wilmott glared at the figure attempting to brow-beat the unfortunate with a withering contemptuous look that usually was enough for men of lesser rank than he.

"Well?" he snarled again.

Incredibly, a winning smile creased the face of the stranger. "Good morning to you. Is it Major Wilmott I am addressing?"

Wilmott's face showed utter disbelief. 'It's an idiot tramp,' he thought, 'How the hell did he get up here, I'll have someone's head for this?' Pumping anger into his voice, he leaned forward, his face close to the tramp.

"I am Major Wilmott!" he snarled, "and who the devil are… " He got no further, as a ripping sensation seared his stomach and it felt as if someone had shoved a white-hot iron bar into his midriff.

Eyes bulging and mouth opening and closing like a

landed fish, he gazed stupidly down in time to see a huge broad-bladed knife withdrawn with a hiss from his belly. Blood immediately erupted from the gaping wound and a glutinous purple strand of entrail began to uncurl. Without thought, he tried to stem the wound with his hands. Blood was already running unchecked down over his breeches and pooling at his feet. He raised boggle eyes to the stranger and noticed now that it did not matter anymore that, whilst the man was smiling, his eyes were glacial, expressionless like a fish.

"Good morning to you," said the smiling stranger pleasantly and turning, walked off down the corridor.

Wilmott felt his legs buckle and he sank to his knees, still attempting to speak through a mouth that would not work. He tried again to shout but could not. The wooden planking of the floor came up and smashed him in the face as he fell forward and his mouth filled with the salty metallic taste of blood. Using the last of his strength, he slewed his head sideways to gaze down the corridor and he caught a glimpse of the sandy grey-haired head of his assailant as it disappeared down the stairs. Then he fell into a bottomless dark pit and greeted oblivion. He never knew who killed him or why.

From somewhere down the corridor, a young voice queried the noise.

The tall officer reappeared outside much too soon for the sentry's liking. He had hoped to be long-gone before that bad-tempered bastard showed up again. Trying to be inconspicuous, he stood up straighter and stared at the opposite side of the street. But the officer stopped and turned to him.

"Your name, soldier?" Once again, that strange voice. "Ezekiel Phillips, sir."

"Phillips." The sentry did not like the way his name was repeated. "Well, Phillips, the Major would like some water, be a good fellow and fetch some from that pump down the street there, would you?"

"Yes, sir."

Abruptly, the menacing officer turned and moved off in the other direction. The sentry watched him stride off up the street, until he turned the corner and was out of sight, then gestured after him obscenely. He began swearing in earnest and with feeling under his breath as he stomped off down the street to the pump. He was almost there when, from the opened now unguarded door, came a high-pitched youthful scream.

Oliver Cromwell's face was red and mottled, sweat ran freely down his cheeks and dripped onto his breastplate. His eyes were deep-set and glittered, evidence of his fever. Irritably, he brushed a fly from his face and glanced at the taller, slimmer figure of Thomas Lord Fairfax who sat his horse next to him.

That his commander looked cool and comfortable annoyed Cromwell immensely. His resentment was not aimed specifically at his commanding officer but at the world in general. Why his God, in whose name he had always worked so diligently, should have decided that he, Oliver Cromwell, his loyal servant, would be burdened with repeated attacks of Malaria was beyond him. The fens and marshes of his native East Anglia bred ill humours and the sickness was quite common amongst his neighbours. He was also aware that many men lived their lives completely untouched by the affliction. He leaned forward to gentle his horse which regularly shook its head to dislodge the ever-present flies.

"I think he means to fall back on Bridgewater," mused Fairfax, his eyes still scanning the church tower of the village of Ilchester some miles distant shimmering in the heat. The two sat atop a small hill, backed by their personal aides and a troop of cavalry acting as bodyguards. The sky above was a cloudless azure blue giving no respite from the sun which beat mercilessly down on men forced to wear leather and metal.

"That is my reading of it too," murmured Cromwell, his voice low in the still air as if he feared he might be overheard. "He will probably feint towards Taunton, hoping to deceive us."

Fairfax grunted an assent. "Edward," he spoke over his shoulder. The tall figure of General Massey heeled his horse forward,

"My Lord?"

"When he sends a decoy south, it shall be your job to deal with it." Massey's reply was calm and assured, his deep voice low,

"Very well, my Lord, it shall be as you order."

Fairfax, despite the situation, was confident and assured. Gathered with him, he knew, were the best commanders Parliament possessed. He was unpretentious enough to count himself amongst them. The west country of late was being ravaged by Goring who, between moments of tactical genius, was becoming ever more the drunkard, aided by his notorious second-in-command, Richard Grenville, a native of these parts. Their rag-tag army was gaining a well-earned reputation for rapine and pillage. On direct orders from the King's nephew, Prince Rupert, the Royalist commanders throughout England were seeking the help of the ever-increasing roving bands of mercenary clubmen, their savagery a blemish on the name of Englishmen.

In contrast, the 'New Model' army flushed by its recent success at Naseby was disciplined and effective. The difference in fighting men of the two sides was ever more apparent as the King's cause began to fall apart. The King himself was rumoured to be in South Wales attempting to raise men. Prince Rupert glowered and watched from Bristol's ramparts, awaiting events.

Cromwell glanced sideways at the imposing, confident figure of Massey and his anger flared anew at his own present weakness.

"You must not fail in this, Massey," he began unnecessarily. "This campaign will effectively finish it and we must allow no part of this last army of the King to escape to the north."

Massey, despite the provocative remark, appeared unmoved and merely inclined his head in agreement. "I will not fail, Oliver, be assured."

A flicker of amusement crossed the face of Fairfax. He always found Cromwell to be somewhat overbearing and he welcomed the unruffled rebuff from Massey.

Cromwell briefly turned his gaze onto Fairfax then looked to his front once more," Tell me, my Lord," he said "Where do you propose to cross the Yeo? 'Tis certain that yonder bridge at Ilchester and that at Load Bridge will be held in some strength."

Fairfax nodded and, standing in his stirrups, squinted downstream. "Down that way at Yeovil itself. My scouts report it is only lightly held and discipline there appears to be lax." He turned and surveyed the group of riders behind him until he found the face he wanted. "Is that not so, Turner?"

Embarrassed at being singled out amongst his colleagues, Major Turner cleared his throat loudly, removed his hat and called, "That is true, my Lord. I had the position reconnoitred once again early this morning."

"Excellent," interrupted Cromwell. "Excellent." He held up his gauntleted hand and balled it into a fist. "Then we have him, Thomas, we have him."

Fairfax held up a cautioning hand. "Be not too confident, Oliver, never forget that it is Goring out there, not some overzealous amateur. We *hope* we have judged his intentions rightly. *We hope*."

Massey, taking some small pleasure in the discomfort of Cromwell, added, "Very true, my Lord, with one of his like one can never be sure. He is a clever fighter and no doubt."

Cromwell shook his head. "Pah," he said dismissively. "I believe he was once, but reports of the behaviour of his army and of the man himself convince me that, as the hopelessness of his cause becomes ever more apparent, he is taking comfort in drink. His men are deserting in droves and the local population have been so harshly treated they are flocking to our banners."

Fairfax removed his broad-brimmed hat and wiped his forehead with a handkerchief. "That may be," he said. "But he has always been a hard drinker and it has rarely clouded his judgement before. I see no reason to expect that it will now. He still has the power to sting us, be in no doubt."

Cromwell would have answered but his words were halted by the upraised hand of Fairfax as he began to turn his horse. "I have seen all I wish to, gentlemen, thank you for your company. Let us return to the army, we move at first light tomorrow. Briefing will be later this evening. Let us away, I'm frying where I sit." He gave a half-laugh and cantered down the hill whilst the assembled company in a flurry of curses and orders scrambled after him.

George Lord Goring spat unceremoniously over the crenellated wall atop Ilchester church tower and gazed at the plain spread out before him like a map. The river Yeo, glinting in the late afternoon sun, looked sluggish and peaceful as it wound its way through the flat replete countryside towards the small town of Yeovil. The willow trees along its banks threw out shadows huge in length as the afternoon sun sank ever lower.

"You're sure, man?" said Goring, his eyes maintaining their scrutiny of the land below him. "They were looking at the bridge?"

The Captain standing beside him nodded and then, realising his commander was not looking at him, said, "Yes, sir. My men report several reconnaissance trips to each of the bridges during the last few days." He glanced behind him at the small assemblage of hard-eyed staff officers clustered around them.

Goring, in shirt sleeves and hatless, scratched his neck ruminatively and grunted. "Then it's tomorrow or the next day that they'll make their move." He sighed and shook his head, "and there is not much I can do about it, not with what I have left."

His fingers drummed an idle tattoo on the stone merlin he leaned against. "Richard!"

Sir Richard Bulstrode, a florid, thick-set man in worn but flamboyant clothes, stepped up beside him. "My Lord?"

"As soon as they begin to cross the river, I charge you to get the baggage and the remaining guns back to

Bridgewater as quickly as possible. Is that clear?"

"But you will need the guns, sir, to stop them surely," protested Bulstrode, his eyes bulging with surprise. Goring turned his gaze onto him

"We cannot stop them, Richard, not with such as I have left."

A chill hand gripped the hearts of all those who were present. If their colourful, drunken, brilliant Commander could not stop the Parliament men, then no one could. It was as if the first knell of doom sounded in their ears.

"Surely, sir," Bulstrode said as much as he dared. "We can do something?"

"Something… yes," continued Goring, a gleam of devilment in his eyes. "We'll not make it easy for them. But, Richard," he touched the portly man's arm to emphasise his words, "I will not be able to hold them for long. You must move with great speed, you understand? If you do not reach Bridgewater before they catch you it is finished down here." He returned his gaze once more to the tranquil scene below him. "Those guns must be saved for his Majesty to make use of. They must."

Bulstrode nodded emphatically. "Yes, my Lord," he said, "I understand. We will not fail you." Several of the men in the group muttered their agreement.

Goring shook his head slightly and spoke quietly almost, it seemed, to himself, "Had you come six months ago, Thomas Fairfax, as God is my judge, you would have had such a fight on your hands." He had faced both Fairfax and Cromwell once before at the great battle of Marston Moor, but he had not been in command that day and neither had they. He had seen the Royalist fighting men wasted by a poor battle plan formulated by Prince Rupert and the Marquess of Newcastle. Fighting that day on the Royalist left wing alongside Marmaduke Langdale amongst others, he had seen many good men, especially those of Newcastle's so-called 'whitecoats' sell their lives dearly to give some element of honour to events that terrible day.

For long moments, he seemed lost in thoughts of the past then, abruptly, he returned to the present and turning quickly, he and his companions moved to descend the circular stairway.

Chapter Fourteen

Somerset, July 1645

Finally, he could keep the secret no longer. It had churned inside him for three days, gnawing away at the little man's conscience. He was not a worldly man and, until recently, had rarely ventured outside of his village. His parishioners told him their mundane secrets,, of course and he did his best to keep them to himself, although it was not always possible. But this was something completely different and far from his experience. He had prayed to his God for guidance but had received none. He was troubled and wrestled with his own feelings which had become more insistent since the mysterious death of Major Wilmott, which itself was the talk and gossip of the army. Several troopers had been questioned, along with an unnamed youth who proclaimed he knew nothing. Whatever methods had been used for the questioning had resulted in a black eye and severe facial bruising to the unfortunate, but still he maintained doggedly that he was completely innocent. The Parson suspected he knew the truth of the matter and felt his part in the murder deeply. If he had been instrumental in the demise of a fellow human being he would go to hell, that he knew. All these emotions churned inside him and he knew he could not keep his promise of secrecy further and must unburden his soul.

The shabby little inn was quiet now. Since the departure of the army two days ago, Yeoville had settled back into its sleepy, somnolent existence once more. The early morning sunlight streamed through the mullioned windows of the large downstairs room, starkly illuminating the wine-stained wooden tables and chipped scratched stools. Dust motes moved thickly in the sunshine and the smell of ale and stale smoke was heavy in the air. The floor, which had constantly run with spilt ale or wine whilst the army was here, was now swept dry. A small pile of broken clay pipes nestled in a corner waiting to be thrown outside.

Parson Roberts and Mary were sat at a small table in the corner breaking their fast with a quick meal of sour ale, bread and a little cheese. Upstairs in their little room, Jacob slept on, and they, glad of his continuing recovery, had come down to this common room lest they wake him.

Mary was looking with concern at the black-clad shabby little figure opposite her. In the harsh sunlight of this July morning, he looked one hundred-years-old, his unshaven chin witnessing their lack of basic supplies. She felt guilty that her decisions during the last few weeks had involved this little old man in danger and privation that he must never in his well-ordered life have known before. 'Well,' she mused, chewing her thumb nail absently, 'with luck, they would leave this place soon and head for home.'

The Parson looked up from tidying the breadcrumbs on his small wooden platter and cleared his throat noisily. She knew from experience that this meant he was about to make a pronouncement and she smiled encouragement.

"Mary," he began, "there is something I must tell you. Something I confess that has been troubling me greatly and is heavy on my conscience." He looked away to peer out of the window at a small cart that was creaking and rattling by.

She felt a foreboding at his words, but managed a smile and chided, "What's this, Parson, a secret, some evil deed that you have kept to yourself for many years? Tell me quick and save your soul." Her mood this morning was lighter than for some time; sleep and the knowledge that Jacob was slowly recovering and would live, having a miraculous effect on her countenance.

She had expected him to return her smile or even to laugh but, unnervingly, he did neither. He was, in truth, deciding whether to continue. He had noticed her lightening of spirit this morning. Gaiety was going too far, but she was certainly less anxious than of late, more prone to smile or even to laugh and he was loath to destroy the fragile flower that was her happiness. Seeing his indecision, she realised how deeply he was troubled, and reached over to lay her childlike hand on his.

"I'm sorry, Parson," she said, "I did not mean to be rude. Please tell me."

Roberts sighed, unhappy at what he must disclose and began to speak. The words came out in a rush, quickly, unemotionally. His voice pitched low so as not to be overheard, but there was no one else to hear.

"The other night, my child, I met a man in a church.... " he began.

She sat very still, watching his face as he told her his story and gradually her expression became as troubled as his. This was a sad tale indeed, but she could not understand his agitation. Finally, reaching the end of his story, he told her who the stranger was.

Mary jumped to her feet, her eyes alive and sparkling,, "But this is marvellous news Parson, Jacob will be so pleased. It will aid and hasten his recovery enormously."

The Parson sat stolidly on his stool and signalled for her to sit down. "My child, have you not been listening to what I've said? This man, Ethan, let us give him his name, this Ethan can help nobody, least of all Jacob. The young man up in our room," he gestured with his thumb at the ceiling, "remembers an elder brother he looked up to. A strong upright youth, who to him was a Hercules off to cure the ills of the world, and though the years have passed, that is still the man he pictures in his mind. The man I met with, the man I spoke with," he shook his head in desperation, searching for the right words, "is a killer, a ravaged husk of a man, on the verges of insanity.

Would Jacob really want to meet that man?"

Mary held out her hands in supplication. "But come, Parson, he cannot be completely lost. He sought solace with you, did you say? Have you not always taught us that a man who acknowledges his sins is half-way to curing them?"

The little Parson raised his eyes to look Mary full in the face. "My daughter," he said, "Who do you think it was that killed Major Wilmott?"

She leaned her elbows on the table and leant forward, her voice little more than a whisper, "My God,." she breathed "So that's who it was, there has been so much talk."

"I have no proof, of course," he muttered, "only suspicions but it can only have been him."

She raised her head defiantly "But Wilmott deserved to die," she hissed, "that... creature. Small loss to the world when he left it. At least twice he tried to murder my Jacob."

"But to kill like that, Mary," groaned the Roberts "without mercy, without warning, without even knowing the man."

"Wait," said Mary, as something occurred to her. "How did he know of Wilmott and what he had done?"

"I told him," blurted Roberts and buried his face in his hands. Mary gazed at him with understanding now. So that was why her little old guardian was so troubled. She felt deeply for him, but her heart was still elated by recent events and her young spirit could not be soured for long.

She stood and moved to put her hand on the old man's shoulder. "You could not know," she soothed. "How could you guess what he would do?"

In the muddy street outside the window, there was an altercation between two women over some eggs. Their raised voices, shrill with anger, had disturbed a mangy dog carried by one of them, his urgent yapping added to the noise. A small crowd was gathering to watch. Mary turned back to face the room, totally dismissing the scene outside.

"I should have known, Mary, I should have seen what this poor, deranged wretch was capable of," said Roberts, "and now, because of me, another of God's creatures is dead, snuffed out like a beetle in the road. Because of me." He turned his troubled old face to look at her.

A thought occurred to Mary. "Parson," she urged, "I must meet with this man, must speak with him, will you take me to him?"

The Parson withdrew a voluminous hanky from somewhere about his person and blew his nose loudly. "You cannot," he said, "He has gone."

"Gone?" said Mary stunned. "Gone where?"

Roberts levered himself up and, walking to the window, peered out at the altercation which was now abating. She had to strain to hear his words over the noise from outside. "He heard there was to be fighting over yonder near Langport or thereabouts. He has gone there."

"But why?" Mary was genuinely puzzled.

The answer was a long time coming, so long that for a moment, she did not think the old man was going to answer her.

"He did not tell me," he said, his voice low and reflective. "I met him again last night, we spoke further, he charged me to look after his brother and after you." He turned from the window to look fully at Mary. "He did not tell me anymore but I think he knew I'd guessed. I could see it in his eyes, you see."

"See what?" Mary's voice was impatient with foreboding. "He's gone there to die, Mary."

"No," her voice was flat, insistent, positive. "No, we must go after him, we must stop him, he must see Jacob."

Roberts looked alarmed. "Don't be foolish, my child, we cannot do that, there would be much danger."

"We must," Mary moved forward to confront the old man. "My husband would never forgive me if I let this happen."

The Parson averted his eyes from the frantic gaze, "Jacob need never know."

"Oh, yes, he does, Parson," her voice was strong with conviction. "I'm his wife, joined together before God and, by his mercy, we will live our lives and grow old together. But someday, soon or late, I will have to tell him that I let his brother ride away to die and did nothing to stop him." She shook her head emphatically, the long strands of her blond hair as usual escaping her calico bonnet. "No, Parson, that will not do." She walked to the door,. intent on climbing the stairs to check that Jacob was still asleep "I'm going to try to find this long-lost brother." It was a flat statement that brooked no argument." Will you come with me?"

Roberts's shoulders sagged as he acknowledged defeat. "You know I must," he murmured.

Hugely outnumbered by the approaching forces of Fairfax and Massey and with much of his force destroyed at Ilchester under the command of the buffoon, George Porter, Goring prepared to make his hopeless last stand at the small town of Langport. There was just the one crossing over the brook, Wagg Ryhne, and with the bordering marshland, it was the only possible position of any strength. It was a last attempt to save his guns for his king. Like a tiger at bay hunted down by beaters, he arranged his forces as defensively as he could and snarled defiance at his tormentors. His men,, he knew still had the capacity to hurt the army of Parliament.

There had been times when he thought he would never escape the nightmare. He reasoned, in the odd lucid moments with what senses he still retained, that it must be the dreams of a fever, but he could not be sure. Lately, he had slept more or less soundly, content in his mind that, whenever he awoke, there would be Mary with a soothing word or a piece of commonplace news leaning over him, her cool hands placing a blessedly cool wet cloth on to his fevered brow.

Gentling his befuddled mind.

Today when he awoke, he felt refreshed and aware, more alive than he had for many days. Yes, he was puzzled why no one was at his side as soon as he called out but decided to lie for a while and wait. The raftered ceiling above him was familiar now and he took comfort from it. He surmised that Mary and the Parson had taken the opportunity of getting something to eat or even taking a breath of fresh air. He could not blame them, he had been a grumpy patient and knew it. Had he been able to, he would have stretched out contentedly but knew that such a small action would bring with it a stab of pain, so he lay still watching the play of sun and shadow on the raftered ceiling and waited.

Half an hour later, he was beginning to feel anxious. Where was everyone? He sighed hugely pondering what to do, then with the self-importance of the young, he raised his head and bellowed. Nothing. He waited for a further few minutes and bellowed again, this time knocking a pewter tankard that stood on the little table beside the bed onto the floor for good measure and added noise.

Slow footsteps echoed up the stairs outside the door and it was slowly opened to admit the ageing landlord, his grey, tousled hair and shrewish face showing over the leather apron that he habitually wore. He was not in a good mood.

"Now then, now then," he scowled. He favoured repetition to add gravity to his words. "What's all this noise, Master Sedgewick?" Jacob was further irritated by the fact that it was a stranger and not his wife or the Parson who had answered his call.

"Where are my wife and the Parson?" he snapped.

"Gone." The landlord was clearly not used to being spoken in such a peremptory tone in his own establishment.

"What do you mean, gone?" said Jacob, wincing as he sat himself up. "Gone where?"

The landlord began wiping his hands on a piece of dirty cloth he had withdrawn from his apron. "They left an hour ago, asked me to keep an eye on you, so to speak. Anything you need?"

Jacob shook his head to clear his wits. "I'm sorry, sir landlord, but where have they gone?"

The Landlord nodded out of the window to the west, "Same as everyone else I expect, gone to see the battle, three wagon loads."

Jacob rolled over onto his side and, lowering his legs to the floor, winced as his newly-injured thigh seared with pain. "What battle?" he managed, his forehead beading with sweat.

"Rumour is that the Lord Goring and his lot are going to meet their end afore the day is out. Fairfax and Cromwell are here in force and looking to finish this bloody war as soon as possible. Should be a sight to see.

Good luck to them, says I. War is bad for trade."

Jacob stood, forcing himself to ignore the pain and began clumsily to dress. "Of all the foolish notions. Why in God's name... " He groaned as he shrugged on his shirt. "I must go to them, where the devil are the rest of my clothes?".

Chapter 15

Langport, July 1645

The ill-kept hedge that they stood behind was low, scarcely above waist-height in some places, and in places thin enough to shove through. As a defence, it offered little comfort to the men who sheltered behind it. Thankfully for them, the ground before it was boggy and tussocked with tall grasses, some deterrent to cavalry.

John glanced left along the line of the hedge, noticing with unease, how few men he recognised. He and the remnants of his regiment had been interspersed with raw recruits from two newly-raised Welsh regiments in an effort to pepper the inexperienced troops with seasoned veterans who had seen action before. But it was a desperate measure and doomed to failure. Martin, standing as ever beside his son, seemed not to notice events around him but stood unheeding stolidly, munching on a hunk of hardened bread that he had scavenged from somewhere. The sergeant, who had strutted down the line a little earlier had told them to 'Keep their wits about them' and could be heard telling the Welsh lads to take heart from the experienced soldiers placed amongst them who had 'seen it all before.' He disappeared down the line, his voice repeating the same litany every few yards. If he did but know it, many of the recruits pressed from farms and villages in the Welsh valleys could not speak English but they nodded enthusiastically at his words, eager to avoid a cuff around the ears.

John screwed up his eyes and squinted across the small valley in front of them to gaze with trepidation at the perfectly-ordered ranks of Parliamentary infantry as they took up station on the other side of the river which flowed peacefully on its way, less than a quarter of a mile in front of his position.

Gazing to his right, he could see the small lane that neatly bisected the opposing armies, crossed the river by a small stone-built bridge and disappeared up over the ridge behind them. He glanced behind him and could clearly see Goring and his staff officers sitting their horses, astride the lane at the top of this small hill, calmly waiting for the fighting to start. Goring himself looked relaxed, chatting amiably to one of his aides.

John was soldier enough to know that this fight would not last long. He guessed correctly that this was a delaying action to slow down the advance of Lord Fairfax and his army. He sighed hugely and shook his head. "You okay, Pa?"

Martin swallowed the last of his bread and nodded across the valley. "We have no chance at all of holding them, you know," he said conversationally. "Not a chance in hell, God save us."

"I know," replied John and nodded his head at the group at the top of the hill. "And I think he knows it too." As he spoke, a grizzled veteran was passing behind them, breastplate dented, clothes muddy and worn and he stopped to chat.

"He knows it well enough, mate," he said, accepting the inevitable as old soldiers do. "We're only here to delay matters to save those blessed guns." He gagged and spat over the hedge. All three men looked up as shouts and commands could be heard as increasingly more parliamentary troops arrived every minute to take ordered station behind ranks already there. The rumble of drums could be heard on the breeze. Mutely, the small, ragged Royalist army could do little but stand and watch.

"Four years I've hefted this cold wife," continued the veteran. "I joined in time for Edgehill, joined, mind, proud to fight for our good King Charles. God bless him." He waggled the weather-beaten pike he grasped affectionately in his gauntleted hands. "I've spitted a few bellies in the years since the Vale of the Red Horse, I can tell you." He chuckled mirthlessly. "Some good times and some awful times, but now, after all that, what's it come to? I'll tell you, sacrificed to save those bloody God-cursed guns." He spat again and grinned wolfishly. "I hope His Majesty remembers me for it. Old Isiah Croft, don't give up his life, such as it is, for just anybody." He peered at them both, looking for reaction. John and Martin nodded non-commitally. Satisfied with this reply, the old soldier moved on down the line and could be heard repeating the same phrases to another group.

"Listen, son," Martin spoke in an undertone, anxious not to be overheard. "When they come, when the firing starts, follow me and keep low."

"What?" said John startled. "Follow you where?"

"I've been thinking," said Martin. "I reckon if we follow the line of this hedge down there," he nodded to their left, "We could probably get across the river unseen. Everyone will be too busy to notice."

John followed the line of the hedge with his eyes, it did indeed seem to slope down through a small wood to the river about a quarter of a mile further on. "You mean run away, desert?"

Martin nodded emphatically. "That's exactly what I mean, unless you want to die here today for a cause you care nothing for." John's gaze apprehensively followed the line of the hedge. "They'll not look for King's men that side of the river," continued his father. "All the killing will be done here or up yonder," he nodded to the top of the rise.

John shook his head uncertainly, "It's risky, Pa. If we get caught by either side, they'll spit us like two pigs and laugh whilst they do it."

"Do you have a better idea?" snapped his father. "Or perhaps your plan was to die here. It will not take long, will it, they'll roll over us in less than an hour."

John thought for a moment longer, then saw the

logic of it. "No, Pa," he nodded. "You're right, let's do it. Let's take a chance and pray to God for his help. Let's go home." Solemnly, they shook hands. They would have said more but, without warning, the ground in front of their hedge erupted throwing stones and earth high and wide, forcing all around them to hurl themselves to the ground. With a thunderous roar, the Parliamentary guns had opened up with a concerted salvo. Fairfax and Cromwell, knowing all too well the weakness of the force facing them, had decided on a quick offensive in strength to gain a speedy victory.

Some yards away, a youth screamed in agony, the idea of impressing his mates by stopping a small cannonball rolling across the ground with his booted foot had paid for his folly with the loss of his leg below the knee. He writhed and shrieked as his mates ran to his aid. Musket balls buzzed thickly in the air and twigs and small branches on the hedge were shredded by their passing.

Crawling to the base of the hedge and peering through the undergrowth, John and Martin saw hundreds of men wading across the small river and advancing up towards them. The small bridge to their right was already clogged with troops forcing their way over and fanning out left and right.

"Have a care," someone shouted needlessly. "Here they come."

Musketry from the waiting Royalist army now added to the cacophony. Men running up the hill were falling, but scarcely enough to make a difference. A young Welsh recruit next to Martin took a ball cleanly between the eyes and, with a look of complete surprise, somersaulted backwards his blood spraying high into the air. Men were shouting obscenities and bellowing instructions. Some yards away, a musketeer shouted, "God save us!" threw down his musket and started to run away up the hill, but he did not get far. A small cannonball hit him squarely in the back and his body exploded in a welter of blood, offal and bone.

A Parliamentary musketeer appeared suddenly atop the hedge and aimed his weapon at them, but before he could fire, John's pike head, twelve inches of sharpened steel, took him in the throat. John clearly felt the blade jar on bone as it bit deeply into spine. The man fell to the ground with a gurgling scream, his hands scrabbling at the blade. A second musketeer arrived but, before he could force his way through the hedge, a musket ball took away his lower jaw. He sank to his knees, his eyelids drooping as if he was tired, then slumped over onto his side. All around was confusion and noise.

John felt a tug at his sleeve, "Come on, son," urged his father, "now's the time, run for your life."

Dragging their pikes by the steel-pointed head they bent double and ran as fast as they could down the line of the hedge. Few saw them go, those that did assumed they were changing position. One officer guessed their intention and fired his pistol at them, but the shot was hurried and the ball flew harmlessly over their heads.

After two hundred yards, it grew quieter, the main fighting left far behind. Still, they crouched and ran. Finally, they were alone, the din of battle far back in the smoke. Together, they crouched behind a holly bush to regain their breath. Around them, the sparse woodland that they had scanned, screened them a little should anyone glance in their direction. Incongruously, a sparrow perched on a branch above them, sang for the joy of living. Feeling certain that someone must surely hear the thunder of his heartbeat, Martin peered owlishly around the bush to see if anyone was following. There was no one. They had done it.

Chests heaving with exertion, eyes rolling with fear, they peered at each other and then, unaccountably, began to chuckle.

"That was sheer bloody murder," said John. "They did not give us a chance."

"Why would they?" gasped his father, still trying to suck great lungsful of air into his body. Sitting up, he started to unbuckle his breastplate. "We'll move faster without these things," he gasped. John nodded breathless agreement and did likewise. "They want this over with as much as we do," continued Martin, "They see a chance to finally finish it now, they're not going to slacken off until it's done. Do you blame them?" As the deadweight fell away from them, they began to laugh in earnest with terror and relief and a host of other emotions. We'll take the pikes for a while in case we are stopped, we can say we were moving position."

Standing, they moved off through the blanketing trees still chuckling without humour, silently praising God for their lives, as the fight raged on, and men died not far behind them.

Finally, after some distance, Martin held up his hand. "Here's a good place," he said, as he glimpsed the glitter of water through the undergrowth. "Time to get our feet wet."

"Now is the time, I think, gentlemen," Thomas Fairfax turned and surveyed his senior officers who were massed behind him. "Over the ford and straight up the lane, if you please, quickly as you can now. Dragoons first, give them no respite, sirs, no respite, I say. Do not let them reform."

In minutes, the earth seemed to shake as rank after rank of purposeful cavalry thundered through the river in an explosion of sparkling water and hammered up the hill. These were veterans of many fights and their morale was high after the success of Naseby. Straight up the lane, they careered, the tough, fighting machines that were the hard core of the Parliamentary army.

Royalist musketeers lining the hedges on either side of the banked lane, poured fire into the leather and steel-clad men as they thundered past, but their numbers were too few to matter. Here and there, a saddle emptied but the now-unburdened horses, unable to stop or swerve in the tightly packed mass, kept running.

At the brow of the hill, George Lord Goring and his

men waited, the dwarf to face the giant, the nut under the nutcracker. Calmly, Goring watched the wave of men and horses coming towards him and drew his sword, a movement immediately copied by his five hundred followers.

"Good luck, gentlemen," he called, almost gaily standing in his stirrups. "For His Majesty King Charles!" The cry was taken up by everyone with him as they hurled themselves forward, horses screaming as spurs were rammed into their sides.

The fight did not last long. Although for several minutes it appeared as if Goring and his men might hold their own or even win the day, eventually, sheer weight of numbers told and, from the milling mass of fear-crazed horses and slashing, cutting men, the Cavaliers broke and streamed away, soldiers no more but fugitives.

At the same moment, huge numbers of Parliamentary infantry hurled themselves across the river and hacked their way through hedges that were by now, virtually undefended. Those Royalist die-hards that still stood their ground were quickly despatched.

Cromwell halted his squadrons at the top of the hill and reformed his sweating cursing men, then they were off again in pursuit along the Bridgewater Road. Two miles on, they found the mauled remnants of the Royalist horse drawn up once more to fight. Goring was making one last desperate effort to save his guns. It was a magnificent but useless gesture. Already badly knocked about and with their morale in tatters, his men gave at the first onslaught of the leather-clad men. It was the last throw.

The King's army in the west, his last hope in this war, was utterly destroyed.

Chapter Sixteen

Somerset, July 1645

"This is no good at all," cried Mary, raising her voice to be heard above the sounds of battle which, even at this distance, were loud. "We'll never spot him from here, we must get closer."

Desperation gave the little Parson strength and his grip on her shoulder remained firm. "I said NO, my child, this is far too close anyway. If I allowed you to get hurt in any way, I would never forgive myself, and neither would Jacob."

They were standing with others beside an ammunition wagon some two hundred yards from the river, downstream and behind the parliamentary starting positions. Their view was interrupted by a clump of standing trees and clumps of sparse brush, but quite clearly, they could see the confused melee at the hedge on the opposite slope. In the distance to their left, they could see the stone bridge. Billowing smoke increasingly blotted any view that they may have had, and for this, the Parson was secretly grateful. The loud percussive reports from the big guns repeatedly startled him and, not for the first time, he realised he was far too old for these escapades.

Grouped about them were two or three dozen townspeople come to see the fight, but their murmurs of discontent were growing as the increasing smoke obscured anything of interest. Little groups were already beginning to move away. He and Mary had begged a lift in one of the small carts that had made the somewhat longer journey to see the fight. Acutely aware of what Jacob's thoughts would be on the matter, the reluctant Parson had done his best to dissuade the determined Mary. Almost they had argued, but not quite, and now Roberts had to content himself with attempting to keep her safe.

Standing on tiptoe, Mary continued to strain her eyes forward, scanning the ground in front of her with increasing impatience.

"What does he look like again, Parson"? she queried. "Remind me."

Roberts gazed at the back of her head with a mixture of exasperation and affection and sighed hugely to register his annoyance.

"Tall and thin," he said, slowly picturing the man he had met. "Battered, travel-worn, dark clothes, long boots above the knee." He squeezed the bridge of his nose as the smoke made his eyes water. "He has a big scar on his face, but you will not see it from this distance."

"We must find him," cried Mary, her tone becoming angry. "We must, for Jacob."

"What must you do for Jacob?" The angry raised voice immediately behind them made them both start and spin around surprised by his sudden and unexpected appearance.

His face was drawn and pale with anger, and pain was twisting it into a mask. His eyes glittered with the remains of the fever and sweat stood out on his pale skin. A crude sling cradled his injured arm and his limp was pronounced.

"By God, Parson!" he hissed, "I had expected better of you than this." His eyes blazed at the old man. "To bring her to gawp at men dying."

"Jacob!" Mary stepped forward and grabbed his arm. "I made him bring me, I gave him no choice, but we came for a reason, for an important reason." Jacob swayed slightly and she held his good arm tighter. "How did you get here?

You'll kill yourself, my love."

Jacob's weakness was a living thing, his head swam and he stamped his foot to keep his balance. In the middle distance, he heard trumpets shrill which meant that the cavalry was about to move and, as a professional soldier, he knew that once you released horse soldiers anything could happen, no one was safe.

Hopefully, they were far enough away to keep them from harm, but they must move back now.

Mary too had heard the trumpets and she turned and moved a few paces forward again, raising her hand to shade her eyes. "I can't see anything," she wailed, "this is no good."

Jacob raised his voice again, pumping anger into his words. "WHAT are you looking for, in Christ's name?" the lash of his voice frightened the old Parson who blanched before his anger. "Tell me!"

There was no answer. "I'm waiting," he hissed through clenched teeth.

Ethan sat his horse some distance off, watching his brother. He was screened from the little group near the wagon by a clump of small trees and his immobility rendered him almost invisible.

Sitting there since well before the battle had begun, he had reviewed his life and his losses as only a man intent on death can do. Many things had passed through his tortured mind, blotting out completely the events going on around him. The faces of old friends long since dead had flitted across his vision and the sudden remembered touch of a child's hands on his neck had made him start and cry out. Above all, the face of a long, dead beautiful woman had appeared and told him to come to her. Yes, he would go, it was time, he nodded to himself.

It was then that he had noticed some way off near an old wagon, the plump, kindly little man who had spoken with him recently and tried to give him comfort. With a shock, he realised that the slim blond-haired beauty with him must be Jacob's wife. He sat as still as a statue and watched, feeling immediately protective towards her brought so near to bloodshed by that old fool.

Then Jacob had arrived and the breath hissed out of Ethan as, despite the passage of the years, he recognised his young brother. His heart beat loudly and unbidden tears filled his eyes. Emotions long since forgotten or cast aside paraded through his head and roughly he raised his gauntleted hand to wipe his face. He knew instinctively he would never make himself known to the group, but this was enough at the end of things to see them this one time. He could not take his eyes off the scene and, as he watched, the lines on his careworn and battered face were softened by flashes of memories from happier times and the knowledge that these two people would survive and be happy. Thank God someone would be happy.

Then a gust of wind cleared the smoke a little and he stiffened, involuntarily jerking up his horse's head. Two pikemen were running straight towards the little group 'Going for the woman,' he thought, 'The bastards are going for the woman.' The red mist veiled his eyes and his sword rasped from its scabbard carving an arc in the air.

"Oh no, my beauties," he hissed savagely. "Not this time, not again." Viciously, he slammed his single spike spurs into his horse's side, it screamed high and shrilly and then they were running flat-out, closing the gap to the running pikemen.

They were soaked through but happy. They were across the river and, as far as they could gauge, away and free. Slumped under a bush at the edge of a clearing they were once again fighting for breath. Steam was rising from their clothing as the heat from their bodies began to dry it.

"Pa," laughed John, "You keep this up and I'm going back to join them lads across the river." His laughter ended with a coughing fit, and he laughed again, "I'll swear I'm dying."

His father lay next to him fighting for breath, but he cuffed John's shoulder with glee, nothing could dampen their spirits now, "I know what you mean," he wheezed. "But we must move again soon, we need to put as much distance as possible between us and this place by nightfall." He stretched out his aching legs, ignoring the slimy feel of his wet homespun breeches. Then, raising himself on one elbow, he peered through the bush that sheltered them "You know, son," he began, "I never thought we'd make it this far, not really I... "

He grabbed John's shoulder, his grip anxious and strong, "Am I going mad, son, or is that Mary and old Parson Roberts standing over yonder near that wagon?"

John gave a half laugh, "Pa, you're raving, what on earth would they be... ?"

His question died on his lips as he too saw the group. They were some ways distant, but his father could be right. Martin continued, "There's a soldier with them as well," he said, "How in God's name... ?"

John razed himself on one elbow, prepared to humour his father, but with a scramble, Martin was gone, off and running. John cried out in panic and, jumping up, grabbed his pike and chased after him.

"Jacob!" screamed Mary, cutting him off half-way through a sentence, she scampered forward a few paces and turned, her face suffused with happiness.

"Look, oh look!" she was shouting and laughing. Both men gazed at her with apprehension.

"My daughter, what is it?" shouted the little Parson and then he saw the distant men running towards them and his eyes flew wide with recognition. He also began to laugh and clapped his hands with childish glee.

"What is it?" yelled Jacob, annoyed at their behaviour his head was still swimming and his shoulder hurt. Mary spun around and threw her arms around his neck. "Oh, Jacob," she laughed again. "It's my father and brother, look, oh look!" Her glee bubbled out of her and she ran a few paces forward again, raising her arms and waving. Then she froze as she saw the horseman thundering down behind them. Her hands came up to her face and she screamed.

The Parson too could see the danger now and was shouting and gesticulating in a frantic effort to warn them, but they thought he was encouraging them and came on, unaware, waving.

Jacob had not moved. With his keen eyes he had noticed the lone horseman at the same instant Mary had, but also in that instant he registered that he somehow knew that man. The way he rode, the shape of his shoulders and head, he KNEW that man, but where from? His frown deepened as he stared forward, screwing his eyes up. Then the veil of the years lifted and he knew.

"Ethan!" he yelled, running forward a few yards, startling Mary and the Parson with the strength of his voice. "ETHAN!" But still the rider came on, oblivious to their shouts.

The eyes of his horse rolled with terror as the spurs dug into him again. Foam flecked his mouth and nostrils. The eyes of the rider were wide and insane, his mouth screaming obscenities.

Ethan could not hear their shouts because he was not there. He was far away in Moravia thundering down on Croats. Bastard Croats, animals, vermin, who had killed his baby daughter and taken his wife. He would make them pay, Christus, he'd make them pay, the filthy scum. His lips were drawn back exposing snarling teeth, his face a mask of hatred and outrage. His razor-sharp sword was held above his head, this would be sweet. He heeled his horse again, the spurs biting deep, the horse screamed again in pain, flattened its ears and ran faster still.

Closing swiftly, Ethan had surveyed the situation with the expertise of a veteran cavalryman. He would take the man in front first, then turn and deal with the second. He raised his voice and laughed, a harsh manic sound. His screamed obscenities in a guttural patois were whipped away by the wind.

Martin did not see the horseman until the last moment, so intent was he on reaching his daughter. At the last moment, he felt and heard the thunder of hooves and a man screaming. Slowing his pace, he turned and looked up and saw the flashing steel coming down at him. Then all went black.

It was a classic cavalry stroke by a professional of many years' experience. The grey-haired head was almost severed from the body, killing Martin instantly. The body, unaware that it was dead, ran on for a few more steps before collapsing in a heap of arms and legs.

"One!" screamed Ethan, hauling on his reins so that the horse slithered to a halt sitting on its haunches. Savagely, he pulled the beast's head around, intending to deal with the second Croat. He was laughing, laughing.

"Ethan!" A voice from the past screamed at him from far away. "Ethan stop!!".

He turned towards the shout and, incredibly, his face softened with recognition. His brother was running towards him. "Jacob," he mouthed. "What do you do here?" he smiled.

It was then that the ten-inch-long pikehead took him cleanly in the side, going in deep under his rib cage. He hissed with pain and felt himself lifted from the saddle, far, far up he went, spitted on the end of the pike like a stuck pig, then with bone-jarring force he was slammed down into the grass, the breath driven from his body. Without conscious thought, he slewed sideways to face his attacker, his instinct for survival automatic.

The burly pikeman some feet away had thrown down his pike and, drawing his short stabbing sword, was marching towards him. 'He's going to finish me with that blade,' thought Ethan, knowing he could do nothing to protect himself. He gazed at the man's eyes, they were murderous and wild. He closed his own eyes, resigned. He wanted to go; this was the end.

There was a shout and a rush of booted feet and he opened pain-glazed eyes to see two men circling each other, each with a drawn sword.

"You don't touch him," screamed Jacob, his sword arm wavering with weakness. "You hear me?"

"Touch him?" snarled John. "Did you see what he did, did you see? That scum, I'm going to cut his bloody head off." With a yell, he lunged forward, the blow parried by Jacob with difficulty. After months in the field on campaign, John was strong. Jacob knew he could not stop this maddened pikeman for long.

They circled each other like a couple of fighting dogs, watching and waiting for an opening, the rest of the world forgotten.

From nowhere, it seemed to the dying Ethan as he lay watching there was a third figure. A plump little old man dressed in black, forcing his way between the circling pair, his hands held above his head in a futile attempt to protect himself.

"Enough," he screamed ."You hear me, there's been enough." Sensing his words were having an effect, he stood up straight and peered at them. "For the love of God, can't you stop?" he shouted, "Enough I say. Jacob, put down your weapon. John, your sister needs you, drop that sword." The anguish in his old voice leant it power and instinctively both men drew breath and heeded his commands.

Jacob almost swooned with weakness.

Seeming to emerge from a trance, John stood from his crouch and the blood-lust died in his eyes. He stared flatly at the Parson, then at the prone figure on the ground and, seeming to reach a decision, he dropped his sword, turned and plodded off to where his wailing sister was crouched over the body of her father.

The Parson turned the full fury of his gaze on Jacob, "Jacob," he spat.

Staggering to regain his swimming senses, Jacob looked down at his own sword then, feeling sudden disgust, hurled it as far away as his strength would allow. It somersaulted in the air, bounced once and stuck quivering into the ground.

Turning, he crouched down over the figure at his feet.

Kneeling with difficulty, he lifted the ravaged head of his brother onto his lap. "Ethan," he sobbed, "Ethan, you came back," and it was the voice of a little boy. He realised there was not much time. Blood was pouring from the huge ugly wound in Ethan's side, the surrounding grass already slimy with it.

The ghost of a smile crossed Ethan's face and he croaked, "Yes, little brother, I came back." His breathing was shallow. "Your wife is safe?"

"Yes," murmured Jacob, glancing across at Mary. "She's safe, Ethan, be at ease."

Ethan made to say more but suddenly his gaze shifted as if someone had peered over Jacob's shoulder and was gazing down at him. The ravaged face lost its careworn appearance and softened to show that it once might have been handsome. "Hello, my love," he said softly. "I knew you'd come," and incredibly he smiled. "I'm so sorry I could not... " His eyes glazed and became fixed, his face bore the look of one who is not afraid of what is to come. He coughed once and his features froze in death. His wife had come for him and he wanted to go.

Jacob's control broke and he sobbed hugely, hugging his brother's head to him.

He was thinking of the last time he had seen this man all those years ago, the arrogance, the brashness, the confidence, and he could not reconcile it to this emaciated, battered figure that lay before him.

The old Parson's hand laid gently on his shoulder. "Jacob," said the old man quietly, "Your wife needs you, my son." Jacob appeared for some moments not to have heard, but then, as if rousing from a sleep, he shook himself, laid the ravaged head back down onto the ground and stood awkwardly, his shoulder severely hampering him. "This is my brother, Parson," he said peering at the little man, "My brother."

Roberts steadied the younger man, his hand on Jacob's shoulder, "Yes, my son, I know." Jacob stared at the little man and wiped his sleeve across his nose as a child would, "How do you know?"

"Go to Mary, Jacob," soothed Roberts. "I will tell you," he said, measuring his words. "But we'll talk of it later, when we have time." he indicated the battered figure at their feet ."I met this man recently. I can tell you probably more than you wish to know, such a troubled soul, God forgive him. But for now," he indicated with his hand the reunited sister and brother some yards away, "You must see to your wife, she has much to bear."

Glancing down one last time, Jacob roused himself and limped off, leaving the Parson alone with Ethan. He stared down at the prone figure, then stiffly knelt and closed the staring eyes, muttering a prayer to his God for the soul of this man.

The sounds of fighting in the distance were diminishing now as the last of the Royalist troops ran for their lives. A desultory cannon boomed in the distance and, as if this were a signal, it started to rain, large drops falling from the lowering cloud. Roberts straightened and with a groan, stood upright once more and gazing down at Ethan, made the sign of the cross. "In the name of the Father, The Son, and The Holy Spirit... " he intoned.

Somehow Jacob made it to Mary before his strength failed him and he sank to his knees. She was crying quietly now, bitter anguished tears that ran unchecked down her face and onto her dress. John was slumped down next to his father's body, one hand on the old dead shoulder as if to comfort.

He gazed across, as Jacob, a puzzled look on his face. "Why?" he snarled. "Why in God's name did he do that?"

Jacob was close to swooning but managed to shake his head. "I don't know," he managed. The faces of Mary and John were moving in and out of focus. He shook his head partly to clear it but also to emphasise his words. "I don't know," he repeated unimaginatively. Darkness enveloped him and he slowly lost consciousness and leaned gently sideways into his wife.

Still stroking the old grey-haired head of her father, Mary moved her other arm to wrap it around Jacob's shoulders. He was a deadweight, but his eyes were opened again.

"Mary," John's voice was hoarse with anger and concern. "Who is this man?" Suspicion and anger clouded his broad face.

Mary's voice was flat, all emotion spent. "He's my husband, brother," she said. "Jacob Sedgewick. I'm married now."

"You're married?" John's voice was tired now, so tired. He sighed hugely. There was something else he needed to ask but he could not think what it was. His mind was befuddled with horror and shock, and the adrenalin still coursed through his body.

Parson Roberts arrived and knelt stiffly down next to Mary. "My child?" he said, his voice full of concern. "What a dreadful, terrible thing to have happened." He glanced quickly down at the body of his old friend. "Is Martin quite dead?" He laid a gentle hand onto his dead friend's shoulder. Mary's gaze seemed not to see him but was fixed on the middle distance. "Yes," she said mechanically. "He's gone, Parson. All this time, all these miles and, just as we find him, he's gone." She sobbed hugely and hugged the inert Jacob closer to her, fighting to maintain her grip on reality.

Groggily, he reached up and stroked her hair, the enormity and speed of what had just happened seeming unreal, a bad dream.

John peered stupidly at the couple and then owlishly at the old Parson, his mind attempting to make sense of the latest happenings. It was then that he remembered the other question he needed to ask.

"How is Ma, Parson?" his voice cracked. "Is she well?"

The Parson rubbed a hand across his face dreading what he must now say. He leaned slightly forward and raised his arm to rest an old, gnarled hand on John's shoulder.

"Martha is with God, John," he said, aware that this good young man must now understand that not only his father but also his mother was dead.

"I don't understand," muttered John stupidly. "When, how? I don't understand?" His control was beginning to unravel.

The Parson's voice was soothing, quiet, but could be quite clearly heard above the furore in the distance. "We'll talk later, my son. There's much we must tell you." He peered sympathetically into John's stricken face. "But for now, we must take care of each other. Martin must be buried; Mary is close to swooning and poor Jacob is in a poor way." He stood up stiffly, his hands on his knees, feeling his age as never before. He leaned down, offering his hand to John. "Come," he said, "I'll help you."

Goring retired with what was left of his cavalry to Barnstaple. He was not sure what he would do now but needed time and space to think. His infantry, such as it was, made their way in small groups to join the garrison at Bridgewater where it licked its wounds. Many had surrendered after the action and faced a hazardous future.

The following day, Lord Fairfax met with a rag-tag representation from the local clubmen who pleaded to be left in peace on the promise that they never again took up arms in the Royalist cause. Their request was granted. Fairfax and Cromwell had other weightier matters on their minds. Later the same day Fairfax wrote to parliament,

"It pleased God on Thursday last by this army to

331

give General Goring a defeat."

Bridgewater fell twelve days later with the whole of the garrison surrendering without a fight. Bristol surrendered just over a month later and with it disappeared the last major manufacturing and recruitment centre of the royalist cause in southern England. No longer able to put a viable army into the field, the remaining Royalist forces had to be content with maintaining garrisons. It was almost the end.

They buried Ethan and Martin two days after the battle, laying them side-by-side in the little churchyard that stood close to where they had died. Roberts had reasoned with the local clergyman and the burial had been allowed, albeit in a quiet unused part of the ancient burial ground, far removed from the village incumbents. It was peaceful there with a small yew tree swaying gently in the slight breeze protecting the crude wooden crosses from the sun.

Parson Roberts took the service, his hat in one hand, his Bible in the other. Quietly, he intoned the prayers for the dead and the rustling leaves of the tall elm trees which surrounded the little grey stone church provided a peaceful background.

Mary did not attend, she was in a laudanum-induced sleep back at the inn in Yeovil. The shock and horror of what she had seen had affected her deeply as they would for many months to come. She had seen both her mother and her father killed before her eyes during the last weeks and, like many in this troubled land, events had caught up with this brave young woman. It was hoped that in time she would make a good recovery, God-willing. But no one could be sure. The love of a good husband whom she admired and trusted deeply would help, maybe.

Jacob and John stood side-by-side, their heads bowed, each deep in their own thoughts. They had reached an understanding during the last two days, Mary, and her well-being the link between them and already the shoots of what would become a lifelong friendship were showing through the distrust. John had grudgingly agreed that the actions of a brother he had not seen for ten years could not be blamed on his sister's new husband. Peering at the two young men as he intoned the prayers, Parson Roberts hoped they would be able to help each other in the years ahead. No one knew what the future held, perhaps this land could recover from the devastation and intolerance that had led to so much violence and death. Perhaps.

The prayers were finished and the dead buried. As the little Parson replaced his hat, his eyes caught Jacobs and, answering the unspoken entreaty, Jacob rested his hand on John's shoulder and turned away.

All three moved silently through the Lych gate and walked away from the peace and quiet of the little churchyard, each of them unable to think of the future for the moment. As they did so, a light summer mist from the river closeby wreathed across the scene and hid them from view. Behind, left in the quiet churchyard forever, Ethan, the troubled soldier of fortune, and Martin, the caring, thoughtful husband and father, each having met their destiny in this war, lay side-by-side beneath the whispering elms.

The End

Epilogue

We know all too well what the fates had in store for King Charles the First and his implacable enemy, Oliver Cromwell. It is still undecided which of the two triumphed in the end.

Thomas Fairfax, The Parliamentary Lord General, retired after the war to once more take up the reins of a country gentleman. Although still involved in politics for many years more, he avoided further pitfalls and lived to grow old with his wife and children.

George Lord Goring, after the collapse of the King's cause, took up the life of a mercenary and adventurer. He left England one grey morning never to return. He died in penury in a Madrid slum.

Edward Massey, despite fighting with distinction for Parliament during what are now known as the first and second civil wars, changed sides in the third and fought for Charles the Second. At the Restoration, he was knighted. He died in Ireland in 1674.

During the period now known as the English Civil Wars, around thirty-four thousand Parliamentarian troops and fifty thousand Royalists died. Over one hundred and twenty thousand civilians, men women and children, died from violence or war-related disease.

The larger European conflict, which raged over most of Western Europe from 1618 – 1648 and is now called the Thirty Years War, claimed a suspected total of eight million lives from warfare and disease. This figure includes the estimated ten to twenty thousand women and girls per year who were savagely tortured and burned at the stake for witchcraft.

"What baffles me is that, despite everything, there are millions of people who still believe God Loves us." Ethan Sedgwick, 1645.